Pride Publishing books by Elle Q. Sabine:

The Second Sons

THE SECOND SONS

ELLE Q. SABINE

The Second Sons
ISBN # 978-1-78430-701-1
©Copyright Elle Q. Sabine 2015
Cover Art by Posh Gosh ©Copyright August 2015
Interior text design by Claire Siemaszkiewicz
Pride Publishing

Published in 2015 by Pride Publishing, Newland House, The Point, Weaver Road, Lincoln, LN6 3QN, United Kingdom.

Pride Publishing is a subsidiary of Totally Entwined Group Limited.

THE SECOND SONS

Dedication

To all the good girls of the world…from Lord Byron—

One shade the more, one ray the less,
Had half impaired the nameless grace
Which waves in every raven tress,
Or softly lightens o'er her face;
Where thoughts serenely sweet express,
How pure, how dear their dwelling-place.

Lord Byron (1815)

Author's Historical Note

The Right Honourable George Canning was the British Foreign Secretary from September 1822 to April 1827 during the period of this tale. Afterward, he briefly served as prime minister until his death on 8 August 1827. He is sometimes known as the 'lost leader', because his death prematurely ended the coalition of Tories and Whigs he led. By 1824, he had four children. George Charles Canning — *appearing here fictionally as Young Canning, aged twenty-six* — actually died in 1820 from consumption. William Pitt Canning was twenty-two, Harriet Canning was twenty, and Charles John Canning — later a prime minister and First Earl Canning — was twelve. In 1824, the Foreign Office was located in the warren of government buildings in Whitehall and had been there since 1782. The Cannings lived at Canning House in Berkeley Square, and this house is still extant today. The author asks you to forgive these few fictional exaggerations related to the Canning family and political history in pursuit of intrigue, romance and fictional consistency.

Prologue

December, 1808

Fiona slipped out through the music room door. She didn't know who left it unlocked in the evenings, but she was grateful. She'd been sneaking out of the nursery at night for years, and since the Worst Day in the country months earlier, the nurses and governesses had been particularly obsessive about not letting any of the four girls out of sight.

Sneaking out was the only way that Fiona could have time alone. They watched her when she studied, when she ate, when she played with her sisters, when she was with her tutors, when she walked in the garden or the park with her inconsolable mother.

Even inside the Mayfair mansion, London in December was suffocating. The air was stale and never just right. It burned hot or froze, from drafts that blew from unheated rooms and fireplaces belching heat waves over her woolen dresses, flannel petticoats and thick cotton stockings. The air was perpetually dark, with windows kept covered to preserve the heat while also preventing natural sunlight from filtering inside. Outside, the air was smoky from the wood and coal fires that kept the houses warm. The stagnant fog smothered the city, obscuring the stars and even the moon, but in the dark void of the gardens, Fiona knew every step of the paths. She'd walked them at night for months, restless from the nightmare memory that replayed in her brain. Early on, Fiona had awoken from her dreams and cried out, but the young women who watched Fiona and her sisters had no help to offer except to assure her that the Worst Day was not her fault and send her back to bed, before they returned to their own slumbers. It hadn't been long before Fiona had stopped seeking them out and turned inward for comfort.

Mayfair was largely deserted, but Fiona's mother had begged to stay in the City, even through the Christmas holiday. The family's ancestral home at Winchester Castle had been tenanted since Fiona's grandmother had died, and the family had no other country estate except Aston Manor. Fiona's mother refused to return to the cursed marble-floored foyer near Chester again, especially not during a week intended to celebrate life. Fiona's father, the Earl of Winchester, had agreed without argument. Fiona rather thought he never wanted to return to the scene of despair either.

The girls, like their mother, still wore black six months later, so Fiona's cape and hood concealed her from sight once she escaped the house and wandered onto the garden paths. It was only in the grim, dark privacy of their back garden that Fiona felt capable of opening the memory of the Worst Day and grieving. She shed her tears alone, so that she could comfort Abigail, reassure Gloria that Johnny lived in heaven now and play with toddling Genevieve. It was certainly true that no one allowed Genevieve to wander or escape. If anyone was more obsessive than the army of governesses and nurses, it was Fiona, Abigail and Gloria when they played with little Genevieve.

Johnny had been so angry that morning. Eight years old, he'd shouted at the prim, sharp-nosed woman who had been their primary governess. Eight years old was too old to be kept in the nursery like a baby. He wanted to go fishing, had even gotten the footmen to agree to take him. But Lady Winchester had been entertaining callers that morning and the earl had been out. Old Mrs. Pringle had said no. He had to stay inside the hot attic rooms with his sisters and read or play quietly until he had permission from his mother or the earl.

She'd made the mistake of leaving him alone with Abigail and Fiona after lunch. He'd been angry, even mean, all through lunch, but when she'd taken tiny Genevieve and little Gloria one room away for their naps, he'd made good on his escape, slipping out through the door quietly while Fiona read and Abigail rocked her dolls to sleep for a nap. Both girls had been relieved to see him go, glad to be away from his cross despondency and ill-tempered manners.

A half hour later, Mrs. Pringle was still absent. One of the younger nurses—still a girl, named Miss Molly—had come to take them for a stroll in the gardens. Fiona and Abigail had raced to the landing ahead of her, hearing the front door open three floors below and the earl's voice in the foyer. With a whoop from a staircase below them, Johnny had raced down the landing from the first floor to the front hall, his stockinged feet sliding on the freshly waxed and polished stairs. A great lark, his face had said—until he'd lost control and tumbled. He'd been unable to stop at the bottom and had flown toward the marble floor. His head had hit hard on the bottom step, then the marble itself.

Fiona's and Abigail's wide-eyed shock and another young nurse's horrified cry—had her name been Annie?—had been nothing compared to the wild horror that had come from the newly-arrived Winchester's throat or their mother's agonizing wails.

Wondering for the first time what had happened to Mrs. Pringle in the aftermath of the Worst Day, Fiona passed the garden bench where her mother often sat in the afternoons and crept into the nut trees that sheltered against the back wall. They'd been packed up by their mother's maid, Frenchie, on that very first evening and taken to Birmingham, returning to Aston Manor only for the funeral. Mrs. Pringle and three young nursemaids had been replaced by eight slightly older nurses, a head governess and two tutors who could run as fast as Gloria did and keep all four girls under constant surveillance.

Fiona paused at the base of the hazelnut tree and looked up. She knew not to leave the gardens. At ten years of age, she was still a child, but she understood London's streets were dangerous to women and children. She could climb the tree and look past the end of the mews to the street beyond. Of course, the governesses and her mother wouldn't have permitted her to risk a fall, so she'd taught herself to do it at night, hanging on grimly and scrambling among the branches.

A shout from the alley attracted her attention and she froze, turning her head, but it was quickly evident that no one could see her. Farther along the mews, but rapidly approaching, the sounds of male scuffling were evident. Behind them another shouted, and his lamp rapidly approached until the three met up directly below her tree.

Fiona hardly dared to breathe. All three were young men, maybe even still youths. In the darkness, the first pair had sounded as if they were fighting. By the dim lamplight, Fiona could see that the oldest youth was dragging a smaller boy behind him. Even with only the bare light from the lamp, it was clear that the smaller young man was bloodied and hardly able to struggle from a beating he'd already taken. "Let Oliver go, March," the lamp-holder demanded, unafraid to intervene. "This is between you and me and it always has been."

To her surprise, March spat in his direction and sneered, tightening his grip on Oliver's collar and coat. "It is about him. You bring him back into my house again, and I'll kill him, Alden. His brother told me what the two of you are doing in private."

"It's not your house—"

"It will be!" The man named March used his free hand, the one that wasn't gripped into Oliver's coat, to swing a punch at Alden's stomach.

Alden, the largest of the three, sidestepped it neatly, set the lamp down in the middle of the mews and calmly drew back to throw a powerful punch at March's jaw. His head jerked and, in his pain, March dropped Oliver.

It was only then that Fiona realized how close the unfortunate Oliver was to unconsciousness. He fell to the ground without even trying to save himself, his head landing hard against the bricks. Fiona clasped her hand over her mouth to hide her cry at the fall, but the two remaining boys were focused entirely on each other. With a low roar of rage, March launched himself at Alden.

The battle was quickly over. Alden responded to March's attack by first blocking then ruthlessly throwing his own punches. Instead of a wild offensive, he delivered four hard jabs to March's stomach in quick succession, then moved upward and hit both sides of March's jaw and the underside of his chin. March stumbled backward. He landed hard on his backside against the back wall of Winchester House, unmoving. Alden turned to Oliver.

At once, Fiona noted, his behavior changed from aggressive to compassionate, even tender. Oliver couldn't quickly limp away, but Alden simply knelt beside him, cradling his head patiently and quietly checking his injuries.

In her silent observation, though, Fiona could not help notice that, behind Alden, March was beginning to stir. He pulled himself to his feet, his hand against the wall. March looked up, and Fiona caught a horrifying image in the lamplight that was March's rage projected as a looming, threatening shadow across the mews. She held her breath, praying that he would simply stagger away, but instead he twisted his mouth in an angry grimace and reached out to deliver a cowardly punch to the back of Alden's neck.

"No!" she yelped. The single word was just in time for Alden to react. March's fist landed awkwardly against his upper arm. In a single second, Alden punched back, and his quick movements took March to the ground, where this time he remained.

Alden looked up in Fiona's direction, but she sank against the tree, grateful for the darkness. "Thank you, lad," he said softly. "But isn't it past time for you to be out here?"

Fiona knew instinctively that she had to protect herself from exposure, even though it meant lying. Luckily the man had assumed she was a boy. "Jus' wanted me some nuts, guv'na," she managed in a loud whisper, anxious for him not to hear her true voice.

"These aren't your trees, I take it," Alden returned drily. He knelt again on the brick, and lifted Oliver into his arms. "My friend is badly injured and I must leave the lamp to take him to safety. Pray keep it as a reward for your warning, but come retrieve it before this mean excuse for a man wakes and catches you. It's a good one. You can sell it for a few pounds sterling."

She couldn't keep the lamp, but if she was brave and quick, she could be certain it was returned to the right household. "Aye," she whispered in the dark, barely breathing. Only when Alden began to walk away did she slide down the tree.

Fiona knew how to open the back gate, but there was no need. It was already unlocked, so she slipped into the shadows and doused the lamp. The complete darkness was easier to navigate, and she didn't want March to see her if he did wake. Farther along, Alden turned into a back gate much like her own, and Fiona clung to the shadows as she followed.

She'd just left the lamp in the shadows at the back wall and returned to the mews when she heard March groan. Her heart beat so painfully that she was certain it could be heard, Fiona pulled the black hood over her face and waited motionless.

It was but a minute before he stumbled past her, cursing a streak of words that Fiona didn't know. She listened, fascinated and distracted for a moment by the vocabulary, before he turned into the gate she'd just left. "Someday I'm going to kill those damnable sodomites," he muttered.

Her heart raced, but she knew she could not stay any longer. Nor could she warn the other two, having no clue where they'd gone or what their roles were within the household. Revealing herself as a young daughter of an earl, even if the house belonged to a duke, would be scandalous.

Fleeing quickly, she raced back to her own gate and slipped inside. Whatever peace she'd wanted to find would not be found in the treetops tonight, and Fiona hadn't even thought to return to her perch. Instead, she went upstairs immediately.

Still, she had no wish to go to bed. Instead, she found herself in the gallery, wrapped in her cloak, trembling as she sat behind the drawn curtains in a window seat that looked over the front of the house. Fiona stayed there a long time, staring at the empty street and the open square of grass beyond it, but eventually she stirred, freezing as a faint noise from the gallery reached her. Ever so silently, she tipped her head to the side and eased the velvet draperies open an inch.

To her surprise, Fiona's own mother glided past. Like Fiona, she was fully engulfed in a black cape and hood, and her head was down. She looked neither right nor left, but moved silently past Fiona toward her own chambers at the end of the hall.

Only after her mother's door closed silently on its well-oiled hinges did Fiona escape the window seat. She'd had too many close calls for one night.

It was past time she was in bed.

Chapter One

Late August, 1824

"Sign this last document and we'll be finished, my lord," the white-haired solicitor directed, shifting a sheaf of parchment from before the Duke to the ink-stained blotter in front of his second son.

Perfectly at ease despite the difficult subject of the papers, Alden dipped his pen and signed below his father's name in a flourish, noting that the elder Collier had already signed shakily in his place as a witness.

Alden would be entrusting his personal business to the younger Collier, but the Duke's son knew well that his father would patronize the frail solicitor as long as the old man could still climb the steps of Lennox House and attend the Duke personally.

The elder Collier, currently packing up stacks of paper at the head of the table, was witnessing the end of an era. The highly respected and often-feared Duke of Lennox was sharing, if not ceding, some of his authority with his only remaining son. Lennox and

Lord Alden Swenson were attempting a new sort of working relationship, at least in the operation of the Duke's business and personal finances. Alden had agreed to not openly thwart Lennox's rule, but Lennox had also agreed not to intervene without first conferring with Alden privately.

Alden well knew that no one would have predicted such a thing a year earlier. Then, Alden had been happily managing the Duke's affairs in Europe, largely independent of his father's direct rule. He'd been content residing in Amsterdam, with occasional trips to the major trading centers of Europe. He'd had a full life there, making a home with Oliver in the diverse community of artists and musicians who flocked to Amsterdam.

The news of his nephew's birth—his elder brother's first son—had further removed Alden from the succession and cemented his residency in Europe.

But within a very few months, everything had changed for Lennox and his family. Alden's elder brother, known by the courtesy title the Earl of March, had committed suicide in a very public and unmistakable scandal. With March's son and Lennox's new heir only a wee babe, Lennox had renewed an old request. The Duke wanted Alden to return to London, and with the louse who had haunted Alden for three decades finally gone, Alden had few reasons to refuse.

"It's done then," his father said softly, sighing and sitting back in his chair. Alden looked up and caught Lennox considering him. "In addition to the business, I'm happy to have it legally established that you shall follow me as one of Eynon's guardians." Lennox examined him carefully, even as the Duke spoke of his daughter-in-law and grandson. "Gloria may be safely remarried now, and I am confident her husband will look after Eynon as he matures, but Eynon will still need you to protect his inheritance when I am gone. And Johna and the girls will need someone to look out for their interests."

Lennox was hardly failing, but he had visibly aged in the years Alden had been in Europe. His face was narrower and the lines around his eyes and mouth had deepened. His hair had thinned, too, and turned a brilliant shade of white that gleamed in the late afternoon sun. Lennox had always been a driven man — full of passion, often moody, overburdened by the combined forces of his financial affairs, government responsibilities, legislative obligations and Court duties. Despite any physical changes, though, Lennox was still that same intense personality that Alden remembered.

The Duke had been rightfully disappointed in his elder son, but he'd also been oblivious to the acrimonious relationship that had defined Alden's childhood and youth. The bitter feud had begun at Eynon Castle and gone with them to Eton and Oxford. As an adult, Alden's sense of self-preservation and protectiveness had taken him as far from March as possible, until March had left his life permanently.

Coming home had been disruptive — disconcerting — in ways far beyond the relocation of Alden's household.

Alden had once acidly said that his father needed to love. He'd only found out in the time since his brother's death that Lennox had loved, did love. Indeed, Alden now understood that Lennox had probably delegated his responsibilities as a parent to nurses and tutors because of his father's tragic love life. Lennox had lost his first love to Napoleon, and his second great love was a woman who could not be

Lennox's wife. In his youth, Alden had assumed that Lennox provided a haven for Johna de Rothesay and Lennox's bosom bow Robert Twicken to indulge their secret passion. Now Alden understood that Lennox, too, had been devoted to Johna. The couple had spent years constructing a web of lies so complete that society still reeled from the revelation of her long-time affair with Lennox. Of course, she remained married to the Earl of Winchester, but Winchester's crimes meant that she no longer had to endure living within his household. Protected from prison by his peerage, the House of Lords had committed Winchester to an asylum and what remained of his estate had been put into the care of the Chancery Court to support him. A divorce was, of course, out of the question, but Johna now lived openly at Lennox House.

Alden well knew that Lennox fully planned to support Johna and her daughters as if she were his widow and not his mistress, just as he'd been secretly doing for the last twenty years. Indeed, Genevieve, the youngest of Johna's daughters, was in truth Lennox's progeny and Alden's half-sister, though Genevieve's parentage had only become public knowledge when Winchester's mental instability had become a sensational affair of the Court and Lords.

"Abigail and Gloria are well provided for," Alden said briefly, naming the two middle of Johna's four daughters. Abigail was married to the Earl of Meriden, and Gloria—who had once been married to March and was the mother of Alden's nephew—was now married to Lord Clare, the Duke of Lauderdale's heir.

Lennox snorted. "We shall see. Fortunes come and go, and I would not have them ever in need. Meriden may be a wizard with pounds sterling, but he is a pariah among the bishops and relishes in it, as well as straddling the aisles whenever he's in the mood to disrupt the Lords. He's really become quite adept at muddling up even Canning's reform efforts. No one knows if the man is a Tory or a Whig, least of all me, and one day politics or war may well be his downfall. As for Gloria, she is Clare's second wife. Even if they have children, she did not produce Clare's heir and she is much younger than him. She's likely to outlive him by decades."

Alden did not need Lennox to spell out the complexities. Alden had met Gloria during the summer months when she had come to London with Clare and Eynon. She claimed to finally be happy living in seclusion with Clare and Eynon at the Scottish border. No matter what that poor woman did, she hadn't been able to escape scandal in London. Her first marriage to March was antipathetic to London's ladies, who had openly despised March. His death put her in the untenable position of being blamed for it, pitied for it and relieved by it, all in the same ten minutes, depending on the gossiper. Winchester had humiliated her again by going to Chancery Court in an attempt to force her to return to his custody after March's death, as a sick revenge in which he desired to keep Johna's daughters in misery and to gain access to Gloria's inheritance. Remembering the gawking girls and gimlet-eyed gossips who had followed Gloria about London during her visit exhausted Alden.

Alden's silence did not deter his father from further speaking. "But you know I worry most about Fiona — and Genevieve."

Genevieve — a sister! — had been a shock to Alden, and her marriage of convenience to the gambler Sir

Peter Devon had taken Alden some time to accept. The couple obviously led separate lives, but the marriage had protected Genevieve from the sort of machinations that Gloria had endured.

Alden had not yet met Johna's eldest daughter, Fiona. According to her mother, the young woman was the antithesis of domesticity and docility. Johna was rather proud of the independent bluestocking, but listening to Fiona's scholarly letters to her mother made Alden's head ache.

"With you here in London taking an active role in the estate and looking after my business interests, and with Lords not sitting until late in the autumn, I've decided it's time for me to attend to duties I've neglected for far too many years." Lennox made the announcement calmly, and Alden looked up, puzzling at his father's tack. "Genevieve is away for the summer with Peter's mother, so Johna is also without obligations. It's the perfect opportunity for us to spend some time at Eynon Castle. I hope the air and refreshing absence of gossiping harridans will be good for Johna's health and state of mind."

Alden's eyes widened. Lennox had resisted the trip to the western coast of Wales as much as possible for Alden's entire lifetime, but especially in the years since Alden had left the Castle for Eton.

As a child trapped there with March, Alden had believed Lennox wanted as little to do with the young brothers as possible. Later he'd been disabused of the notion by Lennox's frequent excursions to Eton, even if those jaunts had proved necessary for hauling March out of trouble with the headmasters. Still later, awakening to tragedy and love in all its variations, Alden wondered if Lennox avoided Eynon Castle as much as possible because it reminded him of Alden's mother, who had died in childbirth there when Alden had been just a tot. As a young man, Alden had postulated that Lennox could not be so far from London and the seat of government, he didn't like to travel or he simply had a dislike of the countryside. But during the last months, Alden had realized that for nearly two decades his father simply hadn't been willing to leave Lady Johna behind in London, alone with her husband. Lennox had spent over twenty years providing a safe haven for the woman—even longer than he'd been her lover—and closing Lennox House would have robbed her of that sanctuary.

"The chance was just waiting to be seized. Johna agrees that now is the perfect time, though she's not thrilled at the idea of traveling in a closed carriage for that distance in August." Lennox shook his head and stood. Alden followed automatically. "Johna received a letter from Fiona in this morning's post. She read it to me over breakfast. Fiona doesn't intend to return before the end of September, when she'll travel down with her Cousin Olivia's mother, Lady Arlington. I expect to be back in Town by then, but if not, she can reside at Arlington House until we return."

Alden inwardly shrugged, not seeing any reason that Fiona should not take up her customary residence at Lennox House even if Lennox and Lady Johna were in the country. He could honestly admit that his own immersion into the Lennox household had been smoother and more welcoming than Alden had expected, and all of London's matrons who oversaw the mores of the rest of society thought they knew him well. Alden had been openly surprised by his own reception in London. Lennox and Johna had welcomed Alden home without criticism. He'd allowed Alden's small household to disrupt the calm environment, and drew back to watch without comment as the household was reorganized to fit Alden's temperament and preferences. But if Lennox and Johna were not in residence—

"With our work today and Fiona's plans in place, it seems a propitious moment waiting to be seized. The servants were bringing down trunks and discussing packing before Johna had finished her tea. We'll leave tomorrow, immediately after breakfast."

Surprised by Lennox's determination to rush from the capital, Alden and his father climbed the stairs to the second floor. He turned left as the Duke turned right. Nearly two months of refurbishing after his return home was finally finished, and a comfortable apartment lay before him, occupying most of the massive wing on this floor, though some smaller suites and bedchambers remained between the grand staircase and Alden's destination. Lennox House was large enough to lose an entire orchestra inside it, but Alden's own corner overlooking a walled side garden was perfectly sized—his own private study, a large sitting room, two comfortably large bedchambers and two massive dressing rooms.

Even as he pushed open the door to the sitting room, he felt the anxious, lifelong drive to impress his father fade. He paused, took a deep breath and closed his eyes for a moment, letting the peace he knew he'd find inside the room fill him.

He entered silently, immediately looking about.

Oliver was sitting in the far corner of the large sitting room, where they had created a space to meet Oliver's needs. His desk occupied the corner itself and his music stands waited within the curved half-circle of windows that looked over the garden. The rose garden below was easily accessible from the ballroom and terrace below but hardly private, as Alden and Oliver could easily see out into it at any time. Gold and forest green striped drapes were pulled back to allow large swaths of sunlight to lighten the room. A white ceiling and cornices provided contrast to the sunny yellow walls, and sturdy oak furniture with plump green cushions sitting on a complementary paisley carpet made the room complete. Landscape paintings of their favorite haunts in Europe hung on the walls, framed in English oak. It was simple, without fuss, but in a style reminiscent of their Amsterdam home.

Despite Alden's pleasure with the space, he ignored it all and concentrated on Oliver. Blinking dazedly as he looked up at Alden, Oliver was a studied contrast to Alden's hulking size and muscular bulk. His dirty blond hair was pulled back into a tight tail, tied with a leather band. His frame was slender, and his height merely average. Obviously the man had been deep in thought as he studied the pages spread on the table. It was large enough to seat six, though only Oliver and Alden ate there upon occasion. It was more important that they had the *option* of privacy than that they actually ate alone.

Alden didn't hesitate, despite the glazed look behind Oliver's dark brown eyes, but paced to a spot just behind Oliver.

Upon examination, he was unsurprised to find the pages were music. "Beethoven," he remarked, checking the title and composer written at the top of each sheet.

"Symphony No. 9. The London Philharmonic Society commissioned it years ago, and he's finally finished it. They just received the sheet music and I dashed over to insist on a copy of the oboe instrumental. You remember it was performed in pieces in Austria just before we left Europe? He's included a choral component, and the Philharmonic Society is in a dither over who will sing it."

Alden rested his thick hands on Oliver's shoulders and rubbed gently, listening to the enthusiastic words. He suppressed an urge to untie Oliver's hair and run his hands down its length, even as he admired his lover's full lips. They trembled, drawing Alden's attention even more to Oliver's generous mouth. Oliver was focused on his music just now, so his eyes were glazed as he twisted to look up at Alden. Oliver's abstracted look always fascinated Alden, no matter the cause. Alden was reminded of the way Oliver looked when Oliver's mind was on his lover instead of his music, and it pleased Alden that he fascinated Oliver as much as music did.

At one time when they'd been young, Alden had been threatened by Oliver's intensity, jealous of any occupation that took Oliver away from Alden's company. They'd coped with the issue, but not truly conquered it until it had come to a breaking point early on in Amsterdam. Oliver had discovered the large population of musicians that lived and congregated there and had enthusiastically thrown himself into a community of people who welcomed him like no one in England ever had. But Oliver hadn't just indulged shamelessly in music and like-minded musicians while in Amsterdam. He'd also invited Alden into his world and made him welcome at his side, a dramatic change from their cautious, secret life together in England.

Even though they'd relocated to London, Alden could never return to those days of secrecy, when he'd been forced to conceal every hint of the depth of his association with Oliver, on the pretext that someone might suspect their affection. In any event, March could never harm or even threaten Oliver—never again. And their relationship was an open secret to upper crust London, though it would have been a graceless breach of etiquette to discuss it openly in any drawing room or at a ball.

He brushed his palm over Oliver's ear. "Play for me," he invited.

Oliver turned from the sheets and met Alden's gaze. In Amsterdam, Oliver had rarely been alone in his music. He'd been surrounded by others just as passionate about their art as Oliver was. Watching Oliver express his emotions in song had been an experience to be endured in public as Alden perfected his ability to conceal his true reaction under the mask of a public façade.

Here, in London, Alden reveled privately in Oliver's passion. Oliver did not hold court in the drawing room at Lennox House, at least not yet. He went to the Philharmonic Society frequently, but he practiced at home, here. Alone.

Alden stepped back and drew an armchair from where it sat in a grouping before the fireplace. He set it down six feet from Oliver and settled into it while Oliver shifted through the pages and arranged them, first on his desk then on the long music stand that waited for him. He would position himself to the side to benefit from the sunlight on the music sheets, where Alden could examine his profile rather than his face, but the view was more than satisfactory. Oliver's dark eyes twinkled sharply in the brightness, and Alden smiled. Oliver wanted to play, to perform the piece. He was excited. His face was slightly flushed, and his high cheekbones pointed to his slender nose that flared when he breathed deeply. Oliver arched his eyebrows as he wet the double reed in the instrument and played a few brief scales.

"Father is taking Johna to Eynon Castle. They leave in the morning."

The words came out abruptly, as they always seemed to do when Alden spoke more than a few of them at a time. Oliver paused in his warm-up and glanced at him with a smile flirting at his lips before returning his gaze to the music before him. "I know," Oliver admitted. "It seemed quite clear from the maids, menservants and footmen scurrying about, but I asked His Grace's valet, to be certain." Oliver moved his long, slender fingers lovingly over the instrument. As if transfixed, Alden followed the play over the keys as Oliver studied the music and silently prepared.

"We will be alone here," Alden teased, semi-seriously, when Oliver lowered the oboe again.

Oliver's gaze traveled from Alden's cheeks down his torso, over his waistline and to his knees. Blessing Alden with a heated look, Oliver slowly drawled out his answer, "Johna's company is pleasant, even when in a fit of the blue-devils. Still, time alone with you is something to treasure these days. The only thing that could possibly improve upon the temporary privacy would be the surprise arrival of our own fated female."

Alden watched Oliver, lust rising in him at Oliver's suggestive words. They had no intention of living life without each other, but the addition of a loving woman would fulfill a dream they both had had independently and together since they were boys. Each had experimented with women when they'd been young. A rite of passage among their class, Oliver and Alden had first visited the Incognitas at

Oxford together. Both enjoyed the physical experience, though they'd never had a woman who aroused them as they did each other. In Amsterdam, they had found a bold, brassy lady who wanted to experiment with them at the same time. It had been interesting in its novelty, but somewhat awkward for both Oliver and Alden, who'd been honestly more attracted to each other than to the female between them. When discussing it afterward, Oliver had voiced a sentiment with which Alden wholeheartedly agreed. It had been awkward because they didn't know the lady's heart. She'd simply been a creature of skin and sensory sensations between them, outside the bond Oliver and Alden had established. They'd decided to save the experience for the partner they both craved.

Oliver settled his lips around the slim double reeds and tightened his embouchure, sucking in his cheeks as he inhaled. Alden relaxed, determined to enjoy the performance before he made any concerted effort to distract Oliver. They had nearly two hours before it would be time to dress for dinner.

Alden lasted until the end of the first movement, his eyes on the passion and intensity in Oliver's face the entire time. The music was lovely, but watching Oliver play roused every one of Alden's passionate and possessive instincts. At first, the music new, Oliver was tentative, but as Oliver absorbed the melody, the instrument transformed into an extension of Oliver's heart. As Oliver finished the last sheet and lowered the instrument to rest on the desk, Alden launched himself from the chair. Oliver, gathering the music, glanced up in surprise, so Alden captured Oliver's cheek in his hand and tilted up his face.

Oliver was a year or so older, but Alden was taller, bulkier and decidedly stronger. "I need you, love,"

Alden rasped, sliding his free hand down Oliver's torso and firmly clasping his hip. Alden's lodged his thumb into the wedge between Oliver's groin and thigh, a position that was guaranteed to awaken Oliver's interest, even through his trousers.

Oliver didn't hesitate. He cupped Alden's cheek in return, stepped forward against Alden's chest and lifted his lips to Alden's.

They were shirtless and shoeless when they stumbled into Alden's bedchamber. "Describe her to me," Alden whispered. He bit Oliver's earlobe, hard, then sucked on it for a moment before asking a second question to incite him further. "Will she look like me?"

Oliver moaned. "Smaller than you, but not a tiny thing," he grunted dryly in reply, fondling Alden's swollen cock through his trousers. Alden matched Oliver's moan with his own. "Small enough that she'll blow your mind when you fuck her, tall enough for me to look her in the eyes when we dance." Obedient to the jerking of Alden's cock, Oliver began to unbutton Alden's trousers, all the while expertly stroking the straining organ with the pads of his fingers and his short nails. "What about you?" Oliver taunted back. "What will she be like? Blonde hair, black hair, ginger?"

Alden closed his eyes and shuddered, even as Oliver drew Alden's cock from the placket of his pants. "If she's any smaller than your tight ass, I'll never fit." He growled against Oliver's ear as Oliver pumped Alden's stiff arousal between them and against Oliver's own navel. "Her hair could be green," he mumbled, "as long as she's wet when she's down on her knees." As if in demonstration, Alden untied the leather band in Oliver's hair, dropped it to the floor and slowly gathered Oliver's tawny mane in his fist and tugged him down. "You?"

"No preference, not as long as she sasses you," Oliver agreed with a low laugh, taking Alden's trousers to the floor as he knelt.

"She sasses me, she'll end up just like this, with her mouth stretched wide." Alden's voice was gruff as he answered, because he was watching Oliver unbutton his own pants and draw out his own impressive erection. Oliver's cock was beautiful, but so very different than Alden's. It was pale and flushed to cherry red as Oliver approached a climax, whereas Alden's golden flesh darkened as it swelled. Oliver's long cock curved, making it perfect for fucking Alden into sensory overload and for shooting his semen onto Oliver's stomach while Alden watched. Now, Oliver took it in one hand and stroked it with his palm, until Alden grunted and pressed the tip of his heavy, thick appendage to Oliver's mouth.

To Alden's satisfaction, Oliver lapped his lower lip in anticipation before opening his mouth just enough for Alden to ratchet forward and past Oliver's warm lips. Alden loved the feel of the pink tissue scraping over his genitals, and today was no different.

Eager and generous, Oliver lapped eagerly then sucked Alden deep inside, his lips stretched around Alden's girth. Oliver brushed the inside of Alden's thigh with his knuckles, and a shiver of anticipation rippled up his spine. Just as Alden needed, Oliver cupped his testicles in one hand, pulled on them gently then released them to drag his fingernails over Alden's scrotum.

Another fissure of delightful sensation ran up Alden's spine. He had no intention of ejaculating in Oliver's mouth, though, especially not so soon. Alden jerked away, pleasure doubling at Oliver's gasp of frustration. Instead, he drew the man up and fisted Oliver's cock firmly in his own huge palm, pumping it into the base of brown curls just below his own erection so that the tip of Oliver's penis pressed rhythmically into the pad of flesh between Alden's balls and cock. Oliver was no small man when fully erect, but Alden's hands were massive and gripped him nearly from tip to root.

Oliver's eyes glazed and he gripped Alden's shoulders. "If her mouth is any smaller than mine, she'll never be able to take you," Oliver taunted Alden, palming Alden's nipples. "She'll have an easier time with my cock."

Alden chuckled huskily. "Make me your promise," he demanded, knowing very well that Oliver craved and delighted in Alden's possessiveness. It was a reality any woman in their lives would have to cope with as well, because Alden didn't think he could share Oliver with anyone but someone he wanted as desperately as he did Oliver. Some days he wasn't certain he would be able to share Oliver with anyone at all, no matter how perfect she was or how much Alden wanted her.

Oliver's lips were red and swollen from having Alden's cock shoved between them, and his chest heaved in anticipation of Alden's touch. Alden had every intention of touching more intimately, though he now ran his hands over Oliver's arms and cupped Oliver's lower jaw in his palms as he waited. It wouldn't be long before Oliver was on Alden's bed and the backs of Oliver's legs pushed against Alden's chest. Alden wanted his cock settled firmly inside Oliver's rear. Anticipation burned in Alden's mind. Once he started to fuck Oliver, Alden would be free to caress Oliver's skin from chest to knees, while Oliver gripped Alden's hips.

Oliver's eyes sharpened and his body tightened, his cock prodding at the juncture of Alden's thighs in his eagerness. "You're not even going to let me have *her* without your permission?" he questioned incredulously.

A surge of arousal pulsed in Alden's cock as he envisioned watching Oliver use his body to love a wanton female beneath him. He rubbed his stiffness against Oliver's abdomen. "No, I'm not," Alden answered, determination forming inside him at Oliver's response. "Promise me."

Oliver groaned and took his revenge by pinching Alden's nipples simultaneously. Sensation streaked through him, followed by fire, then an outraged howl as he realized Oliver had seriously not considered this angle of permanently sharing a woman. He tightened his hold on Oliver's jaw for a moment then spun the man around and pushed him face-first over the side of the bed. The thought of being excluded as the man he loved made love to another filled Alden with aggravated uneasiness.

He had wanted to see Oliver's face as he came, but a little reinforcement would be good for Alden's soul — and for Oliver's. "Who fucking owns your cock?" Alden pressed his palm to the base of Oliver's neck, holding him to the bed. He reached out with his spare hand and grabbed a jar of the specially made cream both men kept conveniently located beside their beds, in their dressing rooms and in various drawers throughout their apartment. He pushed off the lid, dipped two fingers inside, and fisted his cock, smearing the cream over his skin. He reached in for a second dip with his fingers and pushed them confidently against the tight ring of Oliver's ass.

The faint, familiar fragrance of the cream signaled to Alden's body that satisfaction was imminent. It was one of the few luxuries they'd had imported from their favorite London apothecary to Amsterdam, and that gentleman had been delighted when Oliver had appeared personally in his shop upon their return. It had begun as a hasty alternative to the traditional lard older boys at Eton had passed down to Oliver, but both had found the cream tinted with a mild lavender base highly preferable to animal fat. Oliver's finely tuned senses responded to the scent, and Alden had grasped the opportunity to not feel as if he were a rutting barnyard animal. Years later, the apothecary had added a small amount of bay leaf and oak moss to enhance the aroma.

The shopkeeper had once added ginger as an experiment, and the effect on Oliver had been so pronounced and dramatic that Alden still kept that particular jar in his dressing room for the occasional, memorable use. If Oliver didn't relent soon, Alden would be happy to retrieve it and use it now.

As though he'd heard Alden's stray thought, Oliver lifted and relaxed his tight ring, welcoming Alden's thrusting fingers. The groan that Oliver emitted into the pillows reminded Alden of his own growing needs. Alden withdrew his hand.

"Please," Oliver gasped.

"Promise," Alden grunted, guiding his cock to Oliver's waiting ass. He kept his one palm solidly at the top of Oliver's back, holding his upper body to the bed.

"I promise not to use my dick unless you permit it." Oliver gasped as Alden tucked the head of his penis against the waiting muscle. "Now, please. Please."

Alden thrust forward, thankful that Oliver had offered little-to-no resistance. Like Oliver, he wanted a woman's soft curves to rest against. He wanted to caress silken skin, so different from Oliver's satin hair and hard muscles. He needed the fragrant smell of a woman to forget old wrongs. He needed the sound of a melodious voice to contrast with his deep tones and Oliver's baritone. He desired to see the sensual form of a woman stretching in Oliver's arms, her cries of pleasure flooding the room as she begged Alden to taste her and fuck her. He desired the tangy taste of a woman on his tongue while he thrust into her and Oliver came in her mouth.

Instead, Oliver's hands and mouth were empty as he begged for Alden to bring him the same bliss Alden was finding in his body. Alden slid a hand around him and fisted Oliver's cock, jerking Oliver's erection with practiced skill.

"We will find her, someday," Alden promised, rolling his hips to stimulate the place in Oliver's rear that was guaranteed to send Oliver over the edge into orgasm.

Alden's lover reacted just as he expected. Oliver grunted, and cream spilled over Alden's fingers and onto the bedclothes. The hot liquid, evidence of Oliver's response to Alden's dominance was exactly the reassurance that Alden needed. He thrust one final time into Oliver and erupted.

"I love you," Oliver said, the words raw with emotion.

Alden threw himself onto the bed beside Oliver and luxuriated in the sensation of Oliver stroking his chest and abdomen. Alden wiped his fingers on the sheet and drew Oliver's head against his shoulder, then ran his hands down Oliver's body. A long minute of silence passed, then in the quiet room, Alden whispered in reply, "I love you, too. Always."

Chapter Two

Fiona shifted restlessly in the carriage. The busy traffic, noise and noxious aromas associated with the roads into London had already subsided into the restrained, elegant avenues of Mayfair. The sidewalks were mostly deserted in the late evening, though a few gentlemen strolled in the streets, on their way to private dinners and clubs and other masculine entertainments.

Just as gentlemen strolled and ladies glided, so their carriages rolled along slowly, the axles quiet and well-greased. Their coachmen, footmen and maids moved smoothly and silently, at least in public. Young ladies were languid and graceful, elegant in how they disposed themselves in drawing rooms and discreet as they spoke quietly or giggled behind their fans. Boys and girls and nurses might hurry about on their way to Hyde Park, and occasionally a drawling gentleman had been known to rush, but these exceptions were few and far between.

Indoctrinated to the highest standards, Fiona's temporary coachman had slowed to a snail's pace when they'd entered the macadamized and brick-laid streets of Mayfair. Fiona thought resentfully of her maid, riding on top beside him, and sighed at her own inexplicable jealousy. Lucy might be catching the last rays of the sun, but she was also breathing in the sooty, foul air that permeated London, even in the warm summer.

The slow pace was yet another reason that Fiona often felt out of place among the *cognoscenti*. She had never glided properly.

Of course she tried. She'd watched carefully and studied Abigail, Gloria and even Genevieve as they'd taken lessons from governesses and their mother. But even with that intensive training, Fiona simply couldn't remember to glide. Invariably her mind drifted away from the manner in which she walked and she reverted to her customary *brisk* stride. Even worse, when she was worried or angry, Fiona *bustled*.

Fiona's walk was just one of the innumerable ways that made her different from the girls and women who populated London's ballrooms. She'd never flirted with a man under the chandeliers, and her dancing partners were primarily limited to those men with whom she'd established a family friendship. She'd never been asked to waltz by anyone with a personal interest in her.

It was a very lonely existence and a lesson she'd learned over the bitter passing of the years. When her twenty-fourth birthday had come and gone with no change in her life, Fiona had accepted her stature as ape leader and archetypical bluestocking spinster. Publicly, she'd meekly adjusted from wearing pastels and always appearing with her mother to wearing darker hues that better suited her complexion. She'd begun attending events beyond her mother's interests, too. Indeed, when one looked beyond the trite, repetitive script of balls and soirees, London was full of rich culture — lectures, musicales, museums, gallery events, gardens, the theater, the philharmonic, libraries, diplomatic receptions and even church chorales.

A second, small sigh escaped as Fiona watched a well-dressed couple step out of their front door, their black town carriage waiting to whisk them off to some dinner party. The majority of the *ton* may have deserted the stifling air of London until the end of summer, but a few gentlemen remained, and occasionally their lovers — spouses or not — stayed to keep company. Figures essential to government and business couldn't completely abandon London for two months, even if Parliament was in recess. These few bastions of the nobility and merchant classes were still stepping beyond their front doors and gathering to play society's games.

Fiona played a game, too, just not the one her contemporaries pursued. Gradually, over the last two years, she had mostly abandoned the familiar ballrooms lit by chandeliers, the dark card rooms where fortunes were gambled and won, and even the sunlit afternoons gossiping in Hyde Park. They'd been tolerable when her sisters had been her company, but now they were simply a demonstration that Fiona did not belong. She no longer walked through a crowded foyer with hope that she'd meet someone who could appreciate her. These days, Fiona kept up the appearance of social entertainments purely to please her mother and to provide a cover for her actual nighttime activities. Even in such a limited scope, the more time she spent in such venues, the lonelier she felt.

Relieved that it was too late to attend any evening affair, Fiona pondered her upcoming agenda. She would send a note around to Canning House directly, but needed to settle into her rooms before presenting herself personally on Canning's doorstep. Unless they were hosting an evening event, the Cannings would be out anyway, and she'd be stuck scrawling a note for Young Canning or his father. She'd do better to sleep tonight, so she was prepared for tomorrow evening.

The gloom sank into the carriage, but Lady Olivia and Lord Anthony Morewell's driver kept the horses plodding on, turning into Grosvenor Square. At last the carriage rounded the final corner of the square, where Fiona had spent so much of her life. They passed the mansion once known as Winchester House, standing empty and dark. The Earl of Meriden owned the great house now. He was her brother-in-law through his marriage to Fiona's sister, Abigail, and Fiona's natural nephew. Fiona's mother had had a short *affaire* with Meriden's grandfather twenty-seven years earlier that had resulted in Fiona's birth. Meriden was tenanting it out for the Little Season to a prominent laird and his wife, set to arrive soon from Scotland, and Fiona sincerely hoped the mansion was more of a home to that family than it had been to Fiona.

Lennox House was on the far corner, three doors away. Fiona's mother and the Duke of Lennox would be inside.

Two elusive men from Amsterdam were probably also in residence. They had finally obeyed Lennox's summons to return to London earlier in the summer. Fiona had heard of them endlessly over the last few years, since her mother's long-time affair with Lennox had become public knowledge. Years ago, of course, Fiona had worked out who owned that house a few gates past her own via the mews, and Winchester's library had identified the key players in the drama she'd witnessed as a girl—Lord March, eldest son and heir to the Duke of Lennox, and Lord Alden Swenson, his second son. Early on, she'd used a dictionary and a Bible to try to define the word *sodomite* but she'd only successfully deciphered it years later, after Abigail and Gloria had clarified the mechanics involved in the marriage bed. The identity of Oliver, the man beaten senseless by March, had remained a mystery until Fiona's cousin Olivia—Libby—had married Lord Anthony Morewell, a younger son of the Duke of Weymouth. Lord Anthony was the third son. Weymouth's heir was Morpeth and his second son was Lord Oliver Morewell, living in Amsterdam apart from his family

Quite when she'd put together the entire mystery was unclear even to her, but she'd known for some time that Alden Swenson and Oliver Morewell were lovers.

The carriage stopped, and Fiona listened to the familiar sounds of the coachman jumping down and helping down the maid. The front door was standing open and the driver was putting down the step. Fiona hoped feverishly for a cool bath and a quiet night in her room before the next night's work. No doubt she'd formally meet the other two tomorrow, unless all four residents of the house decamped from the dining room to greet her.

A niggle of disquiet struck Fiona as she mounted the steps and found Carrington himself holding open the door. At this time of evening, Carrington ought to be serving dinner and not at the door. Lennox and Johna never deviated from dinner, served at promptly half past seven, and it was nearly eight o'clock.

Still, the butler's eyes were sparkling with welcome and he creased his lips into a smile. London butlers could be fearsome, rigid creatures and Carrington was one of the prime examples of the species, but he had always made an exception for Johna and her daughters. Carrington smiled at them all, even before he bowed. At times, he'd even been known to *beam*.

"I know you weren't expecting me, Carrington," Fiona rushed to explain. "I wrote only days ago and said it would be next month, so I do hope my rooms can be opened and aired this evening. Where is Mother?"

Carrington's welcoming expression faded and concern colored his answer. "I've already sent the maids up to your rooms, my lady, but I regret to say that Lady Johna and His Grace are not in residence. Your mother wrote to you before she departed this morning with His Grace, and we posted the missive today, but it appears you will not receive it until it's sent back down from Northumberland."

Fiona's mouth opened in surprise, but she hastily covered it with a question. "Where on earth have they gone?" she asked, incredulous. Her mother hadn't left London in years, except once earlier in the year with Lennox, when Fiona's sister Gloria and her infant son Eynon had been in danger.

"Eynon Castle, miss. They expect to be gone through the third week of September. I'm sure His Grace would have remained in town had they known. It's unfortunate she didn't have warning that you were coming—"

"Oh, no, they need to be able to have a holiday," Fiona interrupted hurriedly, thinking rapidly. "I suppose there's no harm done. I am hardly in my first Season."

Carrington hesitated. Fiona wondered at his reaction, but a voice from the stairs distracted her. Looking up, Fiona realized why the butler was so indecisive.

"Carrington, don't keep the poor lady standing in the hall," the man chided, descending the last step and approaching them.

Even without an introduction, Fiona knew him immediately. Lord Oliver had the same tawny hair color and face as Anthony, with a clean, firm chin where Anthony cultivated a goatee and mustache. He was, Fiona thought, a few inches shorter and smiled a great deal more easily than his brothers.

She blinked and instinctively began to curtsy, but he reached forward with his hand and waved her off. "No, no. Not to me. You must be Fiona. I am Oliver, and as our loved ones are connected in so many layers I can't even remember them all, it's almost a crime to wait for an introduction. Welcome home, my dear."

With that flourish of familiarity, Oliver lifted Fiona's gloved fingers and squeezed them, then expertly took her arm and drew her to his side.

Dazed by his elegant manners, Fiona forgot what she'd been saying, and absorbed the flurry of instructions Oliver listed instead, blinking as Oliver switched between addressing the butler and providing asides to Fiona. "Carrington, send up a maid to help her unpack and settle. The poor girl out on the front steps with the footmen looks positively exhausted. Traveling is so tiresome for the servants too, no? And they must all be hungry. We were going to dine upstairs but perhaps the family dining parlor would be a better choice. I can't see setting out the formal dining room for three. Send someone up to warn Alden of the change in plans, would you? He's hiding in his office again, waiting for dinner to be taken up, you know. Fiona, I assume you will want to wash up. There's no need for you to change for dinner at this hour and just with our quiet company, my dear. I'm sure you'll want a bath just as soon as your hunger is satisfied. Carrington, if you could arrange for washing water immediately, she can bathe once her rooms are prepared."

This Morewell, Fiona considered, had more vibrancy and energy than the other brothers combined. Morpeth, the eldest, was grave and traditional, a staid and somewhat righteous man who served as an undersecretary at the Foreign Office. Fiona had spent countless hours with Anthony and weeks in Anthony's home, and knew him to be a quiet, dutiful man. Nevertheless, Anthony had defied his family, abandoned the family business of government diplomacy and moved his beloved Libby to Northumberland for Libby's sake. He credited Oliver for demonstrating the courage that Anthony had required to refuse his father's plans to keep Anthony in London, a place Libby could not bear to live for more than a few days at a time. Martin, the youngest son, had only spent a few years working his way up in the Foreign Office, but Fiona knew him well as a reserved, cautious man, unlike the Corinthians, rakehells and sharps of his age but perfect for his eventual roles in the embassies of Europe.

Oliver, while perfectly placed geographically for the last several years, had never been conscripted into serving in the Foreign Office, despite his brothers' careers and his father's history as Foreign Office Secretary. He also presented the perfect hospitable foil against interrogation. His spate of chatter lasted the entire time Oliver shepherded her up the stairs and to her door. Fiona had good reason to wonder if he secretly was a spy, and all the family drama simply a cover.

Fiona knew she should speak, saw the door looming ahead, felt the warmth of Oliver's hand on her arm through the gown and experienced the oddest sensation she'd ever known. A shudder slid up her body from the base of her spine to her head.

Perhaps she had pushed the coachman, and thus herself, entirely too hard.

"I am grateful, but there was no need to change your plans. Mother and His Grace would already have dined so I was expecting a dinner tray in my room," she began, but Oliver shook his head and stopped, turning her to face him and examining her from the hems of her skirt to the crown of her hair under a decorous, dark purple bonnet. Fiona knew exactly what he would see. She was not fashionable or glamorous or beautiful, but her attire was high quality and well-tailored with simple lines, made in London of high-quality textiles. He would find nothing to criticize, even if she wasn't quite accustomed to the open examination of her person.

"Now, now. You've been with my brother and his wife. You can imagine I want to hear all about my nephews?" Oliver asked directly.

Fiona felt a fissure of guilt. Oliver had never met his nephews, but she was not surprised that he asked after her firsthand experiences. He'd certainly never hear them from his family. The Duke of Weymouth and Morpeth had made their disapproval of Oliver exceptionally clear within the family and forbidden him from Weymouth House and all the country properties. He was not to be welcomed back without a white flag of surrender and a vow of filial obedience.

Despite this avowal, Anthony had maintained a correspondence with Oliver for some years and had only recently named his newborn son after Oliver.

"Or do you disapprove of me as well?" Oliver asked directly.

Fiona's eyes flew wide. She shook her head abruptly. "No, that's not what I meant—"

"Then come down for dinner," he said firmly.

"For dinner," she agreed, reluctance coloring her voice. "But after, I think I should remove to Grillions. I have no chaperone here."

Oliver stared at her, and Fiona felt a nervous flutter in her stomach. She couldn't understand it, but panic began to erupt, and she opened her mouth to insist.

"You'd have no chaperone at Grillions either, but we can discuss it at dinner," Oliver compromised. "And here's your maid."

A little chambermaid—was it Carrington's granddaughter?—scurried along the corridor, and Fiona greeted her gratefully, pulling away from Oliver's grip. He began to follow her into the suite's sitting room, but Fiona stopped through the doorway and pointedly shut the panel in his face.

She sensed Oliver Morewell was more of a formidable force of nature than his family understood. Even as unsusceptible as Fiona was to men and as much as she understood Oliver's commitment to Alden, Fiona had felt a curious tingle of awareness where they had touched. Despite the fact that Fiona did not attract attention from men, Oliver had taken her arm in his and claimed the spot beside her eagerly, without any sort of reserve. Fiona had nearly jumped from the energy that seemed to pulse from the

innocuous back of his forearm where her hand had
rested.

Of course, she might just have been tired from the
long journey and off balance at the discovery that her
mother was gone.

Fiona crossed the hall between the bottom of the
stairs and the drawing room at five minutes after
eight, determined to forget any curious anomalies about
Oliver she'd imagined. Carrington was haunting the
front hall, obviously waiting for them to exchange at
least the barest of greetings before serving the meal, so
she waited for him to open the door to the drawing
room and bustled forward with her chin nobly high.

Bustled. Halting abruptly, she slowed and adjusted
her steps just as she entered the room.

Oliver, who had been lounging negligently against a
bureau on the side wall, set down his wine glass and
immediately stepped forward to greet her. As he did,
a second man rose from a chair in the center of the
room. Fiona saw him from her peripheral vision but
the sight was enough. She instinctively recoiled, then
realized her mistake immediately. In recompense,
Fiona turned to face him directly and forced a smile to
her lips, making every effort not to stare.

His identity was without question. As her sisters had
told her, Lord Alden Swenson might have been a
larger twin of March at a healthier, sober point in time.
He was simply gigantic, perhaps the largest man
outside of a circus that Fiona had ever seen. He
towered over his surroundings as he approached her,
his movements restrained despite his broad shoulders
and muscular, proportionate hips. His ebony hair was
impossibly darker than Fiona's black mane, but was
sleeked back and barely long enough to capture at the
nape of his neck in a short, deep burgundy ribbon that

matched his evening coat. The hue was rich and vibrant without being foppishly garish, and under the lamps of the drawing room, it complemented the ivory inexpressibles and waistcoat he wore beneath it.

Breeches? For a dinner party of three?

Fiona had to clamp her teeth down on the inside of her lip to conceal her reaction to the sight of the man's thigh and calf muscles on display before her in the old-fashioned garments. Even covered by the tight fabric, those muscles were simply the most magnificent ones she'd ever seen, an improvement upon the nude, sculpted masculine thighs she'd studied in museum and privately collected statues. No gentleman wore breeches and hose if he could help it, except to Court and Almacks, and now Fiona understood why. Trousers were perfectly acceptable evening attire because they prevented ladies from staring, from ballroom accidents —

"Ah, you've noticed Alden," Oliver broke into her thoughts, unperturbed and smiling. "Lady Fiona, Lord Alden Swenson. Alden, Lady Fiona de Rothesay. Now then, you've met, and don't curtsy, Fiona. That's a dear girl," Oliver breezed through the introductions, coming up just behind and to the side of Fiona as Alden Swenson stopped before her.

Alden's hazel eyes glinted in the light as he took in Fiona from her hems to her hair. It was a comprehensive look, and entirely too similar to the examination Oliver had conducted. "A pleasure," he said briefly, the deep drawl transforming the familiar word into some forbidden, sensual phrase.

He stepped closer and Fiona had to stiffen her knees to prevent her muscles from jumping away. Indeed, even the rigid joints and muscles would not have been sufficient to hold her still, except that Oliver was directly behind her.

At least Oliver was attired much more sensibly in black trousers and an elegant black jacket with a simple ivory waistcoat and snowy white shirt.

The man in front of her wore a white shirt as well, but it was concealed by a complicated cravat that Fiona thought was the Mathematical, anchored with a pin featuring a deep garnet. "Isn't that color perfect for him?" Oliver asked, eyeing Alden as appreciatively as she just had, but with a great deal more affection.

In her surprise, Fiona forgot to speak, so Alden grasped her fingers in his and lifted them high. The old-fashioned kiss to the back of her hand turned her silence into an open-mouthed gape as Fiona stared up into his face.

Bemusement covered his. "Yes, I'm overdressed," he agreed simply and without explanation, then looked past her shoulder to Oliver.

Fiona began to twist away to look at Oliver as well, but just then Carrington knocked on the door.

Fiona quickly found herself out-maneuvered. Before she could quite work out how they'd proceed, she found both her arms captured, with Alden on her right side and Oliver on her left.

If Oliver's presence at her side had been disconcerting, the pair of them together was nerve-wracking. She moved proudly, but her hands and chin trembled wildly. Dressed in a summer gown that left her collarbone and lower arms bare, Fiona experienced an awkward vulnerability and awareness. She wasn't meant to feel so intimately the touch of these hands on her arms, the scrape of their fingers against her skin. They loved each other and could see her as no more than a sister or cousin. Panic gripped her stomach when Alden rubbed his oversized fingers against her skin, offering comfort. Her breath caught, but Oliver settled her hand more comfortably on his forearm and kept it there by the simple expedient of clamping his second hand over the backs of her fingers.

Thankfully the family dining parlor was only a quick walk down the long corridor that separated the front of the house from the back. The table had been shortened as much as possible, but Fiona was still surprised when the men escorted her to the seat at the foot of the table. Alden held out the chair, and Fiona sat, confusion burgeoning.

Oliver gave her a half-smile and took the chair on her left, as Alden seated himself at her right. Fiona shivered as Alden's gaze rested on her face, then lower, and she quickly turned to Oliver. Her sisters hadn't mentioned any distracting tendency of Lennox's younger son to stare at his guests.

"So you've just come from Anthony and Olivia, who I am most anxious to visit, though it seems our reunion must be delayed until His Grace returns to London. The babies are thriving and Olivia is recovering well, yes?"

Fiona drew a quick breath. She had planned to bring up her intent to hire a room at Grillion's Hotel, but the eagerness in Oliver's voice reminded her of how generous the Morewells had been to share their two small boys with Fiona. She recalled how much Libby and Anthony grieved the rift between Oliver and his family.

"Anthony and Olivia—separately—asked me to repeat their invitation to you personally. They'd like for you and Lord Alden to make the acquaintance of little Benjamin Oliver."

Oliver beamed, an unconscious expression so reminiscent of Anthony and Libby's eldest son, Christopher, that Fiona caught her breath and quickly looked down at her plate, grateful when a footman stepped close to serve her.

The meal passed quickly, primarily because Oliver had a stream of questions for Fiona about his brother, Libby, the Northumberland estate in Gallowhill that Libby had inherited from her father, his two nephews and all related concerns. Oliver's rapid-fire enthusiasm was almost feverish and rather disconcerting, but after a few moments, Fiona realized that she was Oliver's sole source of information aside from Anthony's own letters. Northumberland was hardly teeming with friends and family to provide updates.

Indeed, he engaged her so thoroughly that it took Fiona half the meal to notice that Alden's contributions to the conversation were limited to single word responses. She snuck a glance at him while Oliver told a story about Libby shopping in Antwerp when she and Anthony had been on their wedding trip. Oliver had apparently visited with them there.

Fiona forgot to laugh at the proper point, however, because when she glanced at Alden, she discovered that he was examining her as well—and not just her face.

No man had ever ogled Fiona de Rothesay.

A slow flush rose in her cheeks and down her neck, but Alden didn't appear in the least bit disturbed by her reaction, or by Oliver's amused chuckle.

Fiona drew a sharp breath. "I do think I should remove to Grillion's Hotel tonight—"

"No," Alden objected immediately.

At a loss to understand that forceful negative, Fiona gaped at him before Oliver cut into the second of silence, preventing any outraged response.

"It's already very late, and your rooms are prepared by now. Even your maid is off to bed for the night after the exhausting trip down from Gallowhill," Oliver offered hastily. "And I meant to ask. When would be a good time to visit? Obviously we'd need to return to London before the snows start, but Lady Johna would like me to be in London for the Little Season. She's said she likes having an escort and Lennox is often unavailable in the evenings when Parliament is meeting. Early October may be our only opportunity until spring. Anthony tells me that Libby should not travel, and would not wish to leave the lads, in any event."

Fiona's good manners forced her to turn back to Oliver and answer his question, and quite before she knew it, Carrington was carrying away the custard bowls and cream. Beside her, Alden had already risen. As soon as she stood, Alden was there waiting and pulled her arm inside his.

Oddly enough, though, Fiona felt dwarfed by Alden's immense size and his grasp on her arm was firm and unbreakable, she remained calm. He exuded an eerie serenity, as if being within his grasp was where she would be safest. It was nonsense, of course. Fiona had caught him openly examining her collarbone and bodice, despite Oliver's presence, his amused observation and any public belief of Alden's preferences, so she should have been wary. But Fiona could not bring herself to heap suspicion on Alden's head.

Perhaps, she thought, it wasn't that he was angelic, but that he was so very *different* from his elder brother.

She'd never have allowed that cretin, March, the liberty of escorting her anywhere, even in this house, and she'd had to assiduously avoid him during the tenure of March's marriage to Gloria. If March had, for some incomprehensible reason, had the audacity to stare at Fiona's bosom, she'd have boxed his ears and poured his bourbon over his drunken head.

Oliver led the way back to the drawing room, chattering, and though Fiona now recognized Oliver's diversionary tactic, she could hardly take issue with it, especially once Oliver immediately asked that the teacart be delivered.

He pounced as soon as Carrington withdrew and the three were alone in the room. "You must stay. It won't do to be leaving here and heading for a hotel — not this time of night. If we call for a hack, the neighboring houses will take notice, and if a Lennox carriage pulls up at Grillion's, all of London will know. Either way, all sorts of tongues will be wagging in Albemarle Street. No one of importance in London will think twice about you staying here with us. They know all about us — or at least think they do."

Oliver's earnest request surprised her, but she sat back on the chaise and considered the dilemma. She certainly had no wish to cause them grief or give the population of London the idea that she disapproved of Oliver and Alden. Alden, oddly enough, avoided her eyes when she glanced in his direction. "I wouldn't want to disrupt the household, and it seems plain to me that you both have been expecting to be alone here."

"Nonsense, Fiona," Oliver declaimed. "If we truly *needed* the time alone, we'd withdraw to our villa in Merton and leave you here with the staff. We bought it just for that purpose, after all, years ago, even before we went to Amsterdam."

"Why *did* you come down unexpectedly?" Alden's simply voiced, deep question startled Fiona. It had been years since anyone other than Abigail or Gloria had questioned her so directly. Abigail had warned Meriden not to hem her into his expectations, and Anthony knew her secrets. She glared at Alden, trying to ignore the demand in his eyes and his body and in the lines of his face.

Her heart beat faster at the intentness in his gaze. He'd said so little that this question seemed *important*, as if she couldn't simply ignore it—as if he had thought of nothing else all evening. She opened her mouth to deliver the prepared answer she intended to use with the gossips, but suddenly a thin ribbon of guilt erupted in her mind, as if it would be obvious that the words on her tongue would be at best a roundaboutation. She caught herself beginning to blush and immediately stiffened.

Fiona knew her spine was strictly and properly straight, but she couldn't help but lift her chin, just an additional inch. The sparkle in Oliver's eye as he caught hers spoke loudly enough. He'd seen her chin rise, and Alden had, too.

Where Oliver's eyes sparkled at her reaction, Alden's narrowed. Fiona noticed that he didn't stand and tower over her or exert any physical pressure at all. The single-minded focus on his face, coupled with Oliver's silence, was clear enough.

Awkwardness rattled through the room, until Fiona finally cleared her throat and answered civilly enough, "Olivia, Anthony and Aunt Betsy had all asked me to stay, and I agreed. Hence, I wrote to Mother and Anthony posted the letter. But Olivia had some rather urgent commissions — shopping for her and the baby, you understand — and had been planning to send one of the servant women to Edinburgh, anyway. Two days after, I had a letter from another member of the Society of Antiquaries here in London about a lecture being given this week at the Society and decided to attend and handle Olivia's shopping myself."

The letter did not exist, but there were any number of gentlemen who might have sent Fiona just such a missive, and the anticipated lecture was in a few days. Fiona had no intention of attending, however, as she had a particular dislike of Egyptian hieroglyphics. Young Canning or Martin Morewell could summarize it for her so she could speak to the presentation if necessary. It was too bad, she thought, that the Reverend Stephen Weston was speaking on the topic of the Rosetta Stone once again. She'd have been inclined to attend if he'd been speaking on texts in Arabic or Persian. Truly, she'd even have been interested if Weston had been speaking about any of the Chinese languages.

Oliver tipped his head and smiled at her beatifically, as if her answer was as obvious as a divine revelation. "Of course! I had heard Weston was speaking, but I did not know you were a student of Egyptology."

Fiona shrugged, but did not wish to give him any further impressions regarding her interests or expertise. "It is not my primary interest, but one can hardly deny Egypt fascinates English scholars," she permitted. She had no trouble with Weston's claim to glory, though many Fellows of the Society were bitterly jealous of Weston's fame. Allowing her face to fall, she looked carefully at Oliver and briefly at Alden, aiming to deflect them from further inquiry about her academic interests. "And now, it has been a very long day, and I do wish to retire, even if the teacart hasn't arrived. You'll excuse the lack of etiquette as exhaustion, of course?"

Oliver kindly offered to have a cup of tea sent up to her room, but Fiona refused.

To her surprise, Alden said nothing more, so she rose as the two men did. Oliver bade her goodnight first, clasping her hands warmly and kissing each of her cheeks in turn. As a gesture among family, Fiona knew it was perfectly acceptable, though none of the men in her family circle did so, and she'd just met these two men. A sharp, unfamiliar heat passed over her as Oliver met her eyes directly. Even as she blushed, his lips parted and for a moment she imagined that he might kiss her. Her breath caught, half in anticipation and half in fear that he might.

But a knowing smile merely came over his face and, with a familiarity she did not expect, he spoke low and privately, so that not even Alden could hear his words. "Sleep well, my dear, and dream sweet dreams."

Suddenly confused and her mind spinning, Fiona only nodded in reply and turned to escape, jerking free of him abruptly, but Alden moved in front of her before she'd taken two steps toward the door. He was too tall, and she had to tip back her head to look up at him, though she was as tall as Oliver. He was also too broad and muscular, so when he reached forward with a giant hand to capture hers, Fiona shuddered.

She shouldn't fear him, her sisters had said. She frantically reminded herself of it as the heat in his hands lit her skin afire. "We will see you at breakfast," he bade her quietly, bending his head and brushing a faint kiss against her forehead.

Shocked, Fiona shuddered as though his very touch burned.

"Goodnight then," he added, catching her chin with his thumb and tilting up her face so that she could see the amusement and interest sparkling in the depths of his eyes.

The potent combination of the two men was more than Fiona could manage. She stepped back, darted around Alden, and fled up the stairs, even as Carrington rolled the teacart through the hall.

* * * *

Oliver sat unashamedly on Alden's thigh, his feet resting on the floor between Alden's formal buckles and boots. "Thank you for letting me dress you," he began, examining the larger man's cravat with frank approval.

"I felt as if you were hauling me to Almacks to inspect the Incomparables."

"She noticed you, though, no?"

"Oliver, my love, everyone notices me. I'm hard to miss, even without your sartorial attentions."

Oliver chuckled, quite pleased, and placed the teacup on the teacart without moving away. He put his hand directly over Alden's heart and leaned closer, widening his eyes. "She does seem quite outspoken."

Alden met Oliver's gaze, suddenly serious. "She's practically my stepsister, Oliver. Pursuing her is dangerous. My father wouldn't disown me for loving you, but he wouldn't hesitate to cut me—us—out of his life for stepping a foot wrong with Johna's daughters."

"She's responsive to us, though," Oliver countered, closing in on Alden's lips with his own for a firm, persuasive moment. "To both of us. And I know very well that you are attracted to her. We *both* caught you staring at her bosom during dinner. How many women have we met of whom you could even say that?"

"I couldn't help it. She is *pert*, both in looks and attitude, and perfectly proportioned," Alden admitted, clearly torn.

"Let's just take one step at a time. She's hardly the girl who runs crying to Mother, and if she did, she'd end up married to you anyway," Oliver coaxed, his fingers now tangled in the buttons of Alden's waistcoat.

"True," Alden agreed, and gave in to the temptation of Oliver's body. He wound his hands into Oliver's hair, thus ending any coherent conversation for the remainder of the evening.

* * * *

Very late that night, awake in his bed with Oliver asleep beside him, Alden stared at the scrollwork of the cornices along the edge of the ceiling. Moonlight filtered in from the open window, along with the breeze and the faint scent of roses rising from the garden below.

He risked his livelihood, his family and his role in society if he—if they—pursued Fiona and failed. But if they didn't, Alden knew he risked Oliver. He and Oliver had vowed to each other not to turn away from the hypothetical female that they envisioned for their mate, and Alden already knew from what he'd said that Oliver had sensed the potential in Fiona from the moment he'd met her in the front hall.

Of the two outcomes, losing Oliver was the future Alden couldn't contemplate at all.

Chapter Three

Fiona didn't sleep well. She blamed her dreams, but of course it wasn't her imagination that had put the ridiculous thought into her head. Oliver and Alden, together or separately, had managed that feat.

She'd always walked outside the expectations of young ladies of her class, always set herself apart purposely, perhaps even deliberately gone out of her way to avoid attracting the attentions of gentlemen during her first few Seasons. She'd never been interested enough to rethink a decision she'd made as a girl, and Winchester's scheming made any further contemplation of the traditional path expected of an earl's daughter irrelevant. Simply put, the prospect of living her life at the behest of a man who didn't value her or being restricted to the roles of mother and society gossip horrified her. Even later, understanding the real and valuable role that women played in diplomatic and political marriages hadn't been enough to convince Fiona to reconsider.

And no man had given Fiona any reason to reconsider.

So now Fiona was awake in the early morning fog, trying not to think about how she might react to a man — to *two* men, specifically. Even now, this unwanted susceptibility was a painful craving in the pit of her stomach. A bit higher in her torso, the ache wrenched beneath her lungs.

It was lowering to think that she couldn't decide to which man she was truly drawn. It was humiliating to admit that her senses were engaged by a man — by men — who professed to love another. It was soul-destroying to consider that she might be capable of transforming into a woman who could tear apart two people who loved each other to satisfy a lust she found intellectually distasteful. The entire situation was unacceptable, unmanageable and must have been a product of her fatigue.

She'd simply imagined their interest. They were, after all, loving men. They were demonstrative with her, as well. Surely it had been nothing more than sisterly affection in their touches. Her reaction, on the other hand, had gone far beyond appropriate and could be described as embarrassingly wanton.

By dawn, she knew sleeping was impossible. Fiona rose and dressed. She'd go out for an early morning walk to clear her head and leave her note in Berkeley Square for the Cannings personally. The butler knew her, of course, and would hardly be surprised at any sort of unpredictable behavior. In Fiona's mind, it was just as likely that Canning would be at the breakfast table at dawn as at any other time of day. Perhaps she'd even speak to him directly, though there wasn't really a need for such an interview.

Fiona was ready and willing to work, even if she had to wait for nightfall.

More than a year after she'd begun working for Canning's Foreign Office in the dead of night, still no one outside of the Cannings and the Morewells suspected her involvement.

Yet here she was, back in London a month earlier than she'd intended, simply because a red dispatch box had arrived on Anthony's desk via special courier from Whitehall. The message inside had been simple, but it was written in Lord Martin Morewell's elegant Arabic script, so that even if the box had been taken, few could have read the contents. Secretary Canning had personally requested Fiona return to London immediately.

She'd left the next morning and was anxious to get started.

Slipping out of Lennox House was easy, though Fiona moved with extra caution in the upstairs corridor. Carrington's young granddaughter had chattered the night before as Fiona readied for bed, so Fiona knew that the other rooms in her corridor had been transformed into a series of bedchambers, dressing rooms and a study for her unexpected hosts. Gloria wouldn't miss the corner suite she'd commanded at the end of the hall, and Abigail and Meriden could easily be made comfortable in the central wing, so Fiona could hardly complain about a rearrangement that had clearly been needed for Oliver and Alden's privacy.

Fiona knew she shouldn't resent the change, but she did, purely for selfish reasons. She no longer could feel quite as *alone* as she'd done in her rooms previously.

She had no desire to encounter either of them before or after her excursion, though they would be abed long after she returned to Lennox House, in accordance with typical Mayfair hours. Still, there was no reason to take chances. Alden had said he'd see her at breakfast, which meant sometime after ten o'clock by London hours.

Fiona slipped on her half boots after she crept down the stairs. Within moments, she was out of the garden door and into the mews that ran behind Lennox House and Winchester House. With a basket on her arm, she looked no different from any large household's well-to-do housekeeper or the wife of a professional working man out for a morning excursion to the market. Certainly she attracted no special attention.

Along with practical half-boots, she wore a dark brown bonnet that hid the telltale features of her face from those who did not come close. Her gown was russet-colored, common enough in the country but noticeably not *haut ton* in Mayfair in August. Despite the season, the dyed cambric gown was cut conservatively, with the sleeves fitted tight below her elbows and the stiff, pressed collar up about her neck. Olivia wasn't the only one who needed to refresh her wardrobe, Fiona mused. Fiona herself needed a few additional updates if she was to go cavorting about London unnoticed during the warmest part of the summer.

The only belonging she carried that identified her was a flat medallion on a long silver chain hidden inside the collar and behind the narrow opening at her throat. It seemed a simple silver talisman, but the engraved coat of arms was very definitely Whitehall and the Latin text identified it as the property of the Foreign Office. The number on the back would identify her to anyone with access to the right records inside the FO.

Morpeth had presented it to her, to wear secretly, in case she ever had need to claim the protection of the Foreign Office in an emergency.

She self-confessed to a small amount of pride over it. It was a symbol that she belonged to something bigger than herself, almost as if she were again part of a family. Her mother and sisters were still present, of course, but they had their own lives and their own little families, even Genevieve.

Fiona was no spy. She was neither an ambassador nor a bureaucrat who toiled each day in Whitehall to keep the government running. But without Anthony in the Foreign Office, Morpeth had quickly found that his battalion of bureaucrats was not fluent in a number of obscure but important languages. Nearly everyone spoke, read and wrote French and Latin and another Romance language, but very few were able to translate Slavic languages like Sorbian or Romanian, or even North Germanic languages like Faroese and Norwegian. And with the recent war, some of the embassies had taken to encoding their missives to their home embassies in specific dialects of the old languages, like Breton, Cornish and Welsh were dialects of Old English.

Fiona knew many of them—or enough of all of them—such that she'd been infamous among the linguists of London since she'd been in the schoolroom. She'd devoted herself to the study of languages, read them, sought out speakers and writers of the rarer dialects from all visitors to and classes of London and generally displayed an enthusiasm that none of her tutors or mentors ever forgot.

The night more than a year earlier when she'd found Anthony nearly dead from exhaustion and hunched over a stack of documents had been a turning point.

Christopher had been but a new babe then, and Morpeth had arrived ostensibly to meet his nephew. After several days when Anthony and Morpeth had remained locked in Anthony's study from after dinner until dawn, Libby had broken down in tears and Fiona had determined to bring Anthony to heel.

She'd used a stiff hatpin to slip the lock on the door before she'd burst through the door and demanded answers.

The problem was that Anthony Morewell had been one of the few Foreign Office bureaucrats in London who had been entrusted with secondary translation of intercepted documents and letters. Like Fiona, he specialized in several obscure languages, mostly stemming from the period of his childhood when the Morewell boys had taken up studying rare ones in order to communicate with each other and confound their tutors and nurses. In that pursuit, Anthony had explained with a smile, their father's stint as Foreign Secretary and his library had been invaluable.

In time, Anthony's knowledge had been put to use to a more formal purpose. Whenever the British obtained documents — either clandestinely or openly — they were immediately copied in their original language and translated by a bureaucrat in the embassy or by the appropriate agent. Additional copies and copies of the translations were — at an appropriate time — forwarded to the London Foreign Office.

In London, the initial translation was verified by an independent expert as a last protection against treason and simple errors. The approved expert made a second translation and the two translations were, in the final step, compared for discrepancies by the Foreign Office clerks. All the documents were later stored in the massive files kept at Whitehall in neatly organized folios, the pages numbered to guard against theft and chronologically organized.

Before his marriage and relocation, Anthony had been considered the best source for translation for several languages rarely spoken in London. Following Anthony's resignation, the Foreign Office had difficulty in finding a reliable replacement. Anthony had only explained the debacle once he understood his secrets were risking Libby and her recovery from childbed. Once she'd heard the explanation, Fiona knew exactly how to solve Morpeth's dilemma. Still, she hadn't trusted Morpeth would support—or even voice—her offer to the secretary, so she'd written a personal letter to the Right Honorable George Canning, the Foreign Secretary, and enclosed it with a chatty note she addressed to Miss Harriet Canning.

George Canning's eldest son by the same name, generally called Young Canning, had called at Lennox House the day after she'd returned to London. He may have disguised it as a call upon Lady Fiona de Rothesay, an unmarried, practical, well-bred lady his own age known for her scholarship in languages, and thus set the stage for a sober, considered courtship, but in truth they'd frankly discussed her skills, remuneration and the process by which Fiona could accomplish her duties without boldly walking through the front doors of the Foreign Office in Whitehall and attracting the attention of every bureaucrat, ambassador, spy and conspirator in the building.

Fiona thought it was somewhat disgraceful that so few men in London had the necessary education or interest to perform her task. It was even more disheartening to realize that all those who had the skills had either been deemed ineligible or uninterested in the role Fiona would play. Fiona had gone so far as to mention a few names, many of whom had taught her at some point in her education. Several had aged to the point where life in London was untenable and had retired to the country. Others traveled extensively as they added to their knowledge and only resided in London in temporary bouts for rest and planning more adventures. Others worked for the British government in China, India, Africa, Europe and other exotic locations, and were primary sources for translations already.

But Fiona primarily lived in London and went no farther than Northumberland for brief periods. And she spoke fluently, at last count, thirteen languages and could more than adequately read and write in an additional eight, with smatterings of various dialects and related languages.

This morning, however, Fiona was prudent, if not entirely conventional. She arrived at Canning House in her unfashionable gown and reported to the kitchen door. Jameson, Canning's butler, recognized her and frowned, until she explained it was patently too early to be seen ringing the front bell. She stayed only a moment, leaving the note she'd composed the night before.

Fiona made certain to stop in the fish market and buy fresh meat for the kitchens at Lennox House before beginning her trek home. She knew well that the servants would indulge her odd hours and requests if she was kind to them in turn, and if by some twist of fate her hosts were awake, they'd see nothing odd if one did happen to discover her in the kitchen.

She was, after all, merely a female.

Fiona had just delivered her basket to Cook, when Oliver strode through the door into the kitchen. She glanced up, her eyes widening when he approached her with open aggravation.

Unhesitating, he wrapped her arm in his, drawing her close against his side. He took in the scene before them, noting the fish still on the deal table. "Alden and I would like a word with you," he announced succinctly.

Fiona attempted to remove her arm, but found she'd have to make an exhibition of them to convince him to release her. She hated it when anyone stared at her. "If you'll excuse me, I'll freshen up and meet you —"

"Immediately," Oliver refused. "Cook will excuse you."

Fiona couldn't contain her shock as Oliver turned, forcing her acquiescence by the simple expedient of keeping her arm trapped close within his. Biting her lip, she fought to keep silent, not daring to rip up at him in the kitchens. Or the servants' hall. Or the corridor outside the pantry and the butler's pantry, or in the dining room where two footman and an underbutler were polishing the ducal silver. Or in the front hall or on the main stairs, where Carrington was industriously polishing the wooden banisters.

Instead, she remained stoic, shocked by the abrupt insistence of Oliver Morewell. If she didn't know better, she'd have said he was angry, but that was projecting what she knew of his brothers onto him. He had no reason to be perturbed with her. He simply wasn't chattering.

Oliver turned left at the top of the stairs and toward her room. She frowned in confusion. Surely he wouldn't stage what was certain to be a confrontation caused by a misunderstanding in her own rooms?

But no, Oliver pushed open the panels across the corridor, revealing a room at least twice the size of her study that was obviously Alden's office. She looked about curiously, determined not to examine the big man behind the desk after a first quick glance. He was already rising, but one swift impression had been more than enough. Oliver was not the only man in the room who had taken some issue with her.

The space revealed much about its master, despite Fiona's sudden trepidation. The walls were covered in a deep gold, with waist-high dark oak cabinets that ran the long length of the room. The broad shelf that resulted from the arrangement was decorated with only a simple silver platter and a pitcher. Neatly framed paintings were hung at regular intervals along the wall. It was a respectable collection of Welsh landscapes by Richard Wilson, with one notable exception just behind Alden's head.

One of Genevieve's landscapes was in the center of the collection. Fiona focused on it, recognizing her young sister's talent for what it was, despite never having seen the painting before. Something in her heart clenched painfully.

Did Alden know Genevieve was his sister? Surely Lennox had told him. Wasn't Alden set to be Lennox's regent until Eynon was grown? And what, Fiona wondered, would Alden think of Johna and even Fiona, if he learned she had no more de Rothesay blood in her than her sisters? She could hardly be ashamed of her Wessex blood and was ever so glad not to actually *be* Winchester's daughter, but—

"Where were you?" Alden demanded directly.

Fiona blinked, her gaze swinging to him almost against her will. She pulled her arm successfully from Oliver's grip and turned to face his partner. "In the kitchens," she returned baldly, lifting her eyebrows as she drawled her answer in blatant challenge.

Alden's face hardened and his lips clamped together. A low hiss came from him.

"She was in the kitchen," Oliver offered, his voice seemingly deeper than it had been the previous night. "But she'd only just returned. God knows where else she's been while wandering the streets *alone* and on foot, but it seemed fairly apparent she'd been to the fish market."

Alden met Oliver's gaze. "You don't say," he mused dryly. "I suppose it was too much to hope she'd just gone for a stroll in Hyde Park before seven in the morning." He swung his gaze to Fiona and growled, "*The fish market?* What possessed you to go out alone at dawn? I *thought* you were a *responsibly*-minded female."

Already irritated by Oliver's presumption of her person and forced escort above stairs, Fiona's temper exploded. "How dare you!" she forced out, her teeth gritted together. "I am *not* your ward—or his," she added, flinging a hand in Oliver's direction. "You have *no right* to dictate to me, and I will be damned if you stand there and speak to me as if I was your daughter. I *knew* this wouldn't work. I'll be leaving just as soon as Lucy packs my trunk again."

The surprise on Oliver's face as she whirled was obvious, but it was nothing compared to her shock when Alden intercepted her before she could reach the door again. He must have flown across the room, but there he was. He held her in place, stopping her at once with a solid foot of tense air between his massive chest and her gritted teeth.

"Just *what* do you imagine you are doing?" Fiona spat out.

Alden glared back at her without compunction or fear. "I have *every right* to worry about you and to be concerned when you disappear without explanation. With my father absent, *I* am responsible for your welfare. Both society and my own morals demand it. *You* are damn lucky that maid of yours knew you'd left of your own free will, or all of London would have been searching for you, and this little incident would be much worse." Alden's eyes flashed. Oliver stared at Oliver for a half-second before he returned to his scold. "Sit *down*, Fiona, before I give in to the temptation to turn you upside down."

Fiona couldn't help it. Her eyes widened and her mouth opened in disbelief. She hadn't realized he could string so many words together, and he'd just threatened—

"He's not one to mince words, is he?" Oliver said from just behind her right ear. Fiona jerked in surprise, but Oliver steered her back to the armchairs before the desk.

By the time Fiona composed herself, she was somehow seated in the chair Oliver had indicated. She stiffened indignantly when Alden took up a position at the edge of the desk before her. Whether it was to intimidate her by looming over her or to make escaping her seat impossible without brushing by him so close that her chest would touch his jacket, Fiona neither knew nor cared. When Oliver leaned over the back of her chair, his chin coming down nearly to the top of her scalp as he rested his hands on her shoulders, she voiced a squawk of outrage. "What *do* you two think you are going to accomplish by trapping me here and threatening me?" she sputtered, trying desperately to ignore Oliver's heat and the tempting scent of him at the back of her head. Alden's penetrating eyes were difficult enough. She couldn't meet his gaze.

"Spanking is not all that bad, you know," Oliver murmured huskily. "I quite like it. I'd actually recommend the experience."

Fiona's newly persistent gape resurfaced. She immediately looked to Alden, for once seeking an anchor she somehow knew he'd provide. He did not disappoint, his intense glare already focused on Oliver above her head. "Oliver, she wouldn't enjoy this one. Stop with the innuendos until we deal with this situation, or I'll deliver one you won't like either."

A brief silence ensued while Fiona admitted to herself that she was completely out of her depth. These two men were an experience she'd never imagined existed, let alone thought to find herself between.

"Yes, I'm sorry," Oliver murmured contritely, the cheerful note she'd already learned to expect in his voice replaced by a huskier undertone. With a shock, she put a name to their communication, longing exploding deep within her. *Intimacy.* Despite her unwilling brain, her heart leaped. *I wish they would speak to me that affectionately.* But as she recognized the desire, Fiona cut herself off. Oliver and Alden were intimate with each other, not her.

"Fiona." Alden's attention returned to her, and Fiona jerked, responding to his stern tone before she thought better of it. Color formed in his cheeks, bringing out the shape of his jaw and the stiff set of his chin. His nose flared a tiny bit. Fiona felt an unfamiliar pressure on her skin just from this man's voice, and she struggled to understand what was happening to her. The masculine aggression evident in his demeanor should have terrified her. Besides, it was for

Oliver, not her. She had to remember that point. "We are not in Warwickshire or Northumberland. You can't go wandering off around London alone. *You know that.*"

He stopped, frowned, as though he wanted to say more. Behind her, Oliver's mouth hovered just over her right ear. When he spoke a moment later, his voice still low and husky. *Desire*, Fiona recognized, shocked anew. *He's aroused. By Alden.* They must be desperate to finish the painful interview and be alone, and she was practically reveling in their masculinity. Shame and humiliation coursed through her yet again. "You are a female in a city where your reputation would be ruined if you were discovered out without a family escort or, at the most liberal, a servant. Anything could have happened. You might have been robbed, molested, attacked. Why do you need reminding of this? What were you thinking, that your family — that *we* — wouldn't care if you were discovered or, worse, hurt?"

Alden bent forward, only inches from her. Fiona forgot to breathe. "Or maybe you'd not mind if His Grace cast me out of his life for failing you?"

Fiona gasped. "No! They know me. Mother would never blame you — either of you. I frequently go out without her. I've even considered setting up my own house but I thought she and Gloria needed the company at times. And it's ridiculous to think I'd want to get rid of you! I don't even *know* you, or why you're taking such a — a — an *unwarranted interest* in my affairs."

Alden's lower lip curved slightly. Fiona blinked. Had this giant of a man finally been ready to smile at her? Just the glimpse had her aching to see his face creased with happiness.

"Going out with your coachman and a footman or maid is one thing," Oliver allowed from behind her. But then he ruined his admission by adding, "Going out *alone on foot* is an entirely different matter."

"As to why? I have every intention of rectifying that oversight. Immediately," Alden added.

Oliver leaned closer, his breath warm against her ear. Fiona jerked, her body tightening, then heating as Oliver's lips brushed as light as a feather against the shape of her ears.

She might not have believed her own nerves but he sucked the lobe of her ear between his lips. She opened her eyes wider while watching Alden focus intently on Oliver's mouth. Alden bent down, directing his eyes back to Fiona as his lips covered hers.

Fiona's mind blanked. Warmth enveloped her. A finger traced her other ear and a different hand clasped her shoulder, holding her in place. That was Oliver, she realized, because Alden's hands were covering hers on the arms of the chair.

She wasn't breathing. Her entire body was aware, tingling as though she'd been electrified by a Leyden jar. Sharp points erupted in her breasts and between her legs, and Fiona inwardly cursed Abigail and Gloria for their kind-hearted education. She did not need to know this was lust. She ached for a man—for *men*. It was wicked, beyond carnal. Wrong.

But Alden breathed into her mouth and nibbled at her lower lip, so Fiona could inhale the air he'd exhaled. She shuddered violently and listed to the side in the chair, but Oliver was there to steady her. He clasped her firmly around the torso beneath her breasts, holding her back against the chair.

Oliver caressed her other ear with his mouth, before nuzzling the place behind the lobe for a second. "How does she taste?" he asked, trailing kisses down the side of her neck.

Alden didn't pull back, but sucked her lower lip between his and swiped it with his tongue. Fiona gasped as Alden lifted one hand from hers and slipped his thumb between her lips, holding her mouth open.

The heat of his skin in her mouth shocked her, drawing a strangled moan from her throat that Fiona had not known was coming. She trembled.

"Like heaven," Alden grunted. "Hot chocolate and peppermint. Oranges."

"My turn, isn't it?" Oliver groused, pressing his mouth to the nape of Fiona's neck now, though her high collar prevented him from exploring very far. She'd had a bonnet on when she'd arrived home and struggled to think why it wasn't on her head now. She'd left it in her basket in the kitchen.

"When I'm finished," Alden drawled, then fastened his mouth over hers again. This time, her mouth held open by his thumb, Alden invaded her mouth with his tongue until Fiona's body softened and heated. The idea that Oliver would explore her mouth momentarily was nearly as mind-numbing as the thought that Alden Swenson was doing so now and *Fiona liked it*. She couldn't understand why she did or what he meant by it.

"You'll never be *finished*," Oliver objected with a husky, knowing chuckle, pressing soft kisses to the top of Fiona's scalp where her hair was tightly stretched and fastened with the dozens of pins required to keep it neat.

"True," his partner agreed, having withdrawn his tongue if not his thumb or lips. "Should I let him kiss you now, little one? Or make him wait?" Alden murmured against her lips, but Oliver heard every word and groaned, clenching his fingers against her ribs.

Alden lifted his head, reversing his thumb out of her mouth and pushing forward again. She inhaled dramatically, which simply gave Alden more space to press the digit forcefully against her tongue. Almost instinctively she tightened her lips around the heavy extension of bone and skin and blood, and sucked.

Above her, Alden groaned, and Fiona's eyes flew up to find Alden's lips against Oliver's. Alden's free hand was buried in Oliver's hair, and both men were beautiful in their passion. Fiona couldn't stop the moan that rose to her lips at the sight. Had Alden been that beautiful a minute earlier? She couldn't see his entire face when he had kissed her.

Oliver ripped his lips away from Alden and turned, bending down and pressing his mouth to the corner of Fiona's, where she allowed Alden's pulsating finger in and out. When Oliver clasped her ribs again, his palms pressed intimately against her breasts, his thumbs pressuring them softly. He rubbed firm circles with those thumbs over the sides of her breasts, and Fiona shifted forward in the chair, practically offering her body to his caresses.

If he moved his hands just another inch or two, Fiona knew that her nipples would swell against his fingers.

The thought panicked her and she struggled, gasping for breath.

Oliver jerked his mouth away, and Alden quickly removed his thumb, and they watched her closely as she inhaled a desperate, deep breath.

Oliver didn't wait for her to regain her composure or her temper, but spoke roughly and decisively, "In case it wasn't clear to you, we've both just laid claim to *knowing* you, to having an exceptionally *warranted* interest in you. You may not need a father looking after you, but you've bloody well found yourself two keepers who very much want you whole and healthy. So don't think can get away with this sort of exploit again, little one. Because we will find out—and you will regret it."

Fiona stared at him, completely befuddled. When she didn't speak, he snorted roughly and glanced up at Alden. "You have an appointment at the warehouses, and you're already late. I'll keep an eye on her."

Alden's eyes softened and he nodded as Oliver captured his lips briefly in farewell. Alden then brushed an oddly tender kiss on Fiona's forehead. Confused, her head suddenly pounding, Fiona shivered, but she blinked and opened her mouth to speak anyway.

Alden had already disappeared.

"So," Oliver murmured against her ear, "what are you up to this morning? Washing that silky hair so I can brush and dress it for you? That shopping you claimed Olivia wanted done? Napping? Reading? The museum? Or do your tastes run to embroidery and sewing?"

Fiona stiffened. She needed away, to breathe deeply and ask Lucy what these two domineering males had discovered. "I don't embroider," she said shortly. "Ever. And if I nap, it will be alone. In case it wasn't obvious, I've already been shopping, and if you think of touching my hair, I'll chop it off up to my ears."

"You chop off that gorgeous ebony," Oliver growled after a fraught second of silence, straightening abruptly and glaring at her, "and you'll get the spanking Alden threatened, twice. Once from each of us, and I'm the one you'll learn not to cross."

Numb with shock and denial, Fiona stood and pushed past him, dodging him as he reached for her. "I'm going to my study. My door will be locked, and don't even imagine I'll be joining you for luncheon."

If she had her way, she'd be at Grillion's by dinnertime.

Oliver sighed. "Well, you could at least pretend an interest in managing the household. Then you'd have to spend time with me."

"I'm sure you're a better chatelaine than I will ever aspire to being," Fiona said frankly, opening the study door. "And a more effective one than Gloria or my mother, which means I'd rate a dismal failure. The house is beautiful and the upper servants are singing your praises. I've already asked, just to be certain."

Oliver smiled at her brisk, unprepared compliment, but with his eyelids lowered, she couldn't see the expression in his eyes, and she wasn't staying to find out. Before he moved to follow her, Fiona fled. She was leaning against the locked door, holding her breath, when Oliver finally entered the corridor. He paused outside her door, but stayed as quiet as she, and Fiona dared not move lest he guess that she was the least bit susceptible to him.

Only when his footsteps echoed in the stairwell landing did she sit, put her head down on the desk and close her eyes. What in the world was she going to do now?

Her lower lip trembled. She'd spent too much time with Libby and Anthony — or with Abigail and Meriden — not to recognize the fateful and unwelcome sensation in her chest. Fiona wanted a companion devoted to her and her cares, as Gloria and Abigail and Libby had. Fiona had never before prodded the hard lumpy place behind her lungs, but in twelve shocking hours, Alden and Oliver had opened her up and ripped out any opportunity to deny it existed.

Not that she'd admit it to *them*. No, that was impossible. Clearly, they'd intended to forewarn her that they had no plan to argue or compete over her, or even for her to unintentionally separate them. Instead, it appeared they both wanted her and were perfectly content to…share? Was it even possible? Fiona winced, unable to work out how such a relationship would work.

Unless, she thought sourly, one had the task of confining and restraining her while the other went about his daily business.

In the end, their plan didn't make a whit of difference, Fiona reminded herself. Oliver and Alden couldn't be permitted to interfere with her responsibilities. She couldn't tell them the truth, so she'd have to escape them, avoid them or lie to them. She had no choice, not if she wanted to keep working in Whitehall's library of secret documents.

By mid-morning, Fiona's resentment of Oliver and Alden had morphed into new levels of fury. Going out for the evening was not supposed to require convoluted battle plans worthy of the Napoleonic War. Carrington had delivered missives from Canning House, addressed to Fiona in Miss Canning's elegant handwriting and carried to Grosvenor Square by Canning's personal footman, which reinforced the urgency of Fiona's services. However, Lucy had faithfully reported that all the staff had received orders to report to Oliver or Alden immediately anytime Lady Fiona made to leave the house.

At lunchtime, served a cold collation on a tray in her large chamber, Fiona told herself she hadn't ordered Lucy to pack her trunks because she didn't want the carriage drivers employed by Lennox House to be reprimanded for aiding and abetting her escape. Instead, she permitted Lucy to finish settling her belongings and pack her trunks away in the attics while Fiona hid in her office and pretended she could leave anytime she wanted — though how she'd get her trunks back without alerting Oliver and Alden and having one of them outwardly intervene was not a problem to be contemplated.

By teatime, Fiona had given up even the pretense of removing to Grillion's, though she silently overemphasized the secondary reason for staying. Even if her move had no effect on their reputation, her arrival at Grillion's would draw attention, and her every communication and outing observed by any number of people without loyalty to Lennox or Johna or their respective children. Fiona had no desire to attract more notice to herself than she was already going to have to face by going out in society. Returning to Grillion's at dawn was much more problematic than sneaking through the back gardens of Lennox House and in through the back doors as the sun rose.

Besides, she needed access to her own library over the coming days and nights.

Fiona would never admit to anyone other than herself that she had hidden away in her study all day and avoided an exit scene because she knew Oliver and Alden were partly right. Leaving and taking up residence in a London hotel after already spending one night at Lennox House would signal to the gossips that she didn't approve of Oliver and Alden, or that they'd had a disagreement. She couldn't bear to imply either, even if she was furious. Truly, if they hadn't started in with their threats and the subsequent kisses, she'd have been proud to be out and about with them. There weren't many Englishmen ready to buck the expectations of the close-minded people, like the Duke of Weymouth, who influenced society in the direction of their own hypocritical morals.

But in addition to that, Fiona did know well that a lady of quality did not go out with an escort. Even on the safe streets of Mayfair in broad daylight, by all accounts she should have had at least a maid trailing her, if only for the humdrum reason of carrying her packages and helping her with the impossible variety of garments a lady was required to wear. If that point was again raised, Fiona would be forced to acknowledge that she'd gone beyond the bounds of propriety for no good reason. Lucy could well have accompanied her, even in the early morning hours.

She hadn't wasted an entire day, however. Fiona suspected she had been recalled from Northumberland to translate old Slavic languages based in the Early Cyrillic alphabet, so she spent several hours reading the poetry of Vasily Zhukovsky, ostensibly to remember the flow and rhythm of the Cyrillic Russian, though the modern writing was quite different from earlier Cyrllic script. It was a pleasurable reminder of the complexities of the world, and of how language represented such disparate people and places.

Fiona also plotted, because she intended to leave Lennox House that evening come hell or high water, and without two exasperating men in tow. It had taken a few minutes of careful consideration to realize that neither Young Canning nor Oliver's youngest brother, Martin, could call at Lennox House to discuss the details of her nighttime hours without attracting the avid attention of her two rabid keepers, so a series of notes began to pass through Lucy's hands directly to urchins in the streets. By the time Fiona finished her tea and scones, Carrington entered with the required stiff invitation on his salver.

Dinner and a soiree at the Russian ambassador's residence, Lieven House, would begin Fiona's evening. The Countess von Lieven, who had first granted Fiona vouchers to Almacks years earlier, had a soft spot for the girl Fiona had been, even if Fiona would never be quite comfortable with the calculating woman. The countess's involvement in English politics disturbed Fiona, and she knew the Cannings were suspicious as well, simply because Russia's best interests were not necessarily England's.

As she bathed, Fiona wondered what the ambassador's royal wife would think if she knew Fiona was intimately involved in the translation of Russian documents secreted out of the heart of the embassy in London by disaffected Russian staff.

Fiona dressed carefully, aware that she looked best in rich, dark colors that flattered her pale skin and black hair. Unfortunately, it was summer, and pastels were in season, so Fiona felt obligated to add a fashionable paisley shawl in shades of yellow to her dramatic but unfashionable silk evening gown of burnt orange.

In the end, with yellow roses pinned into her updo, Fiona was satisfied. She'd delayed as long as possible, hoping to depart while Oliver and Alden were dressing for dinner, but as the carriage horses had to be harnessed and brought around from the mews, she could hardly escape without warning.

Tomorrow night, she decided as she slipped from her room, she'd sneak out and hail a hackney, then head directly to Canning House. Even if Alden and Oliver tracked her there, they'd get no farther than the Foreign Secretary's impenetrable butler, Jameson. They'd learn to ignore her in short order, or she'd simply pack her trunks and pretend to be heading to her sister, Abigail, in Warwickshire. Canning and Morpeth could arrange for her to stay elsewhere.

Her breath caught as she descended the stairs, because they were both there, waiting for her. Oliver's arms were crossed, his eyes narrowed and his jaw tight from clenching his teeth, but he boldly looked her over from toes to head. Fiona refrained from flinching only by shifting her gaze to Alden, who met her direct look with one of his own. Unlike other men of her acquaintance, he met her stare without looking away uncomfortably or making any caustic comment about an absence of submissive demeanor.

She paused out of their reach, well aware of Carrington waiting to open the door behind them. "Gentlemen." She nodded formally, her eyes jumping to Carrington and back to Oliver. "You'll accept my apologies for not joining you for dinner tonight."

Oliver's lips were flat. "Perhaps you need an escort this evening?" he inquired, the tension in his tone clear.

Fiona almost quailed, but despite her quaking knees, her spine remained firm. "I hardly think Countess von Lieven would be grateful for me adding an unexpected guest to her dinner table." Fiona held up the invitation from her reticule and waved it. "I've been added at the last minute to make the numbers even, and she'll be depending on me to converse in Russian with the embassy's guests from Saint Petersburg. I'll be staying after for the soiree. I suggest you both enjoy your evening together, as I plan to attend Lady Palmerston's entertainment as well before I return and will probably end up blockaded by Mayfair traffic until dawn."

Even though she spoke in her usual brisk, confident tone with which she was accustomed to commanding obedience from staff and her sisters, neither face before her seemed inclined to give way.

Instead, Alden scowled.

Boldly, Fiona stepped closer and spoke in a low tone, to prevent Carrington from overhearing, "You can hardly hold me prisoner, and it would be unwise to attempt it. The *ton* knows I'm in residence. I've already accepted the dinner invitation. What shall the countess think and say if I do not behave normally?" Fiona was unsurprised when Alden's scowl transformed predictably into a reluctant frown.

"Without a chaperone?" Oliver asked doubtfully.

Fiona arched an eyebrow in his direction and replied mockingly, "I'm twenty-six years of age, firmly on the shelf and my own mistress. All of London is aware that the Earl of Winchester is presently unavailable as a suitable chaperone, and Lady Winchester is in the country for a much needed respite. Perhaps you are unaware of it because of your recent return to London, but I have been attending events without a chaperone for more than a year now." She turned to Alden and finished, "Your coachman will ensure I do not repeat my visit to the fish market in my evening slippers and worsted silk and I shall return by dawn." Raising her voice, she tipped her head around Oliver's shoulder and spoke directly to Carrington, "Is the carriage waiting?"

"Yes, my lady." The butler bowed, his eyes on Alden and Oliver even as he opened the door. Fiona saw his carefully blank face, and knew the older man had accurately perceived the tension between the three of them. Whether he knew *why* the tension existed, Fiona couldn't say, but she would not be cowed by any two men, least of all these two.

Alden desisted first, stepping to the side so she could continue.

She swept past them immediately, not daring to pause even when Oliver reached out toward her. Even worse, Fiona couldn't breathe until she was seated in the carriage. She'd seen the stricken look in Oliver's eyes and the fierce look in Alden's, and the confusion in her head was simply too much to bear.

Escape had been beyond desirable. It had been urgently necessary. If only she could remain out and loose on the streets of London until the end of September.

But no. The best she could hope for was to sneak in while they slept, keep the door to her rooms locked and pray for relief from her relatives before she did something foolish.

That was the answer, of course. As soon as she awoke the next morning, she ought to write to Abigail and Meriden, and beg them to come to London and visit. She'd point out their mother had gone to Wales and Aunt Betsy was in Northumberland.

Meriden would try to whisk her away to Warwickshire. Fiona knew he'd pick up the gauntlet of chaperone with a fierce wit that would challenge both Alden and Oliver if she needed. After all, Meriden had proven to be a valiant warrior and he considered Fiona his to protect, by virtue of her sire's Wessex heritage. She'd have more trouble escaping from Meriden's watchful eye than from Alden and Oliver.

It might be well worth the complication, Fiona decided.

Chapter Four

Both Alden and Oliver were utterly silent until they entered the comfortable apartment they shared across the corridor from Fiona's bedchamber and study. Oliver actually winced as they passed the closed panels that led to her rooms. Once they were private, he turned away from Alden to stare out of the window facing the street. "We have to let her go, don't we?" he eventually asked, his voice toneless.

Alden paced, his brow creased and his hands clasped at his back as he watched the carpet at his feet. The emotionless, even words from his lover were a clear indication of how close Oliver was to an outburst of grief and disappointment that Alden hadn't seen in years. He knew well that he was a doubter, slow to believe in others when Oliver was already devoutly faithful to a friendship or an idea. Oliver had a flair for the dramatic, while Alden himself was steady and practical.

As much as Alden doubted that a future for the three of them was realistic — particularly given the intricacies of their family relationships — meeting

Fiona had awakened a passion in both Oliver and his own soul that could not be denied. He wanted to haul her over his shoulder and dump her in his bed, while telling her she was never to leave it. He desired to see her writhing in his sheets, Oliver gripping her hips while he feasted from her. He ached to slide his rigid staff inside her and watch her determined, busy, bright eyes glaze over with pleasure. He could well imagine himself holding her off from bliss because he demanded she speak words that would bind them together. Fiona was terribly dangerous to Alden's peace of mind, and he knew that was one of the cues Oliver had used to judge Fiona as a potential lover, though they'd only known her a day.

Now, though, Oliver sounded defeated. Sad. Alden risked a look at him, finding Oliver pacing himself, walking aimlessly in a circle from his desk to the window to his music stand. Oliver fingered the furniture restlessly. Aimlessly.

Alden stopped. "I wish you could have a piano in this room, but you can play the second movement of that Mozart concerto. *Andante*, I think. It will help me think."

Oliver stared at Alden, so Alden shrugged. He rarely asked for any particular musical boon from Oliver, but Alden knew it was the right piece of music to channel Oliver's emotion. Alden leaned against the wall, head back, as Oliver gathered the instrument and played a few scales to warm up. He listened to papers shuffle as Oliver retrieved the appropriate music. Oliver paused for five long seconds. Alden had seen Oliver's ritual countless times. His eyes would be closed as he brought his attention solely to the music and blocked out all distractions. He'd inhale deeply, filling his lungs—

The haunting melody began, lilting and trailing away with suppressed longing.

Alden loved to listen to Oliver playing the twisting, repetitive notes, but this time the suppressed grief and sadness came through as Oliver's heart, a song of slow heartache. Oliver had never played it so well, and Alden had never loved it so much.

Fiona did bring them an unfamiliar vitality, he decided. Just the one short day of interaction with her had brought a new passion and an unfamiliar edge to them and to every thought of her. They needed her. But did she need them?

His mind flipped through visions as they'd seen her—in the drawing room, the dining room, in his study, her mouth open to his exploration, shuddering in shock and...*arousal?*

The music rose to its final chords. Alden kept his eyes closed when the last note fell away and the rich tone echoed through the room. The haunting note faded but neither spoke as silence and stillness replaced the music.

Eventually, Oliver shifted. Eyes still closed, Alden listened as he set the instrument aside.

"Your heart is already fixed on hers." Alden's tone was husky, reflecting the passion in Oliver's performance. "I've never heard you play it quite like that. Your pain shows clearly."

"When either of us touches her, she resonates with sensuality, even if she doesn't understand it," Oliver replied evenly. "Her breath hitches. Her breasts swell so beautifully. Her eyes lose that owl-shaped analytical lens through which she views the world. We can do that for her. We can give her a safe harbor."

"If she will allow us such a boon. If she chooses to put her faith and trust in us," Alden returned dryly.

He opened his eyes and straightened, crossing the room decisively until Oliver stood before him. Taking Oliver's cheek in his palm, he tilted the man's head and pushed his lips to Oliver's warm, vibrant ones. After a long moment, he lifted his head. "She is headed to Lady Palmerston's after the dinner. Do you have a card for that one?"

Oliver sniffed dismissively, the gesture so reminiscent of the *grandes dames* who so looked down upon him through their lorgnettes with disapproval and yet continued to pen the invitations delivered to Lennox House on a daily basis. Some of these invites were, of course, sincere. Alden and Oliver attended affairs at the Dutch embassy regularly, despite the risk of an awkward encounter with Oliver's father or brothers. The men had befriended the younger sons of the current Dutch ambassador while they were in Amsterdam, and were well liked by the ambassador and his wife. Alden was constantly invited to political dinners and the subsequent soirees in hopes of tapping Lennox's influence. Alden preferred the opera and the theater, even Vauxhall, over marriage mart events, while Oliver naturally favored musical evenings and lectures. These events constituted only a small percentage of the cards. Invites came for come-out balls, for soirees, for musicales with Italian sopranos, for Grand Balls in honor of European visitors, for engagement balls, for art exhibitions and for innumerable other occasions.

Oliver had made a name for himself among the *ton*'s hostesses, as he had regularly accompanied Lady Winchester to summer picnic lunches, to afternoon teas, and even to Hyde Park. He'd stood beside her staunchly even on the worst days of Winchester's madness, when the earl's public ranting had been humiliating but captured in the minutest of details by observers of his trial. He'd danced with debutantes, especially the young ones and those out of their depth, and spoken kindly to all the daughters, nieces, granddaughters and goddaughters that he'd met. He did not cause comment, and dressed fashionably. His manners were impeccable, and at the end of the evening, it was his disavowal of marriage and female companionship that was the cause of any disapproval.

As a result of this sociability, Oliver had his name on the invitation lists of nearly every event of note, with the significant exception of any event hosted at Weymouth House by his mother or sister-in-law.

Oliver blinked at Alden then opened his desk drawer and drew out a stack of cards tied by a ribbon and tugged on the bow. The cards scattered, but he immediately shuffled them, obviously searching. Alden watched him, fascinated even years later by the graceful movements of Oliver's form.

He turned to Alden, a smile on his face and a card in his hand.

"Dear Oliver, would you grant me the honor of escorting you to your evening's entertainment?" Alden raised an eyebrow and held out his hand.

Oliver's face lit and Alden felt a guilty pang in his chest. Could Oliver turn from him that easily, be caught in the snare of woman's sweet smell and soft skin at such short acquaintance? Softly, Alden said, "If you'd rather go alone, I can remain here."

Blinking, Oliver paused before understanding and widened his expressive eyes. "No, no, my heart, no. I want you to be with me. But there is new adventure in store for us now, isn't there?" Alden returned Oliver's smile, but Oliver's gaze was sober, determined. "You are mine, and I am yours. That will not change. I swear it."

"Then it's time to dress for an evening out," Alden said mischievously, pinching his lover's ear. "I hope you have something appropriate in my wardrobe."

Oliver laughed, gripping his hand and tugging him across the room. "Never fear, my lord. I'll have you as elegant as any toff in no time."

Alden grimaced playfully, but Oliver didn't even see it. He'd endure any amount of fashionable torture if Oliver was content with him, and there was no denying that Oliver was an exacting taskmaster, if somewhat bracing, when it came to Alden's appearance.

* * * *

"I expect you two to circulate," Lady Palmerston breezed. "In fact, I'd be only *too happy* to introduce you to any young ladies—"

Alden couldn't restrain the cough, which only made the regal woman pause and glare at him.

"We will find you if the need arises," Oliver hastily intervened, turning away from their hostess and heading for the main stairs.

Alden remained at his back, diligently dodging the mass of skirts and shoulders that pressed around them in the small entry.

"Quite the crush," he said easily, wondering if Fiona had even arrived. He and Alden had dined at home, then had had a frank conversation about the state of their non-relationship with Fiona as they dressed— Alden in a divine turquoise waistcoat, elegant gray jacket, ecru trousers and an intricately tied ivory cravat with diamond winking pin and Oliver in a more subdued outfit of dark blue that complemented his features.

"She does not believe that she belongs to us," Alden had said. "We must tread carefully, until she is as desirous of us as we are of her."

Oliver burned at the thought of not being able to stroke the skin at her wrist or kiss his lips to her eyebrows arching above her expressive orbs. Still, he knew Alden was correct. Drawing a deep breath, he paused past the crowded stairway so that Alden came up at his side. The Palmerston ballroom was a large square space, with columns on the north and south ends, giving it the appearance of a wide arcade with its gilded ceiling. In the alcoves beyond the columns were the musicians, the card room, a room for refreshment and a quieter room for discussions apart from the dancing. Given the time of year, only those of critical importance to government and business were in town, and even fewer of their daughters, but seemingly all of that select company had converged on Palmerston House.

Groups of settees were arranged sparingly in the end of the room where Oliver stood, crowded with laughing, gossiping *grandes dames* overseeing the more capable and exclusive echelon of virgins deemed suitable for marriage to politicians, military leaders, and government statesmen or functionaries. These gentlemen had need of brides who would support and further their careers, and the young ladies were commensurately more educated and subdued than most giggling maidens. Dancing was organized at the far end, where doors to the terrace were standing open to the night air, and the floor was crowded with lines of dancers participating in a quadrille. It was terribly late in the summer for such a crowd, but

Oliver remembered the few cards he'd received for tonight and grimaced. Presumably, with Parliament in recess and many on their country estates, there were fewer hostesses in London to entertain.

It was already warm, and the temperature was still rising inside.

"Check there," he suggested to Alden, tipping his head in the direction of the room where neglectful chaperones and matrons without encumbrances would have congregated and gossiped.

Alden raised an eyebrow and blanched. "I'll dance," he dodged, heading for a gawky, too-tall redheaded maiden being drawn along by a heavy, velvet-clad matron with all the delicacy of an elephant in Hyde Park. Who wore velvet in *August*, even widows? Oliver barely restrained his distaste for the matron and pity for her charge, but headed away from Alden in the proper direction.

He'd taken only a few steps when an imperious voice caught his attention. Turning his head, Oliver swallowed heavily but obediently turned. Lady Sefton, with her vouchers at the ready, was hardly one for any young female to cross, and Oliver knew well enough to be terrified even without any reason to traverse the threshold at Almacks public rooms. "Ma'am." He bowed to the middle-aged woman who reminded him of a less tragic, more vivacious Johna de Rothesay. "How may I be of assistance?"

"Is it true? Has Lennox taken Lady Winchester from London? At long last?"

The question was blunt and Oliver struggled to refrain from flinching. It was true that Johna had not appeared in the ballrooms and popular gathering places over the last three nights, but the couple had departed only a day ago. Still, the matrons would be certain to notice her absence over a period of several weeks. "Her ladyship has accompanied His Grace to Wales," he confirmed, knowing there was no hope of denying it. Still, in the same instance, he gave excuse, "It was an impromptu decision—"

The lady smirked. "It's not of my concern, except that I noticed Lady Fiona arrive. Arlington House is closed. I live on the same street. Lady Fiona *is* staying at Lennox House, isn't she? Why, then, did she arrive alone, I want to know? You have better manners than that, Lord Oliver."

Oliver felt his eyes focus and his body stiffen, but the eagle-eyed mistress was not one to deceive. "Lady Fiona is in residence, my lady, but she had a prior dinner engagement at the Russian embassy with Countess von Lieven. It would have been a long delay to return to Lennox House before coming here, so we planned to meet her here. We were already delayed in traffic."

Lady Sefton stared at him unnervingly for a long moment before she nodded. "It will suffice for tonight," she allowed very softly. Then, glancing at the fashionable throng chatting around them, she added briskly, "I know she came from Northumberland. When you find her, tell her I want to speak with her about Lady Arlington and Lady Olivia. Your brother has kept that girl attached to the nursery up north for far too long."

Oliver bowed again. "Lady Fiona assures me that both mother and son have recovered nicely and greatly enjoy the countryside." He smiled slowly. "Perhaps you could point me in her direction so that I might pass along her comments all the more quickly?"

Lady Sefton arched an eyebrow in return, pleased either by his question or by her ability to answer.

Perhaps she was celebrating both. "She's on the dance floor, you know. Or on the terrace, dancing."

Oliver excused himself, unwilling to examine just why Lady Sefton found his question amusing, but as his back was to the dancing, he would have to make his farewells before deducing what the devil she meant. Indeed, he suddenly decided that he'd liefer have a straight out duel than cross verbal swords with any of the patronesses. They always left him, with their raised eyebrows and knowing smirks, befuddled.

Escaping as soon as Lady Sefton dismissed him, he slipped around the edge of the ballroom, finding Alden dancing with the gangly redhead in a set near the middle of the room. Alden caught his eye and gestured with his head toward the terrace, so Oliver eased behind those who observed the dancers and made his way outside.

The white tiles of the terrace were lit by the reflection of large lamps organized around the stone railing. The terrace opened into a dark garden, and Oliver found his way into the shadowed corner overlooking the steps and settled to observe the swirling cacophony of color. The music lilted and twirled, the familiar cadences of a simple minuet drawing the couples together then apart in a series of prescribed steps.

Fiona, despite her height, was momentarily well-concealed by the height of her partner and the minuet they were conducting on the outskirts of the dancing. The dark shade of her dress among the gentlemanly jackets and trousers made her difficult to track in the shadows, so the dance was ending and she was curtsying to her partner before Oliver found her. His eyes widened as recognition struck him and a surge of long-suppressed anger rippled up his spine. His form stiffened, and he moved purposefully through the crowd.

Despite his best efforts, he had to pause and weave, and greet many of the young ladies whose friendly acquaintance he had cultivated over the last two months.

By the time he reached the place where she had been, the violins were already scraping and she'd been led away by her next partner, a man Oliver didn't recognize from the rear.

The object of his anger remained, however. "Martin," he greeted the younger man directly.

To his credit, Lord Martin Morewell had the grace to look slightly sheepish. "Oliver," he began stiffly, then sighed and whispered, "not here. Morpeth and Melissa are both here, damn his hide."

"I suppose I should thank you for warning me, I didn't realize they were back in town," Oliver returned caustically.

"Let's go into the garden," Martin returned, glancing around him. Very quietly, his voice low as they progressed down the stairs and into the dim paths, Martin continued, "Morpeth came up on business — one of the usual FO panics, you know. Canning and I agreed I had to send for him, even if it was summer. Mother and Melissa were an unexpected complication. Morpeth doesn't know how to say no, especially as they are determined to see me wed this next Season so Canning can raise me to an ambassadorship. But Mother has exhausted herself already and little Morewell has some sort of fever, so they're leaving in the morning."

"So you're ashamed to be seen with me still, then?" Oliver sniffed, digging his fingernails into his palms at the thought of Martin dancing with Fiona, perhaps poisoning her with his family's bigotries —

"Of course not," Martin denied, his voice stiff.

"I've been in London for more than two months and we've not once spoken," Oliver disagreed, perfectly aware of the bitterness that tinged his voice.

Martin winced, and looked at his brother apologetically. He paused and turned, throwing himself down on a stone garden bench.

With other company, Oliver thought disconsolately, he'd have thought the spot romantic. But his youngest brother, who was no longer a baby but the perfectly respectable age of thirty, was not the sort to inspire romantic visions in Oliver. Once upon a time, he'd thought Martin was supportive. They'd exchanged letters and visited when Martin had traveled to Europe. He stared at the man, hard, then looked into an extraordinary stand of hollyhocks that had grown as tall as he. "Why were you dancing with her?" he asked abruptly, turning to face his brother.

Martin actually gaped at him, a schoolboy expression of astonishment that Oliver had little doubt was sincere. Blinking, Martin shook his head. "It's a ball. We're expected to dance," he said dryly. "Anyway, I *always* request a dance with Fiona when she attends an event I'm at, and she *always* accepts. It's one less chance for my attentions to be misinterpreted, and one more time for her to pick my brain over obscure locations in Europe."

"So you don't have expectations?"

Martin, bewildered again, stared at Oliver with a growing comprehension on his face that Oliver wasn't certain he appreciated. "*Me?* With *Fiona de Rothesay?*" Abruptly, he stood and frowned. "She'd eat me for breakfast and be bored by afternoon tea." He paused, squinted his eyes at Oliver and went on slowly, "I get the feeling I should be asking you, brother dear, just what the bloody hell you think you're doing?" He paused and added significantly, "You are not going to try to pretend you have honorable intentions to a *virtuous* young woman of whom even Father might approve, are you?"

Oliver felt a rush of self-conscious shame wash over him, as realization struck him. They did, indeed, have every intention of turning Fiona into their lover, and not for any short-term *affaire*. But what did they intend to give her in return? Could Oliver stand aside and watch her marry Alden, and how would that change everything?

Resolutely, he shook his head. "You're missing the point altogether, Martin," he returned wearily, inwardly wincing at the falsehood. "She's residing under Alden's roof, and we're responsible for her."

Martin raised an eyebrow, and shouted with laughter a second later. "Just the two of you?" he asked in disbelief. Then he sobered instantly and stood. "Brother, Lady Fiona treads her own path, regardless of any guidance or oversight provided by anyone, even by those who have every right to provide it. And don't you dare think that if you damage her reputation, good intentions or not, that there won't be hell to pay. If you and Swenson want to stay in London, you'll make sure that woman's reputation is as white as snow. Not only would Lennox skewer you, the Cannings will make you a social pariah and the Earl of Meriden would bankrupt you and dump you in the Thames and not feel the slightest tinge of regret as he walked away."

Oliver concealed the confusion he felt. Why would Abigail's husband have an interest in Fiona's welfare, beyond the common one any gentleman associated with Lennox might feel? Why was Fiona on close terms with the Foreign Secretary's family? And why would *Martin* of all men be the one to advocate for Fiona's honor?

"As for me," Martin finished briskly, "I was in Portugal when you arrived in London. I returned to Portsmouth three weeks ago and was given strict orders to hie myself to London, stick to business and to stay away from you. I would naturally have ignored those instructions had I the opportunity, but as I've already mentioned, circumstances required me to send for Morpeth almost immediately to handle some sensitive issues at the Office. Of course, once Mother and Melissa came up to London with him, I had no chance."

Oliver nodded, needing no further explanation. His sister-in-law, the duchess-to-be, held absolute sway over the servants at Weymouth House, her rule even more absolute than the duchess herself. Martin would not have been able to so much as send Oliver a note without the kitchen boy's delivery of it reported to the house's mistress.

"Not even time to write a note and send it from the Office, then?" Oliver mused, glancing up to the house. "We'd better return, the supper waltz has finished."

Martin shrugged negligently. "So, do you want to know about little Benjamin Oliver?" he asked, a sly grin on his face. "Father was nearly apoplectic when he heard the name, but he has no influence over Anthony these days. Instead, he describes poor Anthony alternately as 'that cursed boy' or 'hen-pecked dreamer' and swears he'll disown him. Anthony doesn't appear unnerved by the threats."

"Fiona," Oliver said curtly, "has told me all about the baby, and Anthony has invited me to visit and meet the prodigy."

"Excellent. We should plan to be there together, so that I don't have to come up with excuses to see you," Martin pondered. "You do know that Morpeth swears he'll have me playing secretary to some poor sop of a territorial governor in an African backwater if I so much as speak to you in public? I might add that I don't have the good fortune to be married to — or the lover of — a partner of generous income, so I'm rather dependent on his goodwill."

"I'll go up first if you don't wish to be seen with me," Oliver muttered, the resentment in his chest swelling. It had been many years since he had felt guilty over the allowance Alden gave him, let alone the support that came from sharing a household. He had no wish to revisit such a period of pointless angst.

"Nonsense," Martin objected. "They've all gone in to supper. We'll separate on the terrace. I want to visit the card room anyway."

True to Martin's prediction, the terrace was empty, except for one man. Alden waited, scowling at the brothers as they climbed the stairs. "Where is she?" he demanded immediately.

"She was dancing, when we went into the garden." Oliver frowned. "The waltz —"

"Yes, her partner was Canning," Martin supplied helpfully. "Young Canning, I mean."

"She's not in the supper room or the withdrawing room," Alden growled. "I thought she was with you."

Oliver shook his head, perturbed. "Young Canning, you say?" he asked Martin, remembering Martin's warning. Oliver's eyes narrowed, and he turned and headed down the terrace stairs and toward the garden gate. "Let's be sure she didn't escape through the garden gate." Alden paced after him, but Oliver was aware that Martin remained on the terrace, watching them.

To their mutual disgust and concern, Fiona was nowhere to be found. Lennox's carriage had disappeared and after a few minutes of searching, Alden discovered that Canning's phaeton was also missing.

Oliver didn't like it at all, and he was even more displeased when they arrived home at Lennox House at midnight to find that Fiona had sent her carriage and driver home from Lady Palmerston's directly. The driver, roused from his sleep, revealed that Lady Fiona often left her evening engagement early to visit at Canning House. "She 'n' Miss Canning are bosom bows," the driver mumbled, before Oliver and Alden sent him back to bed.

At one o'clock they remained in the drawing room, and Fiona had not returned.

At two o'clock, they dismissed the servants and sent the butler to bed, and Fiona had not yet returned.

At three o'clock, Alden lifted his head from perusing a biographical sketch of the Foreign Secretary that he'd found in a book in Lennox's library and snorted elegantly. "Harriet Canning is a mere twenty years old, six years younger than Fiona."

"Gloria's age." Oliver groused. "Not even close to Fiona's age. And I know I saw Harriet Canning on the dance floor when you were scouring the supper room that last time—after Fiona and Young Canning had left. It's hardly an age difference to inspire such a close friendship then, unless Harriet Canning is an ape leader, and I've heard her described as an angel."

At four o'clock, Alden inhaled a shot of whisky and glowered at the fireplace. "Is she Young Canning's lover? They *are* nearly the same age."

Oliver considered the matter, his eyes on Alden's exhausted features, his heart remembering Martin's warning. "If she is, they've kept it very secret." He remembered the sensuality they'd seen in her the morning before and shook his head, his voice betraying his uncertainty. "I thought she was untouched, but it's possible."

"I'm going to spank her so hard she won't step foot in a carriage for a week." Alden paced.

For once, Oliver had fewer words to say about the matter than Alden. His words were directly to the point. "Only if I don't put her across my knee first."

* * * *

Fiona was dizzingly weary. The exhaustion, aggravated by the darkness and the steady *clop-clop-clop* of the carriage horses, tugged at her consciousness until she merely existed in a daze.

Wrapped in a thin black cape to hide her features, she was barely visible in the corner of the nondescript black coach. Morpeth might be charged with following up on any questions created by Fiona's work, but managing the documents library in the FO was Martin's responsibility, and it was Martin who had kept her company through the darkest hours when Young Canning had given up on his own work and returned to Canning House. It was Martin who had supervised the small cadre of translators the FO kept available. Now he sat slumped, as weary as Fiona, in the opposite corner of the unremarkable carriage. Arms across his stomach and chin down, all she could really see of him was a faint gleam from his eyes in certain places.

It was nearly dawn, so close that the carriage was not as dark as when she returned from a ball and so early that even the early morning social traffic of Mayfair had dissipated to a few half-drunken men stumbling home from brothels or the high-class townhouses of their mistresses.

Around her neck, Fiona once again wore the FO medallion tucked inside her chemise. Fiona thought it was exciting to be granted the privilege of one, even if she was constantly chaperoned by Young Canning and Martin Morewell. Of course she couldn't wear the thing openly, but had kept it in her reticule until she and Young Canning had snuck down the terrace stairs and out of the garden gate at the end of the supper waltz.

Martin had helpfully distracted Oliver, and Alden had been inside. They'd waltzed through the doors once and seen him, trapped in a conversation with the inveterate gossip, Lady Jersey. The woman had clasped Alden's arm tightly, as if she had no intention of releasing him. Young Canning had immediately turned her and danced her back out to the terrace, where they'd deliberately fallen behind the others when the waltz ended and remained to stroll. Of course they'd truly been keeping a close watch on the garden and on the crowd headed to the supper room. At the first opportunity, the pair had headed to the garden gate and disappeared into the maze of carriages.

Inside the bedchamber upstairs next to Harriet Canning's, Fiona had changed her gown into a dark, serviceable cambric one and pinned an apron to guard against ink stains. Donning the hooded cape to conceal her identity, she had been escorted into the mews by Young Canning and driven directly to Whitehall.

Her earlier instincts had been correct. She'd spent most of the night painstakingly translating Russian letters from Saint Petersburg to the Bavarian Prince of Thurn and Taxis, whom she had deduced to be Princess Esterhazy's father.

In daylight, it would have been a meticulous, time-consuming task, made worse by the small, cramped Cyrillic script and the large amount of irrelevant, vicious gossip contained within each missive. By the light of a lamp after her early morning outing and the day's events, it had been absolutely draining, particularly when the subject was the possible assassination of the Russian tsar, Alexander I.

The carriage turned into the mews and Martin shifted, raising his head to peer in her direction. "I don't dislike them, you know," he said clearly. Fiona cast him a curious glance, but focused abruptly on his form when he added, "Oliver thinks I hate him. I could never hate him. I'm envious, yes, admire—"

"*Envious?* His family has cut him off, shunned him, made him dependent on Alden Swenson's generosity and wealth, even endorsed him being beaten to unconsciousness, and you're *envious*?"

Martin's eyes flashed in the dark as he jerked to Fiona. "*Beaten to unconsciousness? When?*"

Fiona pursed her lips together, understanding she wasn't supposed to know what had happened to Oliver fifteen years earlier. "Why are you envious?" she asked again.

"'Because," Martin paused, cleared his throat, and proceeded carefully, "he had the opportunity and the courage to defy Morpeth and my father, to walk away and damn the consequences. Anthony did it too, if in a more socially acceptable manner. I admire Oliver—both of them—for that, even if they are dependent on the wealth of their loved ones. They have the courage to seize the life they want for themselves, regardless of the consequences."

Fiona stared, but while she tried to work out his tack, the horses came to a stop in the lane at the back of the garden. She shook her head in his direction, and Martin opened the door. "Until tonight," he whispered.

The chill of the morning intensified as she repeated his words in a low voice and descended the steps. He slipped back inside the black carriage and the door closed noiselessly behind him. The driver, well trained in delivering the FO's operatives to all manner of places and atall times, said nothing to the horses but let the reins loose so that they plodded forward.

Fiona pulled the hood of her cape further over her hair and slipped into the garden. In short order she entered the terrace doors to the music room, to which Lucy had helpfully absconded a key some months earlier and had it copied.

Shivering in the dark room, Fiona paused to lock the door behind her and return the key to her reticule. Her toes curled tightly inside her dancing slippers and as she moved silently through the house, she wished she had been able to organize ahead of time for her half boots to be waiting at Canning House.

In the upper corridor, she glanced at the closed doors that led to Alden's study and the rooms that he shared with Oliver. She grimaced, forced her mind back to a more mundane consideration, and decided she would buy herself an extra pair of boots and have them delivered to Harriet. Most days, when resident in London, Fiona's maid, Lucy, would go out for errands and meet with Harriet's maid, Goldie. The girls were sisters, and Lucy had worked in Canning House before Canning himself had suggested Lucy fill the role as Fiona's personal maid. The arrangement had made communication between Fiona and Canning House much more convenient. No one looked twice at the two maids together, even in Bruton Street, with their lists of errands in hand. Lucy would return to Lennox House with whatever belongings Fiona had left at the Cannings, and Goldie would return to Canning House with whatever materials and attire Fiona felt would be necessary for the coming night.

But this morning would not end as perfectly as Fiona expected. She opened her mouth in dismay as the door jerked away from her. She was caught. Fiona felt him seize her forearms and tug her forward.

Impressions pushed into her consciousness then — the turning of the tumblers on the door behind her, the scrape of the key as it was drawn from the keyhole, the width and breadth of the man behind her and the stiff fury of the man in front of her.

A faint aroma of bay leaf caught Fiona's attention, but only for a brief second. Oliver took her out of Alden's arms and lifted her against his chest. Though they were nearly equal in height, her feet left the floor. She gasped against the warmth of his neck and reached out to balance herself in his embrace.

Chapter Five

Alden came up behind and pressed against her, pushing her even more intimately against Oliver. In that moment, Fiona's exhausted brain and body failed and instead of thinking consciously, she simply reacted.

She raised her head, brushing her mouth along Oliver's jaw. Surprised by the roughness there, she tried to draw back, only to find that Oliver anchored his hands against the back of her head.

She was immediately fascinated, drawn to the exquisite taste of him. She acquiesced to the insistent demands of his mouth, opening hers slightly. Oliver slid his tongue in only far enough to trace her teeth. Fiona raised her palm and brushed his jaw, absorbing the texture of the small hairs that were erupting from his skin. Behind her, Alden moved even closer, so near that he held her hips in each palm.

His mouth, like Oliver's, fascinated her. He breathed kisses along her temples, and she shuddered between them, a fissure of surprise flickering inside her when Oliver groaned and moved his lips across one cheek and softly bit the lobe of her ear. Instinctively she turned to grant him easier access to her ear, and Alden shifted. He raised a hand and clasped his palm against her open cheek, tilting her chin up forcibly with his tongue to kiss her as well.

Stunned, she wiggled her shoulders. Alden's tongue was more invasive than Oliver's had been. He plunged inside, held her taut and open then withdrew to thrust again, a blatant display of possession that Fiona had no trouble interpreting, despite her shock and exhaustion.

She wiggled her shoulders harder and tried to shake her head.

"What's wrong?" Oliver murmured against her ear. His teeth scraped at the joint of her jaw below it. "You are so delicious. Absolutely delicious."

Alden used his tongue to demand her submission. She couldn't answer, wasn't certain she even knew how to answer. The faint aroma of bay leaf she associated with Oliver reached her again, and shame hit her as she remembered who they were, who she was.

Apparently sensing her emotional withdrawal, Alden lifted his head and met her gaze, until she dropped her chin and stared at the floor. The sudden subjugation of her physical response caused a sharp convulsion to pass over her frame, before she straightened and brutally reasserted control over her body and her mind. Decisively she stepped back.

Both waited, silent, as she stilled and focused simply on breathing. They didn't speak but simply held their positions, until the locked muscles of her legs and arms unclenched. Finally, eventually, she sank to the settee behind her.

Fiona's mind raced as they took seats, Alden on the settee beside her, Oliver in a chair he pulled close to her knees. What would they want to know? Where she'd been all night? With whom had she spent the last hours? When would she be leaving so that their lives would be peaceful?

"Why are you in my rooms?" she finally managed to ask evenly, hoping that taking the lead in questioning would deflect them. They had to be as exhausted as she was.

"Who is he?" Alden snarled into her ear.

Fiona didn't understand, so she continued to avoid their gazes and ignore their questions, still trying to work out what to say.

Oliver — *Oliver?* — growled. "Who were you with, Fiona?" he demanded. "Whose bed were you in? Young Canning? Or the Foreign Secretary himself?"

Baffled by the question, Fiona looked up at Oliver and shook her head. The lamps were lit. They'd been here, waiting for her. Dismay followed bewilderment, the surges of emotions as unfamiliar as the kiss the three of them had shared the previous morning. "I— I—I wasn't—" she began, then stopped abruptly. Denying a lover would only prolong the questions, and how improper was that embrace with them assuming she'd just come from another man's bed? Inhaling quickly and firming her jaw, she defiantly met Oliver's eyes. "I am not in your care," she enunciated slowly, so there would be no confusion. "Neither you nor Alden has any reason to concern yourself with my behavior or activities."

"No reason?" Oliver frowned, using a single finger to turn her head enough that he could challenge her. His brown eyes were sharp and twinkling, unlike the softness she had seen in them previously. "You will find you are mistaken," he warned her.

"I thought I was clear enough this morning," Alden interjected fiercely, sliding a possessive hand from her scalp and down her spine.

With that last word whispered against her ear, Fiona blinked and began to pull away, but Alden cupped her jaw with his palm and his lips met hers.

At the heat of his mouth on hers and the hand he moved from her waist to cup a breast, Fiona shuddered and found herself sinking trustingly into Oliver, who crowded up against her side. Alden was again behind her, at the edge of the settee, pressing against her right shoulder and twisting her head so that they could kiss. Oliver caressed her ear and tugged at her lobe again, then trailed his lips down the sliver of skin revealed by Alden's open palm against her jaw. Fiona shuddered when Alden settled his lips to one corner of her mouth and Oliver found the other corner. With all three of them connected at their lips, an unfamiliar urgency woke inside of Fiona.

"Do you love him?" Alden asked starkly, barely lifting away enough to express the question.

Fiona blinked, trying to work out his direction, but her attempt to focus only made her realize that Oliver cupped her breast. Shocked by the heat and the sudden tingling that erupted across her nipple and down her spine, she jerked in their arms, reaching out blindly and clinging to the first bit of fabric she found.

Before she could assimilate the sensation or process Alden's question, Oliver spoke, his mouth so near and low to her mouth that she had to hold her breath to catch the words. "He can't be making you happy. You looked miserable when you opened the door."

Suddenly, Fiona didn't have to think. She shook her head negatively. No, she didn't love Young Canning or Lord Martin, and neither loved her. They didn't make her happy. They made her feel important and useful —

"We'll take better care of you than this," Oliver promised, the heated breath of his words washing over her cheek and into her ear.

"You are ours, now," Alden muttered. The guttural words shocked her, and her mouth opened. Oliver captured her, his tongue against her lower lip and pushing it inside. Alden slid kisses over her cheekbone to her ear and sucked the lobe, much as Oliver had done on the other side. She swayed but the two men whose arms were wrapped tightly around her prevented any sort of withdrawal.

It was Alden whose lips lightly brushed over her eyelashes, the feather-light contact shattering her senses. To Fiona, it was almost as intimate a gesture as Oliver's hand at her breast and his tongue inside her mouth. "You're beautiful," he growled. "Even exhausted, you're absolutely perfect."

The strangeness of it all — the intensity, the masculinity, the exhaustion, the tenderness — was too much.

Fiona jerked away from Oliver's kiss, and tears welled in her eyes.

The emotional response only confused her more. *She never cried.* Why now? Why here? Why them? Nearly twenty-four hours of being awake and busy was clearly too many hours.

Both men must have sensed her distraction, her shifting focus, though she didn't struggle further. She was too worn to fight, to argue with them or with their presumptions. She wasn't sure if she ought to feel offended or honored. She didn't know how to react to their apparent belief that she'd spent the night with an unsatisfactory—or at least inconsiderate—lover.

In any event, her acquiescence was apparently a clear warning to all of them that she was too far gone to think clearly.

"You need to sleep, to rest, before we pursue this further," Alden murmured regretfully, lifting her away from Oliver. She felt the loss of Oliver's warmth, but Alden moved forward and they entered her bedchamber.

When Fiona found her feet again, Oliver was pulling back the bedcovers. The room was cool, a welcome relief from the August afternoons. Lucy would be coming up shortly with her washing water and to put her to bed. The thought made her shudder, because then Oliver and Alden would truly know her secret. If they suspected her maid was aware of her deceptions, Oliver would be relentless in dragging out all the details from the poor girl.

"You need to go," she managed to say, but the words were listless. "Both of you," she tried again. Even to her ears, the objection sounded unconvincing. It was a secret relief to have her cape untied and removed as she was settled onto the bed. Oliver sifted through her hair, and she felt the hairpins tugged. He tangled his long fingers in her braids, smoothing out the dark locks with his fingers.

She should stop that, she thought, but Alden's hands distracted her. He was unbuttoning her bodice, an action shocking enough that her heavy lids flew open. "What—"

"You can't sleep in this dress," Oliver reassured her. "We'll take it off and you can slide under the coverlet in your chemise. Don't be afraid."

"I'm not afraid," she whispered, "but it's not proper."

"You need someone to care for you," Oliver murmured soothingly. He pushed he fabric of her sleeves down her arms. Before her, Alden was silently kneeling at her feet, and she blinked. He was picking the knots from her dancing slippers.

"Where is your ballgown, Cinderella?" Alden spoke gruffly, looking up. His gaze drifted over the cambric gown—thankfully she'd left her ink-stained aprons at the FO—and frowned disapprovingly. "Why have you been with someone who lets you walk away in this condition?"

Fiona stared at him blankly, still understanding that they believed she'd been with a lover, but unable to process exactly how to disabuse them of the notion, or even if she ought to do so. Maybe she should let the fiction stand, to explain her nighttime absences.

Instead, Oliver urged her back against the pillows and her slippers disappeared. Beside the bed, Alden was easing her skirts over her hips, but her apprehension had faded. She was simply too exhausted to argue, to tell him he didn't understand. She would explain, she decided, after she'd slept. She'd explain she hadn't been with a man, that she didn't have a lover. She didn't want them to think she was a woman of loose morals who would turn to them so easily, having just come from the bed of another.

She wanted them to like her.

Like her? Fiona was simply too tired to think clearly or make any wise decisions, and the low voice of

Oliver against her forehead, bidding her to sleep well, was all that she needed to shut out the world.

* * * *

Fiona rolled in the bed to get comfortable and stayed still, absorbing the quiet atmosphere of the room with its shades drawn and permeating silence.

She was still in a state of shock.

She'd slept, of course, but it had been a fitful sleep after the first hour. Now, she simply wanted absorb the shifting world beneath her feet. The whirlwind effect of being around Oliver and Alden disturbed her, but in her secret heart, Fiona could admit she was flattered by their open admiration and attraction to her, even by their assumption that she was desired by another—that she was desirable enough to attract the attention of other men.

Fiona was less impressed at the notion that they clearly considered it right and proper to seduce her, even as they believed that she had shared another's bed.

She'd done what no one in society believed possible for a woman—that is, kept their attention for more than a few minutes at a time.

Why her, though? Heaven knew that she'd never be a successful candidate as a gentleman's wife. She had little interest in domestic affairs beyond how they affected the comfort of her bedchamber. She had never felt any compulsion to reproduce, and though Libby and Anthony's children were adorable, Fiona had not a single wish to create or raise one of her own. Not even the detailed discussions she'd had with her sisters, Abigail and Gloria, about the mating process had moved her beyond academic interest. They'd confirmed the accuracy of various male statuary that Fiona had both seen personally and in books. They'd explained how pleasurable mating was when with the right partner. Even then, Fiona had resolutely and privately labeled the discussion abstract knowledge, unrelated to her actual life.

Now she wasn't so certain.

Fiona already suspected that Oliver and Alden— either individually or together—would most definitely qualify as the 'right' partner that Abigail had once decreed necessary for intimate pleasure. And that meant she might be able to enjoy the experience and find out for herself if Abigail and Gloria were right.

It wasn't as if they'd expect her to marry them. They'd been lovers for years and society well understood the pair intended to be together forever. She could explore while she was here in London, while she was conveniently under the same roof as they, effectively limiting the possibility of scandal, with even her mother absent. After a bit, any lingering awkwardness would wear away. She wouldn't be alone with them once her mother returned from Wales anyway.

Except, as her lovers, Fiona knew they would never accept her inexplicable all night absences.

The thought was barely in her mind before her bedchamber door opened. Fiona lifted her head, expecting Lucy, but it was Oliver who breezed in, a pitcher of washing water in his hands.

Gasping, Fiona sat up, but Oliver spoke before she could organize her wits. "Good morning, beautiful," he greeted her, eyeing her intently from her forehead to where she gripped the blanket around her torso. "You look better, if not quite recovered. You should rest today so you're prepared for later."

"Later?" Fiona choked out, watching him closely as he drew back the heavy drapes and tied them open. "Where's Lucy?"

"She apparently had a shopping list from you and asked one of the chambermaids to wake you and help, so I've come instead. Did you not ask her to go out?"

"Oh, that's right." Fiona sighed, chewing her lower lip. Lucy had gone to meet Goldie and retrieve her ballgown and any missives for her mistress from Canning, Morpeth and Lord Martin. "I need gloves and ink. And she was picking up a package for me from Hatchard's bookshop."

Oliver started to chuckle then glanced at her, still holding tightly to the coverlet. "Are you rising?"

Fiona swallowed, then gathered herself and said tartly, "I'm waiting for *the maid*."

"I'll help you wash and dress," he returned implacably, folding his arms over his chest as he stood at the end of her wide bed.

Her eyes widening, Fiona shook her head.

"I help Alden every day, and you see how fashionable and well-groomed he is," Oliver drawled. "I won't turn you out in trousers and a morning coat, though. Never fear."

"What rot!" Fiona spat out, her eyes wide.

"Eventually you're going to have to come out from beneath the coverlet," Oliver warned. "When you walk out into the corridor, whether it's to eat or to confront us, we're going to sit down and have a chat. You are going to behave like the honorable lady I know you to be and make us a few very important promises. First, you won't go off alone with other men, no matter the past. Second, you won't let anyone—even us—treat you badly, which includes keeping you out all night and returning you at dawn exhausted and in a damp air. Sleep is important to your health and to your very fine brain, Fiona. Third, you will not deceive us. Argue all you like, even throw things if you must have a temper, but do not lie to me. Understand?"

Fiona felt her heart beating against her ribcage. It echoed in her ears and her blood clogged her throat as her arteries and veins swelled.

What sort of commitment were these two asking for?

How could she possibly promise not to lie to them? A promise of lifelong fidelity was more realistic.

"And why do you think I'd make such promises?" she asked, letting her incredulity show in her voice and in her words.

"Because if you don't," he said simply, placing one hand on the poster at the foot of the bed, "I will keep you in this house until you do."

Fiona's eyebrows shot as high as they'd ever been in her life. "Just *who* do you think you are?" she sputtered, then added in a very slow, deliberate voice, "Forcing a promise from me does not obligate me to keep it."

"Is that what you think?" he mused. "Let me tell you what will happen, then, if you have the audacity to lie to us, to sneak out without a proper chaperone and spend time alone with other men or risk yourself in ways as you did yesterday. If either Alden or I find out you are not taking common-sense measures to assure your safety and reputation, you will find yourself bent over, your dress pulled up, and your bottom spanked in a way you won't forget. You may be an independent young woman, Fiona, but your behavior reflects on everyone else in your extended family, Alden and I included. We won't permit additional humiliation of your mother, allow you to worry Lennox or anger your sisters and their spouses. Independence does not mean that your actions do not have an impact on others. Just last night, Lady Sefton observed you arriving alone at the Palmerstons' and made haste to take issue with me over it. You are *not* as free as you would like to think."

Fiona burned. Oliver's lecture was too accurate and too well intentioned to miss its mark in her honest heart, but she still resented it. The threat to spank her was ridiculous, too. "Frankly, Oliver Morewell, you could do with a lesson in manners. First thing in the morning, while a lady is still abed, is hardly the time to read her a lecture better suited for a six year old. Now get out of my chamber and send in the maid."

"Remember what I said, Fiona," he warned. "If Alden had come in here this morning, he'd already *be* spanking you, and I am only slightly more under control."

"*Out!*" she demanded.

Oliver shrugged his shoulders and turned. "It's not as if we're making you promise to share our bed, Fiona. We just want you to be honest with us — and with yourself."

He didn't even bother to close the chamber door, so Fiona waited until the outer door of her sitting room closed before she let loose the scream building in her throat. "*That cad!*"

Fiona was getting out of the house without a confrontation with those two forces of nature if she had to climb out of the damn window and down the tree outside.

It wasn't actually that difficult, though she did have to bribe Carrington's little granddaughter, the chambermaid, to stay in the room until Lucy returned. After the girl had bounced away, Lucy opened the door, peeked into the corridor and waved to Fiona. "I'll just be a minute, miss," Lucy returned aloud, even as Fiona dashed past her toward the stairs.

Fiona was half down the stairs before Lucy shut the doors and walked at a sedate pace in the opposite direction past Alden's study door and Oliver's sitting room door.

In the end, Fiona had to confess to Carrington that she was walking out to call on two ladies having at-homes and to a luncheon. She needed no chaperone other than her maid for those outings at midday, and Lucy met her on the front steps.

* * * *

"What now?" Oliver asked, disgusted. Lucy, shaken by his questioning, admitted that she had walked with Lady Fiona to Upper Brook Street, where Lady Fiona had called on the Countess of Camberwell and sent Lucy home. Carrington had not even blinked at Oliver's aggravation, but reported that Lady Fiona had gone out walking—as was apparently her custom—to make calls and to a luncheon at Lady Sefton's on Park Lane. Oliver and Alden could hardly check up on her at those engagements and indeed, they were perfectly appropriate outings for a lady of her standing and age.

Nevertheless, Oliver was anxious, and Alden's intense focus on Oliver meant that Alden knew it. He cradled Oliver against his chest and kissed him, pressing him into the sitting room door. "She'll have to come home before any evening engagement," he reminded Oliver. Alden wanted his tongue inside Oliver's mouth and he wanted to work his big body to Oliver's leaner one. Knowing Oliver loved having

Alden's size and weight used against him, Alden traced Oliver's sides and used his fingers to grip Oliver at the top and backs of his thighs. Physical affection moved Alden too, and Oliver rubbed against Alden in response to the hardening flesh prodding Oliver's diaphragm. Above him, the complex irises of Alden's hazel eyes were shot with a dark blue, a color evidenced only when Alden was focused on the passion between them.

Oliver craved the exultation of knowing Alden still responded to him after all the years they'd been together. Oliver arched and moaned when Alden clasped Oliver's hips in his large hands and rubbed his thighs on the raised placket in Oliver's trousers. "Let me help you relax, Ollie," he offered.

Oliver moaned, so Alden slipped to his knees and undid the placket, using his mouth on Oliver's staff when it popped free of the buttons and confining fabric. Oliver whispered Alden's name, and the sound nearly cindered Alden's control over his own flesh.

Hot and fully erect, Oliver's cock filled Alden's mouth, tasting and smelling of the soap Oliver used to bathe. Alden tugged on it tightly with his lips, letting his bottom teeth scrape over the vein on the underside, hardening the flesh in the way that Alden well knew Oliver craved. He didn't speak again, but rubbed his thumbs into the tight space between Oliver's thigh and the sac below his cock, one on each side.

Oliver groaned again, jerked as he undulated, pushing his cock farther back in Alden's mouth. The warmth of his semen splashed satisfyingly and slid down the back of his throat, the experience comfortingly familiar in the face of all that seemed to again be changing.

"I'll think of something, Ollie," Alden comforted his lover, after he had carefully arranged Oliver's cock inside his trousers and buttoned up the placket. He rose smoothly to his feet, tipping Oliver's chin up and resting his lips on Oliver's, to share the taste of Oliver's seed. Oliver hummed appreciatively, so Alden kissed his forehead and his cock to Oliver's stomach and sighed. "I have to go."

"I could—"

"I'm already late," Alden denied regretfully, pulling away. "But you'll make it up to me."

"Yes," Oliver agreed. "Yes, I will."

* * * *

It was several hours later when Alden crossed the Westminster Bridge, passing Parliament Square to turn on Horse Guards and round St. James's Park on his way back into Mayfair. Driving a phaeton through the teeming streets of London wasn't his idea of a joyful afternoon, but being confined inside his father's too-small town carriage all the way to Southwark and back was a needless torture. He was too big for that box, and the August sun would have made the carriage stifling. He'd ordered a larger town coach to fit his bulk—the winter months to come certainly required the services of a coachman—but it was not yet finished, so he was making the best of it.

He navigated the curve past the Horse Guards parade ground and almost lost control of the two bays he'd bought only a few weeks earlier. The street paralleled a walking path not twenty yards away. Through a stand of ancient heavily leaved trees, Fiona de Rothesay was walking.

Alden had only seen them a second, but he was certain she was arm in arm with Martin Morewell. His head was bent down to her. He was speaking earnestly —

Alden clenched his teeth, trying his best to restrain his reaction. He knew well that she'd disappeared with Young Canning only the night before while Martin and Oliver had been in the gardens, and she didn't outwardly appear to be loose with her affection. If anything, she seemed *demure*. Innocent. She'd been shocked by their caresses, but not fashionably missish or even knowingly flirtatious.

He'd have wagered his quarterly ducal allowance that she was a virtuous woman.

First Canning, now Martin Morewell. *Why Martin?* Alden knew perfectly well that both men were eminently eligible bachelors, and their ages would soon make marriage a requirement if they wanted to remain in the government ministries or Parliament.

And Fiona was undeniably educated in the languages and cultures of Europe, with a fluency in languages that probably met or exceeded both of them.

Alden managed to turn onto The Mall instead of proceeding up Marlborough Place into Mayfair. He drew the phaeton to the side of the street in front of Carlton House Terrace. Sparing a brief moment to look at the royal excess and its decaying façade, Alden hopped down as his tiger dashed to take the heads of his team.

By the time Alden entered the park through the stand of trees on the north side, Fiona and Martin had changed direction and were heading back toward the Birdcage Walk.

Alden approached them easily by virtue of his long legs. He had no reason to rush, but strolled naturally. St. James's Park was *haut ton* but hardly crowded by the ladies of high society. As the park was mostly used by gentlemen in the surrounding government buildings for fresh air and to stretch their legs, there were few people nearby to distract him or even nod to as he trailed the oblivious couple in front of him.

They were no longer talking amicably.

It took Alden longer than he would have liked to realize but from behind, he could see Fiona's stiff posture. She was upset. She shook her head, again and again, tried to pull her arm away. Martin kept a firm hold on it, she tugged a bit harder.

Alden did not like the implication that Martin Morewell was somehow restraining her. At all. It was bad enough that she was walking in public with Oliver's half-estranged brother when the two had seemed cozily intimate. But to see her resisting Martin? Ire struck him, and his temper was as sizable as his body.

Without hesitation, he turned into the trees and hurried, knowing the path met a crossroads not far ahead. He'd meet them there.

* * * *

"It's impossible, Martin. There must be some other way for me to do this other than sneaking around and staying out all night, constantly arguing with them. It's only been one night, and I'm exhausted. Maybe if I lived alone, I could live nocturnally and just start my day with dinner, but you must know it's impossible to simply decide to break out on my own and set up a household immediately, with both Lennox and my mother out of town. Oliver and Alden are already suspicious—"

"I knew they had something to do with it! You haven't told them—"

"Of course not! But neither can I slip off and stay out until dawn as I did before. Oliver insists I need a chaperone to go out in the evening, and both are hovering over me while I'm home, knowing I'm apt to sneak out like a thief."

Fiona felt her voice trail off in a huff at Martin's exasperated look. She nearly choked when he drawled, "My brother is hardly one to stand on propriety."

"Well, he is this time," she snapped.

"He's hardly *chaperone* material, and you're already staying there without your mother."

"You're the one who called me down to London, while Aunt Betsy stayed up north," she groused, trying to pull her arm away. "You need to think up a better plan. And you do *not* get to be judgmental. Even Lady Sefton made it clear to me today that if I'm to stay at Lennox House and appear to approve of Alden and Oliver — *which I do* — then I have to behave as if they have my support, and that means appearing in their company in society—not moving out, not avoiding them, not creating scenes the servants might hear or see, after I've come home at dawn."

Martin snorted. "It's not like you're an eighteen-year-old debutante looking for a husband."

Fiona stopped abruptly, the dismissal in his voice striking her. "I see," she said coldly, jerking her arm away. "Because I'm on the shelf, have an academic turn of mind and my last name is de Rothesay, my reputation is already in tatters and I should flout society to my heart's content and your convenience?"

Martin grimaced, shaking his head, and grabbed for her arm. "That's not what I —"

"Let go of her," commanded a deep voice at Fiona's rear. "Now."

Fiona felt the blood drain from her face. She shuddered, but still stepped back from Martin. A second of bewilderment flooded her at her instinctive trust in Alden, particularly a furious Alden. Eyes wide, she began to turn but he stepped between her and Martin, his large form blocking her view of the two men facing down each other.

Alden clearly had the advantage of height and muscle.

"What the hell are you about, Swenson?" Martin exclaimed. "We're in St. James's Park, for the love of God."

"Reach for her again at your own risk, Morewell," Alden drawled, not as loud as Martin but certainly loud enough. Suddenly sure that Alden's right fist was going to land against Martin's jaw, Fiona stepped up to his side and slid her arm inside his bent elbow, claiming Alden's escort. He didn't hesitate to step closer to her, but neither did the fierce frown on his face ease. "I'm not the lad your brother once thought to beat into submission. I won't hesitate to step between the two of you."

Martin's brow knitted in confusion. Fiona, also confused, almost opened her mouth to speak, but Martin got in first. "Firstly, what the hell are you talking about? And secondly, Swenson, I was hardly accosting her. We were having a civil discussion —"

"Just keep away from her," Alden snarled, turning her up the intersecting path. Fiona bit her lip, concentrating on walking properly as he hustled her along, but she couldn't glide quickly enough. After a few minutes, Alden stopped and stared down at her. "You can walk faster if you take bigger steps, you know," he said disparagingly.

Gasping, Fiona glared at him. "Ladies," she bit out, "even angry ladies, do *not* stride about as if we're late for a vote at Westminster. Nor, I have been assured on multiple occasions, do we ever *scurry*. Ladies *glide*."

Alden continued to peer into her pinched face for so long that she nearly lost her courage and flinched. "I've never strolled in a park with a lady," he admitted grudgingly.

"You're not off to a good start," Fiona returned. "What *was* that about?"

"You needed to be rescued," he grunted, moving forward again, this time at a more leisurely pace. "Mostly because you are once again out without a proper companion. Martin Morewell is an unmarried gentleman and *you were alone with him*. You weren't *supposed* to leave the house at all. What were you thinking?"

"That I won't be confined against my will?" she spat out, trembling when they passed the trees and she sighted Alden's phaeton. "And if he's an improper companion as an unmarried gentleman, how exactly would you describe yourself?" She looked about for the Lennox carriage and stopped abruptly. "I'm not getting in that," she gasped, staring at it. As high-perch phaetons went, it seemed stable and the horses controllable, but Fiona had seen several tipped over. The high, precarious seat was dangerous.

"How would you have gotten home?" Alden derided.

Fiona drew herself up proudly. "Martin would have had the Morewell carriage out," she claimed, withholding the information that she'd intended to avoid returning at all and dress for evening instead at the Cannings. The Morewell carriage would have taken her directly to that address.

Alden stopped again on the sidewalk, his hazel eyes fading to a dark color. "You do not *ever* inflict such a pain on Oliver, do you understand me?" he uttered furiously, the color rising in his cheeks. Turning to his tiger, he ordered the young man to return the phaeton and tugged Fiona along beside him, pausing a few paces away to wave down a hackney cab. One promptly halted, the black job horse clopping to a stop before them on the cobbled street. Alden lifted her into the cab without putting down the step. He followed her up into the dusky interior after tossing their direction at the driver and tugged the door closed even without a walking cane to assist him. His arms were that long.

Fiona trembled. The inside of the cab was completely inadequate in size, so they were sitting hip to hip on the cramped seat. She could barely move.

Alden kept his face rigidly forward and did not look at her, but Fiona could not let that last protective comment between them go unaddressed. Her pride, and her heart, were both at stake. "I wouldn't have hurt Oliver," she returned acidly. "Do you think I'm such a two-faced, backstabbing fishwife that I would be so cruel?"

Alden pinned her with another furious expression, as if she could've escaped the tiny hack by clambering over his lap and tumbling out the door. "I don't know what to think," he said bluntly. "After your performance last night and now this. *With Martin Morewell.* What am I supposed to think?"

Fiona felt the oddest sensation in her chest and in her head, behind her eyes. She nearly whimpered, fought against a foolish urge to beg his forgiveness, and brutally hardened her heart. He couldn't know how much she wanted to acknowledge that she was important to them and would do so except that it would give them the aegis they needed to direct her movements. He couldn't know how she alternately loved and envied his defense of Oliver's well-being, how she admired that he recognized and accepted Oliver's interest in her without jealousy or recriminations.

She couldn't forget how he—how *they*—had kissed her.

"You're to think that I had—have—a life that does not concern you," she demanded. "I have responsibilities, friendships and family here, too."

"Everything about you concerns me," he nearly bellowed, raising his hands to cup her upper arms. "So tell me about these damn *responsibilities*. Now."

Fiona wanted to shrink back, but she held her ground. In any event, she was already pressed into the corner of the seat with nowhere to go.

Oddly enough, despite nearly being crushed in his arms and by his rumbling fury, Fiona wasn't the least afraid. "No," she said, meeting his eyes and lowering her eyebrows stubbornly, steeling herself for an additional manly display of temper.

Alden growled furiously, a noise she almost expected, but instead of shaking her, or bellowing, he kissed her.

This kiss was not exploratory or even claiming. This kiss demanded. Alden did not hesitate to insert his tongue inside her mouth and abrade her bottom lip with his lower teeth, pushing it down to open her mouth wider. Fiona tipped her head back as he laid claim to her, his upper lip scraping against her. Fiona felt her body swell and soften and lean into him in betrayal of her better intentions to resist him, as her skin tingled with awakened nerve endings.

She had no choice but to submit. She had no choice, not because he took away the choice, but because she wanted him to continue.

Even as his tongue held hers down, she opened her mouth for him, welcoming his claim. Fiona knew the truth. She couldn't fight him or this aggressive conquering. She didn't want to.

If she could have spoken, she would have begged him to pull her closer, to cup her breasts beneath her bodice and squeeze them, to hold her within his arms and not let go. She wanted to plead with him.

She wanted to push him away and make him let her go about her business.

The horses drew to a halt, the hackney stopping abruptly. Alden lifted his head, and Fiona came to her senses in a rush, shuddering violently in his arms before he released her. "We can't be seen like this, getting out of a closed carriage at your house," she hissed as Alden opened the door.

"That was your choice," he snapped back. "I would have put you up beside me in the phaeton."

He jumped down and Fiona went to follow, only to find that he hadn't set the step down. She glared at him, but he simply paid the driver and came back for her. To her outward horror, he lifted her into his arms as if she was his bride instead of a prospective step-sibling and carried her up the steps. "Put me down," she furiously whispered.

"Stop wriggling," he ordered shortly. "If I put you down, you'll end up making my reaction to you obvious to the entire household."

Fiona gasped and stilled obediently, then felt her cheeks and neck heat as embarrassment struck. It only doubled when he swept through the front doors, held open by Carrington, and Oliver entered the front hall. "Is she all right?" Oliver asked, even as Alden paused.

"Yes," Alden answered, delivering her immediately to Oliver's arms. Shocked, she grabbed onto Oliver without thinking. "Take her up to my study. You and I need to discuss something before I deal with her."

"Deal with me?" Fiona squawked indignantly.

"Hush. It will be fine," Oliver assured her, turning obediently at Alden's directives.

"Put me down, Oliver," Fiona ordered, squirming again, but Oliver just grunted and climbed the stairs, tightening a hand on her thigh and the other around her shoulders. "I'm too heavy. You'll hurt yourself," she tried again.

"Just close your eyes and don't panic," he murmured. "I'm enjoying this a bit too much to disobey the big man downstairs. What kind of trouble have you gotten yourself into?" he asked.

"I didn't do anything wrong," she practically spat out.

Oliver hit the study door with his hip and it popped open. "If that's true, then you have nothing to worry about. He'd never truly *damage* you, even if you deserved a serious spanking. You know that, right?"

Fiona had had enough of Oliver and Alden's innuendos. "What is it with these threats? For what?" she objected. "I am hardly a schoolgirl."

Oliver sighed. "Just stay there and think about whatever you've done," he returned seriously. "Or about your foolish behavior from this morning. Running out without speaking to us first was most definitely a signal that you were ashamed of whatever confession you need to make, and you well knew it."

"Fiddlesticks," Fiona argued.

Oliver shrugged, kissed her forehead then smiled. "Let me go see what I can do to calm him down. Don't try to escape again, because we will catch up with you. We'll be back in a few minutes."

Fiona knew better than to agree, especially once her eyes caught sight of the door behind Alden's desk.

No matter what they said, she had a job to do, and one she couldn't tell them about. She knew Martin well, and they'd argued about telling Oliver what she was doing. Rushing to the window, she watched and smiled as a second hack pulled up to the house. Martin jumped out. The front door opened.

By the time they came back upstairs, she'd be out of the house and in Martin's carriage, which she fully expected would be waiting in the mews to sneak her away. If she couldn't resist Alden with his tempting kisses and Oliver with his persuasive words, Fiona would simply have to run.

Chapter Six

"Why are you here?" Alden snapped, following Oliver into the drawing room.

Martin stood before the fireplace, arms crossed. He'd barely looked at Oliver, but faced Alden's abrupt question squarely. "You were out of line," he stated evenly. "There was nothing *illicit* going on. We were strolling in a public park, for the love of God. She was simply delivering a letter from Anthony."

Oliver looked to Alden. "Where exactly did you find Fiona?" he asked Alden, his heart beating slightly faster. "And what did you do?"

Alden snorted. "She was strolling in St. James's Park with him, and he was being a prick. I had *every* right to interfere."

"She was delivering *confidential papers* to the Foreign Office, you arsehole. To Me. From Anthony. Because of your totally inexplicable behavior last night at Palmerston House and my idiot brother, I couldn't simply call here this morning and pick them up from the safety of Lennox's drawing room," Martin exploded, slamming his fist down on the back of a chair.

Oliver straightened, suddenly understanding. He knew well what Martin did at the Foreign Office. Once upon a time, he'd been slated to run Martin's library, before Morpeth had gone to their father complaining of Oliver's relationship with Alden. Before his father had issued the ultimatum that had required no thought from Oliver at all.

"Then why was she trying to break free of your grip?" Alden challenged, moving closer to Martin.

Alarmed, Oliver stepped between the two men, his eyes narrowed. "You're putting her in danger?" he asked softly. "Isn't that what dispatch boxes and the official courier service are for, brother?"

Martin blanched and shifted uncomfortably. "The occasional dispatch box is perfectly acceptable, given Anthony held an important post in the FO, but if they are frequent or rushed, people might begin to wonder," he eventually conceded.

Alden growled. "So what were you arguing about?" he repeated.

Martin sighed. "I hardly think that's any of your business, Swenson," he objected.

"Fiona is my business," Alden grated out an answer.

Oliver looked at him nervously. He hadn't seen Alden so angry since the night... Well, since that night years earlier that Oliver didn't wish to remember.

Martin flinched. "With Lennox out of town, perhaps. But there's nothing nefarious to concern yourself." He shrugged. "We sometimes disagree. I am supposed to escort her to that hieroglyphics lecture tomorrow night at the Society of Antiquaries. It's fairly widely known that Lennox disapproves of her going about Somerset House without a gentleman escort. And

Anthony didn't want her going alone. But Fiona listens even less often than Oliver did as a youth, even when it's in her best interests. Most of those clever gents are in awe of her, but there are a few of them who strike me as conniving and clever, rather than intelligent, and I've seen the looks she gets when her back is turned, even if she is oblivious to their interest. Naturally, Fiona was trying to refuse my escort, thinking no one would harass her if she went alone, not with Lennox out of town. She doesn't want me calling here and antagonizing you, but I happen to agree with His Grace and Anthony. She needs a male escort at Somerset House."

Oliver watched Martin carefully. His brother was still keeping something secret, but Oliver couldn't tell how serious Martin's evasiveness was. He knew from sharing a long childhood with his brother that Martin's right eye blinked when he lied, and the man was having trouble now keeping it still. "I will be her escort," he volunteered. "She will not find it easy to leave in a Lennox carriage without alerting me to it."

The Morewells would want to be sure Martin's bride was fully capable of all the relevant duties of an ambassador's wife — the appropriate European etiquette would be reviewed, she'd be tried and tested on all the related responsibilities of a hostess, her virtue would be closely watched. Martin might even be required to produce at least one child first, as proof that his bride was dutifully compliant.

Fiona was unquestionably fit for the role, with the possible exception of organizing and hostessing political events. Martin had both acknowledged his need to marry and decried Fiona as a possible candidate. But had he been completely honest the previous night?

If Martin was seriously considering her for the role of his wife and if Fiona was inclined to respond, Oliver knew he and Alden would have to draw away. His stomach clenched unbearably at the thought.

Martin just stared at him, his gaze inscrutable. "I don't pretend to understand, but you're neither interested in Egyptology or ancient languages. Still, if you insist, I won't argue, Oliver," Martin finally replied.

Alden snorted, but Oliver kept his eyes carefully on his brother. "I insist," he drawled. "Now, in the future, please remember she is a virtuous woman and not to be pawed at like a damned flower seller."

Martin stiffened. "Don't be crude," he sniffed. "I am perfectly capable of minding my manners, and I know my duty, even if I dislike it."

"Good," Oliver said equably. He glanced at Alden's frozen face, and noticed Alden's fist wrapped tightly around the back arch of a nearby chair. Quickly, he faced Martin again and moved toward his brother, stepping in front of Alden as he did so. "I'm so glad you called, even if the circumstances are challenging. You do know you are welcome at any time?"

Martin drew a deep breath, and responded as Oliver expected. They exchanged the usual niceties and discussed the desultory topics of relocating from Amsterdam to London before Martin straightened. "I need to return," he sighed reluctantly, glancing at the drawing room door. "You'll let me know if I can be of assistance in watching out for her, won't you?" he asked.

"Yes," Alden said shortly.

Martin paused at that abrupt answer and met Alden's glare steadily. "Don't make the mistake of thinking that I am my brother," he challenged the larger man. "Or that I have the same rigid narrow thinking. If you'll excuse me?" He bowed slightly to Oliver before tugging open the corridor issues.

Oliver watched him depart, sober as he stared after his brother. "What are the chances Fiona is still upstairs?" he asked Alden.

"She's had enough time to be in Chelsea by now," Alden growled.

He had another question. "Do you think Martin's untimely call was a distraction, so she could get out of the house?" Oliver questioned, hating that he had to suspect Fiona's underhanded behavior. Carrington reported that she'd left by the music room door and the grooms reported that they'd seen a black carriage waiting. She'd climbed in without assistance and the driver had immediately whipped up the reins.

"I'd wager that as soon as I put Fiona in the hack, he ran back to St. James's and called for his carriage."

"He left here in a hack."

"That's because *Fiona* left our house in *his* carriage."

Oliver stared at the ceiling in Alden's office, both angry and frustrated by Fiona's evasions. "What are we going to do?"

"We're going to dress for the evening, then comb Mayfair. There can't be that many evening events tonight."

"I have no compunctions about searching her desk. She must have an invitation somewhere. But even if we bring her back here, how will that help? She'll use the first excuse to run again."

"We're not bringing her back here," Alden said determinedly. "Not until we've established some level of understanding with her. We're taking her to the villa. She won't be able to run from there."

A fresh burst of energy swept Oliver. Alden was right. The London house was too easy to escape from and the servants could be relied upon to accommodate anything Fiona asked of them. She was, after all, Johna's daughter. But in Merton, hidden away in their private villa, Fiona would be unable to escape them. "If we leave directly from wherever we find her, it will be dark and she won't even know where we've taken her," he contemplated aloud.

"I trust you can pack bare essentials and a few changes of attire," Alden said briefly. "You'll know what she needs."

Oliver smiled at his orders. "I love you."

"I love you too," Alden answered, a wicked glint in his eye that Oliver appreciated so much more, because it had been absent for so long.

Fiona wasn't hard to find. The invitation to the soiree at Canning House was sitting in full sight on her desk, leaning neatly against the lamp. Despite Lucy's shocked objections, Oliver packed three of Fiona's most flattering evening gowns, a morning gown, a walking dress, drawers, petticoats, a nightgown, her brushes, her soaps and her house slippers.

He had a moment of guilt about the Egyptology lecture and reminded himself to ask Alden if they could bring her back to London for just that event. After all, it was the reason she'd come from Northumberland.

"She's been on her own, figuratively, for far too long. Your father may make small requests of her, but she's not been accountable to anyone and flouts authority to suit her own ends."

Alden grimaced. "She's taken it too far."

"She's taking it dangerously far. She's too thin. She's exhausted. She's going to fall ill at the pace she's maintained, presumably since she left Anthony's. We haven't really slowed her down at all."

Sending their baggage with a driver directly to Merton, the pair continued the conversation once they'd left the house in the phaeton. Alden drove, both men wrapped in their great coats despite the warm weather, to protect their evening clothes from the dust in the streets. Neither wanted a Lennox coachman to witness Fiona fighting them, and though they left it unsaid, Oliver knew quite well that she was likely to object to being appropriated.

Alden parked the phaeton himself in the mews behind the next corner and hopped down. Oliver followed him, watching dispassionately as Alden offered one of the waiting urchin lads a coin to hold the horses until they returned.

Neither had been invited, and this was the house of the Foreign Secretary. Fiona hadn't taken her invitation, but both men understood she was known at the house and they did have her card for the event. They slipped inside through the unlocked garden gate and up onto the terrace at the far side, startling a German bureaucrat and a little French matron whose eyes widened in fear. Oliver made certain to smile at the woman in understanding, even as Alden politely looked away, and they escaped into the light spilling onto the terrace even as the woman squealed in indignation at her lover.

A loud smack echoed in the silence behind them, followed by a masculine grunt of pain.

Oliver flinched and glanced up at Alden, who was trying desperately to keep his face straight.

"Poor man," Oliver muttered.

Alden started to speak, but froze instead as he examined the scene through the terrace doors, standing open to a long music room. At least for the moment, no one was dancing. "Do you know the house?" Alden asked.

"Yes," Oliver affirmed, watching as Martin and Morpeth argued some point at the far end of the room. He waited, watched Morpeth's shoulders stiffen in agitation, just as they'd done when he was a child. Martin shifted, turning away from the room as he spoke, and Oliver knew the time had arrived. "Follow me if you can. Your height makes you impossible to conceal."

Behind him, Alden humphed, but Oliver collected himself, donned his social mask of personable charm, and moved confidently into the room. All they had to do was cross it and meander through the card room to the door to the front corridor. Simple.

* * * *

"I'm certain I saw Lord Alden, Fiona," Harriet whispered, drawing Fiona's arm inside hers. "He's hard to mistake, as tall as he is."

Fiona shivered. She knew neither Alden nor Oliver was in the main rooms. At Harriet Canning's whispered warning, Fiona and Harriet had strolled through the reception area, searching for Oliver and Alden. "They aren't here now," she returned, hiding her puzzlement. Surely they wouldn't cause a confrontation *here*, in the Foreign Secretary's own house?

"I think we should warn Papa and my brother," Harriet said clearly. "What if they hurt you?" Harriet was a tiny creature, prim and proper in public with a sharp chin and flashing blue eyes. She looked as though she was still a child, and many men had made the mistake of treating her as such, when in fact she was startlingly perceptive and direct.

Fiona shook her head, denying that they would hurt her more than that Harriet's concerns should be shared, but drew Harriet out of the main rooms and into the anteroom at the top of the grand staircase, which was surprisingly empty. "Neither Lord Oliver nor Lord Alden would hurt me, Harriet. They both want to *protect* me. They are worried, you know, because I was out all night. They think I'm having an illicit *affaire*, and of course Martin told them nothing of how I spend my time."

Harriet pursed her lips in disapproval. "Still, they weren't invited—"

Fiona nearly sighed but it was already after ten o'clock and she needed to start on the true night's work. "I need Lord Martin or your brother to escort me to Whitehall anyway. I'll go up and change now. Will you please inform Young and ask him to help me out of the house? I will go down the service stairs and meet him in the kitchens."

Harriet grimaced. "That would probably be best. I'll go now." She pressed Fiona's hands and smiled. "Thank heavens you aren't one to panic."

Fiona agreed and turned into the main gallery. It was dimly lit with deep shadows in the window bays, and away from the main guests, but the guest bedchamber she used when in Canning House was at the end of the corridor, past Harriet's apartment and just before the concealed door that led to the service stairs.

Alden stepped out from one of the window recesses just before she reached her chamber door. Gasping, Fiona stopped abruptly and started to back away, but Oliver was behind her.

"Wh – what – ?"

Alden covered her mouth and he lifted her against his chest. Too stunned and confused to struggle and shocked by the response of her body, Fiona required a full ten seconds to assimilate that Alden was following Oliver down the narrow back stairs, and she was firmly grasped in his arms. When they reached the dark service corridor at the bottom, Alden hoisted her even more tightly against him.

"Hush," he grunted, before Oliver led them quickly but unerringly through the lit, bustling kitchen. Fiona saw it flash by, realized no one had seen them and squirmed, only to have Alden shift and palm the back of her derriere to hold her still.

Even through her silk ballgown, two petticoats, chemise, garters and stockings, Fiona felt her skin burn from the heat of his hand.

Suddenly she was much more aware of how he held her close, wrapped below her breast with one forearm and jacket sleeve between her breasts, the warmth of his palm against her lips, the tingling of her skin where he touched her.

Half-formed thoughts and emotions raced through her when Oliver pushed open a service door to the gardens. The night was warm but a cool breeze had begun to drift over the city. Fiona felt the tendrils of air on the nape of her neck, felt her pins come loose where they were rubbing against Alden's waistcoat. She had to stop this, she told herself. She couldn't let these two men, nearly strangers, walk away with her. She couldn't *want* them to, could she?

The answer, the *longing*, was startling enough, and distracting enough, to keep her silent as she struggled to think.

Ahead of them, Oliver flipped coins at two boys holding the horses and Fiona realized —

"Umph," she grunted, suddenly remembering all the reasons to fight. She would be missed. Martin and Young Canning would come looking for her, and the Foreign Secretary himself would want to know why she'd disappeared.

"You'll be perfectly safe as long as you don't try to jump down," Alden snapped, tossing her up onto the phaeton's seat.

Fiona gasped as the seat tipped, swayed, and she grasped the low back and stabilized herself, especially when Alden followed her onto the perch. It tipped again, until he slid more to the middle, leaving only a small space at his side where Fiona could sit close to him. Her thigh was up against his, and his long legs were warm, even through his superfine breeches. She looked down, blinked at his unusual fashion *faux pas*, and by the time she recovered, Oliver had jumped onto the tiger's seat behind them and the phaeton turned and clopped sedately down the dark street.

By all precedents, he should have been wearing black or gray linen trousers, not Court-appropriate ivory superfine.

Fiona blinked. They'd come out of the service door onto the side street. The carriages and drivers from the Canning House event had been left behind and they were on the gas-lit street facing Berkeley Square. The night was quiet, with very few people about on the side streets, and Alden was already turning onto a larger street where he could pick up speed.

They were not returning to Lennox House.

She shrugged her shawl up over her shoulders and debated, putting her lips together tightly. She could scream. She'd attract attention even from Mayfair's cadres of servants out for the evening and strolling home, cause a scandal, possibly get Alden or Oliver arrested, definitely humiliate them.

She could also acquiesce, secure in the knowledge that the Morewells and Cannings would definitely be rescuing her in short order. They would soon deduce Oliver and Alden were responsible for her disappearance. However, no way would anyone know where Alden and Oliver were taking her. Fiona didn't even know where the phaeton was going, but she suspected that Oliver, at least, would not set out baggageless, which implied that it had been sent ahead or was following behind, so the servants at Lennox House would know their destination.

Both Martin and Young Canning knew that Fiona was sympathetic to Oliver and Alden's concerns. Still, they'd search for her.

A small voice inside Fiona's head suggested she might also want to actively participate in her disappearance. How many times would she have this chance, to explore intimacy with *anyone*, presuming that was their intention?

No one spoke, not while Alden maneuvered the horses through the streets, carefully but without any confusion despite the dark night. He knew, Fiona realized, precisely where he was going. Behind them, Oliver passed up a covered lantern. Fiona took it and hung it on a high pole provided for just this purpose before she even grasped her own complicity in the action.

Glancing at the large bulk of the man beside her, Fiona shivered a bit. He didn't seem angry, merely doggedly focused. She openly examined his features — the shape and set of his jaw, the line of his lips dimly visible from the pale shafts of light emanating from the lantern. She debated asking as to their purpose, but neither did she wish to distract him from the cattle and his examination of the dark road.

Far better to wait until she had their full attention, she told herself decisively, knowing she was clinging desperately to the notion that she was in control of the evening's outcome.

When the phaeton crossed Chelsea Bridge Road and continued to roll along, Fiona realized where they were headed.

Alden and Oliver had a Merton villa, presumably one of the gated, private properties between the sleepy village and Cottenham Park. Many noblemen kept their mistresses in those homes along the river. The long properties stretched down to the river, hidden from each other by hills and high fences. Groves of fruit trees protected guest houses. Fiona had once been to a picnic at a villa owned by the Castlereaghs, and she'd gotten lost in the thick maze of formal gardens and overhanging arbors.

Merton's villas and their adjoining grounds were designed to shield occupants from the prying eyes of neighbors and servants.

She suppressed the urge to shiver, her heart beating faster, keeping her lips together as they proceeded steadily.

Her stomach lurched when the phaeton turned, and they faced a tall, wrought-iron set of gates. Alden halted the horses, allowing Oliver to hop down and open the gate.

Alden walked the horses forward through the posterns. Fiona couldn't help but twist and look back, and she inhaled sharply when she realized that Oliver was actually locking them inside.

She turned to Alden, who watched her now. With the hour drive from London completed in the darkness, her eyes had adjusted to the shadows, enough for her to see his lips twist. "Only our caretakers are in residence, and they have separate quarters above the carriage house."

Oliver returned to his seat, and the carriage rumbled along the bricked drive for two minutes, passing through a grove of trees that hid the house from the road. Pulling up in front of a circular drive, Alden halted the horses and waited while Oliver jumped down and moved around the carriage to help Fiona.

She eyed the distance to the ground and decided to accept his assistance without fussing.

To her surprise, instead of steadying her as she descended, he reached up and grasped her waist, holding her against his chest for a stunning moment of contact before her feet touched the ground.

Her long-resisted shudder was unavoidable, as was the small noise that came from her throat.

Alden sent the horses forward without remarking on the scene, and Fiona couldn't read the emotions in Oliver's eyes in the dark. She only felt his arm tighten around her waist. "Come inside, my dear. We have much to discuss."

Fiona stilled, paused, and looked at the wide double doors before her. Fiona inwardly noted the doors were constructed of heavy oak, probably able to withstand most frontal assaults.

With a sigh, Fiona stepped forward. "We do need to *discuss* this nonsense before you take me back to London," she finally conceded. She glanced at Oliver, but he simply met her eyes evenly in the dim light and used a key from his waistcoat pocket to open the doors.

The villa was comfortable, the luxury understated and subtle. Oliver led her into a marble-tiled foyer. To her left was a drawing room with a high ceiling. An arched opening within revealed dim hints of the dining room beside it. To her right, doors opened to a music room with long windows covered with white drapes. The hall was lit with wall scones that led them forward, and the drawing room with white-glassed lamps. To her surprise, without comment, Oliver ushered her into the drawing room and settled her into an arm chair. "I'll get tea. We can talk when Alden comes inside," he announced quietly.

Fiona inhaled carefully as he disappeared, marshaling her thoughts. Her first thought was for her evening's work. Tonight, the letters from Saint Petersburg were written in Kashubian, a Slavic language from a region between Poland and Russia. During the late afternoon, Secretary Canning had summoned her to his study at Canning House and made particular mention of his interest in any hint of plans for a coup or assassination of Tsar Alexander I.

Given the seriousness of the subject, Fiona pondered how quickly a rescue mission would be launched. She suspected it would be as quickly as Young Canning could discover where she'd be taken, and that would likely be in the morning.

Fiona concluded she had at least several hours and more, probably, into the morning before anyone from the Foreign Office discovered her location.

As for escape, she supposed she could get out of the house, but what good would it do? She could find the stable and take one of the horses, but she could hardly ride astride in a ballgown into the heart of London. She could hunt down a neighbor, but given the neighborhood, known for homes occupied by the mistresses of noblemen, it might be difficult to find anyone at home or with servants willing to answer the door. Witness Alden and Oliver's own house. The caretakers were not in the same building, and she couldn't have passed the gates.

The likelihood of a successful and respectable escape in Merton, so late at night in an unfamiliar area, was nonexistent.

So she'd stay in the house. And...

To her surprise, Alden pushed a small mahogany teacart into the room, with Oliver following closely behind him. Neatly and efficiently, Oliver set the tea to brew while Alden settled himself on a chaise. Unblinking, Fiona watched them, considering what she might say and what she could do. What she wanted to do.

What she would do.

"Are you planning to run again?" Oliver eventually asked, looking up and meeting Fiona's eyes.

Fiona considered, but conceded, "Not tonight. I can't see the point."

"Precisely why we're here," he returned. Beside him, Alden frowned and crossed his arms over his chest.

"What I do tomorrow, however, largely depends on you," she murmured, lifting a hand to take a cup of the hot tea from Oliver.

"Aren't you curious?" Oliver asked, gesturing between the three of them languidly. He poured a cup for Alden and added in two large lumps of sugar before he prepared himself a cup of the brew.

"Curious?" Fiona frowned at him.

"Of what could be," Alden murmured deeply.

"Would you take me back to London tonight?" she asked, tipping her head. "If I asked?"

Oliver and Alden looked at each other, obviously considering. Eventually, Oliver sighed. "No. It's already after eleven. Unless you have some compelling reason to return, I can't see why we should return to the City until at least tomorrow morning, no matter what happens or doesn't happen between the three of us tonight."

Fiona sighed, audibly. She had a compelling reason but she did not have leave to explain. Silent, she sipped at her tea, watching Alden cradle the delicate cup, incredibly gently despite his size. She watched Oliver's long, elegant fingers as they worked but then she peeked at his face and found that he was watching her, too. She didn't feel as if she knew him *intimately*, but his first concern that morning had not been propriety, but her well-being. Such things were good portends, especially since she'd known Martin for years and had still been shocked when he'd physically constrained her in the park.

Where else would she ever find a man so considerate, let alone two of them together? When else would she have such a chance?

"Yes," she admitted hesitantly. "Yes, I'm curious."

A sharp noise came from Alden. His hands shook as he carefully placed the teacup and saucer on the lower shelf of the tea cart. "But?"

Fiona thought, glanced at both of the men, and returned her cup to the teacart as well. She whispered, "I don't know what to do."

Oliver sipped and watched her, until she straightened proudly and glared back at him. Gently, he set his cup aside and stood, holding out a hand to her. "It's late," he murmured, and Fiona shivered at the deep tone. "You don't have a maid, and you need some time to learn to be close to us. Come with us, and let us care for you. You can call a halt the moment we make you uncomfortable."

Alden stood. She had to look up, but he stood beside Oliver and extended his right hand as well. "Please," he said.

The light wavered, and the lines in Alden's face glowed. A memory erupted, of the tender way in which a much younger Alden had carried Oliver through the mews. Fiona was surprised at the sudden longing that hit her, a desire to be touched with such raw fervency, a desire to be *known*.

How would she ever know unless she—unless they—tried?

"Yes."

Chapter Seven

They led her, Alden with her right hand clasped in his left and Oliver with her left hand in his right one, through the front hall and down the dark corridor, past the music room and a set of closed doors to French doors inset with an intricate stained-glass design. Fiona wanted to stop and study the image, but it was too dim to see properly and Oliver was pushing open the doors and leading them inside.

Fiona held her breath as Alden closed the door behind them and snubbed the lock. She exhaled slowly, evenly, controlling the panic rising in her chest.

The large room was stunning even in the dim light, but the centerpiece was a giant Elizabethan bed positioned in its center in front of Fiona. Two posters framed the ornate carving of the headboard that extended up to the wooden canopy. Two more thick posters supported the wooden canopy from the foot of the bed. Heavy burgundy velvet drapes were roped back at the front corners, but sheer, rich white shimmered from the canopy and fluttered to the floor.

The counterpane was burgundy silk, intricately embroidered with gold thread and with a collection of billows in various shapes and garish colors piled near the headboard. On each side of the bed, tall sets of white double French doors with diamond panes stood open to a garden terrace, allowing small sprays of moonlight in, to spill onto the polished floorboards. To the left was a fireplace with a seating area around it. Lit by two lamps, Fiona briefly admired the ivory upholstered chaise and two leather armchairs, and a fine rosewood escritoire in the far corner. To the right of the bed was an open area clearly intended for dressing, with a dressing table with stool, full length cheval mirror, appropriate bureaus and an open door into a wardrobe.

But for all Fiona's curiosity over this wondrous room, her attention was immediately caught and focused on the brilliant ceiling, painted in a gorgeous swath of golds and dark red hues within the traditional white cornices that merged the walls and ceiling.

"Robert Adam," Oliver murmured briefly. "We bought the villa for the ceiling. This chamber was the original library."

Alden released her fingers and moved through the room, lighting extra lamps and candles to brighten the space, revealing the ivory paper striped with a regularly spaced burgundy ribbon. Beside her, Oliver squeezed her hand and tugged. Still distracted, Fiona followed him, studying the graceful design of circles and squares that spread out from the central chandelier hanging between the doors and the foot of the bed.

"Come, sit," Oliver murmured, adjusting the upholstered rectangular stool so it was perpendicular to the vanity. He guided Fiona to the seat and Alden lit the oil lamps on each side. Fiona glanced into the mirror, and her eyes widened helplessly as she took in the sight of the two large men behind her.

"I'm going to take down your hair," Oliver murmured.

Fiona trembled, her heart racing. She twisted slightly to watch him, surprised that he did nothing more than simply brush the pads of his fingers over the nape of her neck.

The touch startled her. Such contact, gently against skin exposed by the mound of hair fashionably piled on her head, was novel, scattering sensation from her neck and down her spine. She shivered. What other man had brushed that sensitive patch of skin, pulled taut by her topknot? None. Oliver repeated the innocent caress, scraping the short ebony tendrils that had escaped.

Alden had retreated through a door in the far wall of the room, but now he reappeared, a length of white draped over his arm. She opened her mouth to object, but fidgeted slightly, shifting to watch him in the mirror. He spread the garment over the foot of the bed and expertly turned down the counterpane. He'd dispensed with his jacket and waistcoat and was garbed in only his trousers and shirtsleeves. Approaching from behind her, his size again startled her, but he only brushed a tender kiss against Oliver's lips before circling them both and kneeling before her. Without comment about her shaking fingers, clenched in her lap before him, Alden lifted one elegantly shod foot onto his thigh.

Like the ballgown she'd worn that evening, the dancing slippers belonged to Harriet Canning. They had been a touch too small, pinching her toes inside silk stockings, but they were little more than low-heeled sandals, with wide white ribbons wound over her ankles and knotted at mid-calf, designed to protect her white stockings from being frayed on the ballroom floor. Alden set to work picking at the knotted ribbons, brushing his palms against her stockings. At first, Fiona thought the occasional touches were accidental, but when he deliberately lifted her skirts and folded them back on her knees, she gasped and held her breath.

"Lean back against me," Oliver murmured, bending forward to feather the words over her ears. Oliver was exploring her hairline and had carefully located the pins holding up the coiffure. For each one he pulled out, he caressed some sensitive spot along the edge of her ears, behind her lobes, at the hairline along her neck and lower, where her shoulder bones connected with her spine.

It was an evocative, sensual experience that Fiona hadn't known enough to expect. Barely able to absorb the sensations, she blindly obeyed Oliver's injunction and leaned back. Oliver pulled the last remaining pin from her hair and removed his fingers, allowing it to fall around her. Deliberately, he fingered the tresses, arranging them over her shoulders and down her front to flow over her breasts.

Caught up in the spell they were carefully conjuring, Fiona had no thought but to follow his directive. He stepped closer and she settled back, resting her neck and the back of her head against Oliver's stomach. At her feet, Alden circled her ankles with his massive hands, soothing with rhythmic motions of his palms and fingers. His sensual massage eased any lingering pain from the pinched shoes, especially when he moved his hands farther down and caressed the arch and sole of each foot in turn.

"Are you frightened?" Alden asked, his voice rumbling over her, husky. Fiona considered briefly but denied it with a restricted shake of her head.

The movement returned her attention to Oliver. He had laid a single lock of hair from her right temple down his forearm and over his palm. With his other hand, he pulled her brush through it, a movement that was as much a caress as part of any toilette. He repeated the motion again and again, studying the strands carefully until, apparently satisfied, he draped that lock of hair over her bosom and used his fingers to separate the next lock in turn, repeating the process.

"So lush," Oliver whispered, after a few moments of silence.

"Absolutely," Alden agreed.

Fiona blinked, then focused on Alden again. He'd released her stockinged feet, settling them on a ruby-hued cushion, and sat back onto his heels to watch the spectacle Oliver was creating as he brushed her hair. Quite without thinking, her nerves reacted. Previously clutched together then relaxed in her lap, she clenched her fists in the froth of her petticoats, revealed when Alden had flipped them up to her knees.

"Shhh," he murmured, catching the barest exclamation of disappointment that Fiona voiced as she exhaled. "I'm only going to fetch warm water, for washing you."

The provocative phrasing accelerated Fiona's heartbeat until it pounded furiously in her ears, but Alden was already standing and moving away.

Oliver chuckled, but it was a quiet, masculine amusement. "If you enjoyed that," he murmured suggestively, "imagine how it will feel without your stockings in the way, with only his warm hands working directly on your velvet skin."

Fiona jerked, desperately trying not to imagine any such thing. Against her spine, Oliver shifted, pressing his body into hers until Fiona could identify the outline of thighs on either side of her spine and a strange hardness between.

A full minute passed before she could deduce just what that unfamiliar pressure was, and when she realized, Fiona blushed as brightly as any schoolgirl, grateful for the dimness of the candlelight.

"You are likely accustomed to wearing your hair up at night," Oliver said, drawing her mind away from the sudden preoccupation in hers. "But it is stunning. I—I suspect *we* – would greatly prefer to see it falling so charmingly over your shoulders." He turned Fiona's head slightly toward the mirror.

Fiona blinked. Still attired in Harriet's ballgown of mulled indigo silk embroidered with silver thread, her hair swirling about her shoulders, Fiona nearly didn't recognize the woman before her. The gown was cut across her cleavage, and her modest bosom was lifted and displayed charmingly by lavender ribbons wrapping around the bodice and threaded through the laces at the back of the garment. Her long locks tickled the exposed skin, and her face was partially concealed by the low light, though an unusual color in her cheeks could be easily discerned.

"We've somehow discovered an Aphrodite—a muse." The voice was Oliver's, but it was Alden who loomed into the space beside her, settling a pitcher and bowl onto the vanity table. Alden examined her as well, lingering on her for disconcertingly long minutes. When, discomposed by the study, Fiona began to shift, Oliver rested his hands on her shoulders to encourage her. "Let him look," he murmured. "Let him appreciate having you here, with us. Alden enjoys…watching."

Fiona sucked in a sharp breath, lifting her bosom abruptly and capturing Alden's instant attention. She met his gaze and didn't look away, even when Oliver brushed his hands over her back, loosening her laces.

"We're going to take off the ballgown now," Oliver stated evenly. "There's no reason to be afraid, none at all. Do you feel excitement in your stomach and even lower? Are you curious what it will feel like to wear only a chemise and stockings while you are with us?"

If she hadn't wondered before, she did now. Fiona trembled, her eyes still on Alden as he brought forth thick cotton squares, poured a teaspoon of liquid into the water bowl, and carefully filled the bowl with the ceramic pitcher. Alden dipped the fabric into the water, still so warm that wisps of steam rose from the bowl.

Oliver released the last lace and the fitted bodice loosened. It was the work of a few seconds for him to draw the brief sleeves down her arms and over her hands, and for Oliver to urge Fiona to stand so he could push the silk skirts down past her hips. She'd been through the familiar process of undressing thousands of times, and her instincts took over as the petticoats dropped as well. She simply sat back down, garbed only in her chemise.

Almost as if he were a lady's maid trained to the duty, Oliver drew the skirts and petticoats down and off her feet, leaving Fiona dressed only in a silk chemise tied a bare inch above her nipples.

Awareness struck.

Panic blossomed.

"Look at me," Alden demanded, and despite her keen desire to flee, Fiona managed to do so. Alden stepped closer, trapping her on the stool as she straightened her spine and looked at him mutinously. "You are beautiful, designed by the Creator himself to attract men such as me. There is no shame in sharing your beauty with us, just as there is no shame in sharing your very fine mind with the scholars of London. You, Fiona, are utterly spectacular, and hiding yourself against a ballroom wall doesn't diminish it for an instant."

Oliver returned while Fiona's mouth fell open in astonishment, his arms empty of her gown and petticoats. "He's absolutely right."

Fiona pressed her lips together. She didn't trust herself to speak. If she spoke, she would cry — and she *never* cried.

What followed was an education for Fiona in the nature of intimacy. Alden took charge of her hands, wrapping hot wet cloths around them. Oliver tipped her face toward him, tucked her head between his torso and his left arm, and used a third cloth to carefully wash her face.

If she had imagined her first acquaintance with intimacy, she would have said it would have involved the more secret parts of her body, but when Alden unwrapped her hands and slowly, silently, traced every line of her fingers and palms with the blunt tips of his own digits, Fiona finally grasped the true nature of the experience. Both Alden and Oliver were creating a fascination for their touch, a longing that was growing in her heart and her womb to experience more. They were offering her a tuition which she would not have found elsewhere. Intimacy was not only nudity, but an emotional and tactile openness to another.

Thankfulness — *gratitude* — and admiration crept into her heart.

Alden turned her palm over and bent down, touching his lips to the center, even as Oliver set aside the cloth and drifted down her front to tangle in the ribbons that kept her chemise in place.

Subsumed in the moment, driven not by curiosity but by an unfamiliar desperation to simply see the expression on their faces as her breasts came into view, Fiona made not a single demur when the ribbons were pulled free and the chemise fell to her waist.

Their reaction was all she could have wanted, if she'd had time to form expectations. Alden, eyes wide, focused intently on her bounty — the globes firm and high with nipples slightly angled upward. He fell to his knees beside her, reaching out and tracing a circle around each one.

The touch shocked her and she arched, driving her head into Oliver's side. Without hesitation, he absorbed her abrupt movement and lowered both hands to cup the outsides of her breasts, lifting them and squeezing them together. A single glance in the mirror confirmed his fascination, confirmed when he bent to her temple and nuzzled hotly over her temple. "Treasure," he managed, the single word almost strangled.

Her breasts displayed by Oliver's hands, Alden ventured farther and scraped over Fiona's nipples, one hand to each nipple simultaneously. She gasped, the noise turning into an unfamiliar moan as he squeezed those delicate nubs between his thumbs and index fingers. Alden's eyelids drooped and he firmed his digits against her skin, tugging slightly until Fiona moaned.

"Later, just like this, with her sitting between your knees and laid back against your chest," Alden grated. "With me between her legs, bare everywhere for me to explore."

"Why not now?" Oliver asked directly, shifting against Fiona.

A needy noise left Fiona's throat.

"Indeed, why not now?" Alden asked, bending forward and tweaking his lips around her nipple. He sucked in deeply and Fiona's shock splintered into a million shards of glass, the eruption sending waves of static electricity across every nerve and emptying her mind of any rational thought.

Alden caught her as she listed to the side, and lifted her against his chest, surprised by the spontaneous orgasm that had rocked her. Oliver hurried to undress, uncharacteristically flinging his clothes to the floor before rushing ahead and taking his place in the bed. Just as Alden suggested, he sat back against the headboard, gloriously naked, his erection rising proudly from the nest of gilded curls at his groin. Alden deposited the dazed bundle of female in his arms to Oliver's lap before she could come to her senses.

He stripped as he watched Oliver arrange her, his lips twisting in amusement as Oliver tucked his cock between the curves of Fiona's bottom, where she could cradle and caress his erection simply by reacting to their attentions. Naked, he mounted the bed at the foot and lay forward, parting Fiona's legs, still clad in silk stockings. Alden moved between her knees until she had little leverage to conceal her charms.

Only then did he allow himself to examine the treasure revealed before him. She was beginning to stir and blinked lazily at him when he rested his hands to her thighs above her garters and traced their swells up to her mons. Black curls thickly covered that pad, but Alden forged a path downward with his fingers as deliberately as he could manage, learning her form and folds. Above his head, Fiona emitted a senseless moan, and he glanced up to see Oliver exploring her breasts, as fascinated as he had been by their plush promise. Of course, Oliver could not taste the delicious nipples from his position behind her, but both men could now see the dusky rose hue revealed by the light of the bedside lamps. Alden watched avidly for a moment as Oliver explored them with the patience of a golden god, experimenting with how Fiona responded to his tugs and pinches.

Alden raised his eyes and met Oliver's. No words were needed for Alden to know that Fiona, between them, was the fulfillment of Oliver's deepest fantasies.

He could hardly concern himself with the thought, as consumed as he was with the woman herself. Leaning forward, he bent his head again, pleased when Oliver squeezed and offered him the treat.

This time, Fiona's cry of pleasure dissolved into a moan as he sucked in the nipple and rubbed his upper front teeth against the aureole. She suddenly clutched his hair, not pushing him back as he had feared, but to hold him close.

Alden sucked gently and pushed one blunt middle finger inside the opening between her legs.

Beneath him, Fiona's body arched in offering, pushing against his finger and presenting her nipple to his grateful mouth. He inserted his finger an inch farther inside, and he found the hard button blossoming just above her sex with his thumb. He flicked it, not quite sure what to expect, and Fiona erupted again. He lifted his mouth, aroused beyond his expectations to see the shuddering convulsions and to feel them around his finger where he continued to stretch the tight walls that gripped him.

"Mother of God," Oliver grunted beneath her, catching his attention. As Alden watched, Oliver's biceps convulsed and his eyes rolled. He struggled for control, and Alden realized with a burst of sensual appreciation that Fiona's bottom must be clenching against Oliver's stiff cock.

"Jealous, my love?" Alden smirked.

"Fuck no," Oliver returned hoarsely. "I'm desperate."

Fiona blinked, no doubt astonished by the crude reply from Oliver. Alden shifted, refusing to even consider removing his finger from the hot tunnel he was so carefully probing. Instead, he slid his hand beneath Fiona's bottom and under Oliver's erect staff, cupping that hot arousal in his palm. Above Fiona's head, he met Oliver's gaze. "Mind your mouth," he admonished.

Oliver tensed before hips bucked at the warning, his cock thrusting hard up into the valley between Fiona's cheeks. Alden dug his fingers into her sweet skin, trapping Oliver even more tightly between Alden's hand and Fiona's ass.

Fiona shuddered, drawing his attention down to her svelte curves. Her eyelids flickered open. Cloudy and dark in the lamp light, the orbs were a heady distraction. Alden wondered how long he could simply lie there and drown in them, but knowing Fiona, it wouldn't be nearly long enough to satisfy him. Experimentally, Alden stroked his palm upward over the underside of Oliver's cock, scraping Fiona's bottom with his fingernails. Fiona squirmed and moaned appreciatively, but Oliver's eyes rolled into the back of his head and he struggled again to restrain his climax. Encouraged, Alden repeated the movement.

The stimulation was simply too much for Oliver, whose hips moved out of his control. He pumped his cock against the tight cavern Alden had made between his hand and Fiona's velvet curves until the cream spilled out over Alden's wrist and along Fiona's labia and thighs.

Alden's thighs tightened and his own nerves flickered as he struggled to control the sudden lust that gathered in his groin. Intent on the erotic vision before him, watching Oliver's glazed eyes and Fiona's rapidly clearing ones, Alden deliberately withdrew his finger from Fiona's flowering pussy and ran it lengthwise through Oliver's creamy ejaculate. Coated with Oliver's juices, Alden thrust his finger deeper, pushing higher inside her until he found a natural resistance he hadn't expected.

Surprised, he looked up and surveyed her.

Beneath him, Fiona was shaking, her eyes glittering as she watched him. She clenched Oliver's hips beneath her. He held her gaze and withdrew his finger two inches, then thrust in again, pushing farther. "Your maidenhead," he grunted, unable to express the multitude of emotions he felt in words. He hadn't imagined it before, had truly thought she'd spent the previous night with a lover, but now? Now, Alden wanted to be the one to take her. He wanted to keep her sweetly innocent of any man's touch. He wanted to see her shimmer and glow in the blissful throes of orgasm as he thrust his cock high up inside her. He wanted to see Oliver rocking into her pussy and against her clit as he slid his cock into her mouth. He wanted to watch Oliver enter her from behind while he knelt before her and sucked on her clit until she screamed their names. He wanted Oliver to acknowledge his claim upon the gorgeous creature spread out before him. He wanted to see her asleep in his arms, satiated and safe, not just tonight but for many nights to come, for as long as she would stay there.

Hauling his mind back to the moment at hand, Alden swallowed a curious lump in his throat and tried again, catching Oliver's eyes with his this time. "Hold her close," he managed, savagely satisfied by the way Oliver's eyes widened at his words, and how his love tightened his arms obediently around her torso, both supporting and restricting the unconscious little movements of her body as she artlessly responded to their touches. Shifting and bending a bit, Alden brushed his lips over Fiona's mouth as she inhaled a shallow breath. "I don't know how to keep it from hurting while I do it," he muttered, knowing full well the tinge of regret in his words.

Oliver knew quite well—and Alden had never denied—that Alden derived a certain pleasure from causing a small level of erotic pain, and he fully expected to pursue the same with Fiona. Why would he shy away from this one moment, this one opportunity?

Alden couldn't imagine hurting her by driving his cock up inside her. She was achingly tight, and he was startling in girth and length. It would be some time before she could easily take any rough penetration from his cock, and he wasn't ashamed to admit he looked forward to watching—to helping—Oliver enjoy pumping into her.

But first, Alden intended to breach the constriction that stretched against his fingertip. He withdrew it an inch and thrust upward again, but still cautiously.

Fiona's eyes widened. "Just finish it," she begged, her body fully taut as she stretched, shaking with nervous anticipation. "Don't worry. I'll survive."

Oliver growled, a purely masculine sound that, even as long as they'd been together, Alden had never heard from him. Alden glanced at him, surprised, but the picture of the two of them together, clearly waiting on him to accomplish the difficult moment, galvanized him.

He withdrew his finger completely again, drawing a frustrated moan from Fiona's lips, but reverently coated his finger in Oliver's cream and Fiona's own juices, then repositioned his finger and thrust it up inside her as high as possible.

Fiona uttered a small sound of distress, which she quickly swallowed. Even so, both men couldn't help but hear it. Oliver smoothed his hands over her breasts and whispered some words of comfort directly into her ear. Alden watched as Oliver traced the delicate curve with his lips. At the sight, Alden couldn't help but lean down. "I'm sorry, *roosje*," he murmured, sliding his tongue between her teeth and tracing the sharp edges. He began to extract his finger, but she clenched around it and shook her head frantically.

"No, no, I know there's more," she denied. "I—I—I need *something*," she pleaded.

Lust, suppressed beneath the tension of the previous minutes, struck him squarely in the chest, no doubt encouraged by her aroused helplessness. It was wholly at odds with her usual assured and brazen self, and the sight of it nearly undid him. If he hadn't already had his finger deep within her, Alden knew he would have lunged into her immediately, without regard for her comfort level.

Instead, he grimaced as his hips acted without his conscious permission, thrusting against her thighs. Dragging his hand from where it still cradled Oliver's cock and her bottom, he knelt up and framed her face, tipping up her chin while struggling to get his base urges under control. "Yes, there's more," he gritted from between his teeth, "but I'm going to need my hands for it. Stop clenching, *roosje*."

The mere fact that Fiona had to concentrate to relax and let his finger escape nearly splintered Alden's mind, but he didn't hesitate. Once free, he lifted his hand and wiped it clean on the edge of the sheet behind him. Lifting his hand, he licked his thumb and thrust it into Oliver's mouth. Alden clasped Oliver's jaw, holding his mouth closed around Alden's thumb.

It was hardly the first time Oliver had had one of Alden's fingers in his mouth but surprise etched Oliver's face for a moment before he sucked on it eagerly.

Fiona, between them, waited, barely breathing, her eyes squarely on Alden's face, so he forced his mouth to open and said, keeping both of them in his gaze, "I want to watch Oliver worship you—love you as you deserve."

Wonder colored Oliver's expression. Alden retrieved his finger, knowing Oliver wanted to speak, even as he watched Fiona re-direct her eyes down his body and absorb the unmistakable size of his erection. She swallowed, an action that left a visceral reaction in Alden's gut. "Yes, that might be for the best," she finally whispered.

Alden raised an eyebrow, openly smirked at Oliver and bent forward, grasping his cock in his own hand and rubbing it against her mons as he spoke. "Soon, *roosje*. Soon you will take me, too."

"What about you?" Oliver asked directly, though he wasn't about to turn down the boon that Alden had offered him. He had watched in complete fascination as Alden had used his cum to supplement Fiona's natural lubrication. The moment had crystallized for Oliver an urgent desire—to claim her more explicitly. But he'd expected Alden to want that privilege. Instead, his lover had found ways for them to share this first intimacy with the treasure in their arms. Alden may have broken her virginity, but Oliver would love her first and take great pleasure in it.

He inwardly thanked Alden for the earlier climax, recognizing that he would have been unfit to pay proper attention to Fiona's pleasure if he'd been in his earlier state. Brushing out her hair, washing her, seeing to her physical needs was the stuff of Oliver's fantasies, and he had been frantic by the time they'd even approached the bed.

Now, though, he was prepared to draw out the moments. As Alden lay down in the bed, he helped Fiona shift to lie in the circle of Alden's embrace, her head on his upper arm and his cock tight between her thighs. Alden was partially on his side, and Fiona slightly tipped, but this position allowed Oliver to lie on his side and settle her body half beneath his. With one of her small palms curled over his shoulder, he stretched her other arm behind her to stroke the side of Alden's torso. Oliver trailed his lips over her hand and up her arm to her collarbone, unsurprised when

Alden curled his hand past Fiona and clenched his scalp.

Alden had to be in *extremis.*

The thought brought a smile to Oliver's lips, even as they fastened to Fiona's. She shuddered beneath him. He felt the tremors against his bare skin from his lips down to her shaking knees. He adjusted to clasp one of Fiona's sweetly rounded breasts in his palm and with his free hand set himself to exploring the curves below her navel that he'd been unable to learn while behind her.

He'd been fascinated and eager while only able to see her profile and ear. Now, watching her fight to contain the little moans that rose to her lips while she watched him stroke her, his cock hardened with a vengeance. She was a siren who had lured them out of their complacency with each other, however unwittingly, and Oliver was suddenly and impulsively eager for her to understand just how important she would be to them.

Meeting her eyes, he smiled and tugged his head from Alden's grip, sliding down to lick her nipples and rub his chin against the underside of each nipple until she twisted and Alden had to grip her to hold her in place. Then he sank lower, anxious to bring her to the same state of bliss that Alden had twice witnessed.

The skin at Fiona's hip was as luxurious and velvety as the delicious flesh at the nape of her neck. Oliver nearly moaned himself as he licked her and nuzzled the dip from her hipbone down to the curls at her pubis. Without even thinking, he cupped and lifted her buttocks, spreading her open.

The vision before him was captivating, but combined with the pulsing lust from Alden's body, his tortured face and Fiona's reawakening hunger, Oliver could hardly breathe. Several long heartbeats passed before he managed to mutter, "Heaven on earth," and dropped his mouth to Fiona's curls. They adorned her pubis and farther down over her labia, guarding the cavern Oliver sought, but he was careful to only take small sips from her. Oliver didn't want her to come again until he was inside her.

Of course she was still dripping wet from Alden's exploration, so Oliver rose to his knees and rubbed his stiff cock in her juices, thrusting back and forth enough to coat the long, heavy organ. He'd fought the earlier orgasm, holding back as much as possible in anticipation of this moment, and Oliver's cock was almost at full attention. He was well aware that he would be easier for Fiona to take inside her than Alden, but Fiona still seemed suitably impressed — impressed enough that she suddenly reached out and stroked him with her fingers.

Oliver was forgetting to breathe. He paused to take in air, then grasped her wrist for a moment. He redirected her hand to tighten about him. Oliver freely admitted to being selfish enough to accept the moment, even if he was already covered in her lubricant. Still clasping her hand around his erection, Oliver jerked himself twice, only to find that Fiona wasn't inclined to let him go.

He grimaced, lowering his hips to hers, angling into her until she was forced by the contact of their bodies to release him.

Oliver's first thrust entered Fiona only a few inches. He felt his face contort with the effort to hold still and not ravish her. Behind her temple, a raw noise came from Alden, who had lifted up enough to watch Oliver's first possession of Fiona. Oliver followed

Alden's fascinated gaze down to the sight at his crotch and nearly lost control of his body again, undone by the vision of Alden's arm between Fiona's breasts, and his large hand splayed over her navel. Fiona, by now frantic, struggled in Alden's arms, pushing to lift her hips and deepen Oliver's penetration.

He obliged her demand, and sank in farther, nearly overcome by the tight squeeze around him. Repeating the movement, Oliver thrust again, not breaking contact but reversing briefly only to drive further forward.

Behind her, Alden's erection strained up between her thighs, poking Oliver's sac. Oliver started forward again, and inched even deeper, struggling to hold back until Fiona came apart in his arms.

Loving the sensation of Alden's hardness against his thigh and scrotum, he lifted Fiona into an angle at which he could penetrate her fully.

She urged him on by spreading her hands over his chest and stroking, even as she tried to articulate her own needs. "Oliver, help me, please, just—just—just *more*," she whispered.

The need echoing in her voice was more than Oliver—or Alden—could withstand. He pumped hard, and repeated the motion, until he was fully seated inside her, looking into her face just as he withdrew and thrust all the way to the edge of her soul.

She convulsed around him, the walls of her sheath trapping and massaging his cock. Unable to resist the evocative evidence of her pleasure coming from her mouth or from her pussy, Oliver shoved his hands into the mattress and gave one last powerful stroke before the blood left his head and he shot off inside her. Even as the bliss flooded him, he knew Alden, too, was climaxing against them, spraying his semen over Oliver's balls and Fiona's labia.

Alden made a guttural noise, but Oliver turned his head from Fiona's closed eyes and slack face to look at his first love. Alden's tension was already easing, and he was curling his arm protectively around Fiona to move her into a comfortable position.

Oliver smiled, and Alden's lips twitched. "Rest," Oliver murmured, brushing a kiss over her forehead and bending to press another one against Alden's hand, where it now rested on Fiona's hip. "I'll go heat some water and clean us up again and settle the sheets and blankets."

Alden nodded, the expression on his face conveying the same satisfaction Oliver felt. Oliver smiled, lifted himself off them, and strolled across the floor, perfectly aware that he was far happier than was wise. But he fully intended to enjoy his final privilege of the day before crawling into bed beside the two people who might possibly satisfy every desire in his life.

Chapter Eight

Fiona woke slowly, confused by the satiated sluggishness of her arms and eyelids. But soon enough she realized she was unusually warm, and she forced her eyelids to open to find out why.

The sight before her ended any thought of closing them again.

She was lying on her side and Alden faced her. The blankets were, thankfully, tucked around her up to her shoulders but he was outside them, and utterly shameless in his sleep and nudity. The enormous expanse of his chest rippled as it beckoned for her to touch him, but Fiona clenched her fingers where they rested and restrained herself. Even closer, his face was open for her perusal. His face was smooth and unlined, free from the control he retained over his expression when awake. He was not watching her, as he had so often in the last unnerving days, so she cataloged the sculpted angles and curves. One arm stretched over the pillows above her head. She tipped her head to the side just enough to recognize Oliver behind her, and to see that Alden's fingers were tangled in Oliver's hair. Alden's other hand rested heavily at Fiona's hip. Even through the thin blanket, she could feel the heat from his palm, reminding her of his more intimate touch.

His touch had been a wonder, glorious. He'd caressed, at times gentle but a moment later firm and insistent. And, at the end, he—they—introduced her to the bliss that her sisters had assured her was possible with a loving partner.

Except Fiona, who had always eschewed any interest in a conventional relationship with a man, had again managed to flout all precepts of normal *moral* behavior and leaped irrevocably into a bed two men already shared.

Of course, Fiona reminded herself, the leap was irrevocable only in the sense that she couldn't reacquire her virginity, even if she had the desire to do so. In truth, she still couldn't fathom how a relationship between the three of them could work. Every time she tried to imagine it, the thought that she might be the person that finally separated Alden and Oliver was impossible to accept. They had thrived despite criticism, ostracism, scandal and violence, but would fail because of some great passion with Fiona de Rothesay?

The notion was beyond ridiculous.

Behind her, Oliver slept as deeply as Alden. Dawn had long since fled and no clock was located conveniently within the reach of her eyes, but she knew he was sleeping heavily. He was so close that Fiona could feel her hair rustle gently when he inhaled and exhaled in long, even repetitions. Just thinking of his body heat pressed to her back through the bedclothes caused ripples in her womb that echoed up her spine. Who could have thought a man's body could do what Oliver's had and *she would love it*? She tried to imagine such a thing with some other man — *Martin?* — and her mind seized. *No.* Young? He was not such a taskmaster as Martin, but her distaste for the idea, even having known both for much longer than either Alden or Oliver, was marked.

Although, in truth, she had known Oliver and Alden longer, or known of them. She knew, even without the reassurances of her sisters, that Alden Swenson was loyal and devoted. She'd seen and never forgotten his tenderness at a much younger age, and quite possibly that was why she so easily trusted him.

If Alden had transformed her opinion on the value of an intimate relationship with another human being, Oliver had broken down every stereotype she'd had about the purpose of a man in her life. Both Alden and Oliver had been forward about claiming the role of protector and Oliver had demonstrated thoroughly to Fiona's mother and Lennox that he was fully capable of acting as the chatelaine of Lennox House. But Fiona had not truly grasped the satisfaction Oliver derived from overseeing her physical well-being until the wee hours of the morning. She'd fallen asleep in Alden's embrace, but woke to Oliver slowly swiping away the remains of her maidenhead and their subsequent coupling with a warm cloth. In addition to the effort required to leave the bed, he'd have had to heat the water necessary to perform such an intimate service, when he could have simply remained abed.

He hadn't been doing it to arouse her, to capture her attention, or even to garner Alden's praise and appreciation. She had studied him beneath hooded eyes, not wanting him to guess she was awake, watching his careful attention to detail, to the pleasure that lit his face as he'd performed the mundane tasks of gathering up her garments and hanging them in a wardrobe for later airing, washing and ironing. He'd emptied the basin, neatly lined up her brushes on the vanity and settled the bench in its proper place beneath it. He'd left the room and returned with fresh washing water, and draped Fiona's own dressing gown on a straight back chair next to the foot of the massive bed where she could easily retrieve it. He'd even positioned her slippers on the floor beneath the chair.

Oliver had meticulously drawn thin blankets over Alden and Fiona, arranging them to perfection then, still nude, had circled the bed and climbed onto the opposite side of Fiona. Kneeling on the bed, he'd leaned over Fiona and brushed a kiss over Alden's eyebrow before performing the same office for Fiona. Only then had he consented to settle beside Fiona on the feather tick and close his eyes.

Was he always so generous in caring for others?

Wrapped in the warmth on each side of her and the imposing wooden canopy of the bed over her head, Fiona thought it might be easy to push away society and choose to remain within the narrow world they'd fashioned in Merton.

But how long could she remain so secluded? Fiona was certain that the Morewells and Cannings would be actively searching for her and that Lucy would be their quickest way of finding her. The maid would know that Oliver and Martin had spirited her away, and from there, Morpeth was likely to know of the pair's retreat. But suppose he didn't? The staff at Lennox House would believe Fiona was with Alden and Oliver, but did they know where? And if they did, would they tell even the Foreign Secretary himself if asked?

Fiona guessed that, Lucy aside, they would not speak, though the carriage driver assuredly knew the villa's direction. After all, they had proved loyal to Lennox in the past.

Anthony would guess immediately, but he was in Northumberland and it would require several days to send to him and receive an answer. Fiona supposed that no one in the Foreign Office would want it widely known that they were searching for her.

The Egyptian hieroglyphic lecture she had supposedly returned to London to see was tonight.

She would need to convince them to return her to London for the event. Once in London she stood a much better chance of disappearing into Whitehall. As much as she wished to stay isolated with Oliver and Alden—as much as she would enjoy it—she couldn't abandon her responsibilities.

If she was important to Oliver and Alden today, she would still be important to them a week from now, when she would have finished translating the series of letters about the Russian tsar. No conscientious diplomat could ignore the time element suggested by an assassination plot.

And in the meantime, she had the day to spend with her two lovers, and no obligations beyond returning to London by late evening, unless of course she was retrieved before then.

Fiona blinked, sighed and closed her eyes as she considered what she would choose to do with her day. She couldn't see any way to remove herself from the bed, with both Alden and Oliver lying on the bedding. And yet, to be lying between them while the sun indirectly lit their nest, bare beneath the bedclothes, was almost more intimate than what they had experienced the night before in the darkness.

It would be much easier for her to meet them over the breakfast table than across a pillow.

It was not dark now, and Fiona did feel a degree of awkwardness. She felt her cheeks coloring even as she thought about it, and squirmed, turning over to hide her face. Her face hidden in the pillows, Fiona felt Alden stir beside her. Instinctively, she closed her eyes. He stiffened, as if he had woken enough to grasp the notion that all three of them were bare in the big bed, and to feel the same degree of awkwardness Fiona felt. His breathing sped up slightly. She lay still and quiet, barely breathing, wondering what he would do if he knew she was awake.

But all he did was scoop an errant curl of hair off her cheek and tuck it behind her ear. She barely managed to restrain her squeak and covered it as a sleepy murmur, biting the pillow beneath her. Fiona heard his chuckle. To her surprise, he slid off the bed and walked away. She listened as the door at the far corner of the bedchamber closed. Presumably it led to some sort of bathing or dressing chamber, but Fiona had no intention of investigating or following him. Instead, she rolled face down on the bed and turned her head toward Oliver. She spent several long seconds listening and looking at Oliver's less than graceful repose — his jaw hung slightly open and saliva pooled at the corner of his mouth, though that hardly made him unattractive. He had thoroughly kissed her, and she remembered the flavor and touch of that mouth. She'd like to experience it again, she decided. The kiss — and all else they'd done.

Not immediately, however. At the moment, Oliver still slept. She crept away from him, through the still-warm depression in the bed Alden had left. Completely silent, she slipped the dressing gown over her body and fastened the buttons, then retrieved her slippers so that they didn't tap on the floor and glided on her bare feet toward the French doors that led to the corridor.

The stained glass set in the doors formed a brilliant scene of a tree with golden and red leaves. Completely opaque, it was an intricate design that coordinated with the beautiful ceiling over her head in both color and theme.

Fiona felt a physical tug of regret as she opened the door and slipped out, closing it behind her. But truly, she had no idea how to wake up with one man in bed with her, let alone two.

The house was quiet and still, so Fiona stopped in the front hall. She had a ribbon from some previous morning in the front pocket of her dressing gown, so she smoothed out her hair and hand-combed it into her familiar bun, then tied the ribbon around it to hold it in place and examined her face.

She didn't *look* as if she'd spent half the night in a decadent, illicit experience that fit more with classical Greek depravity than English morality. She didn't see any difference in herself at all, at least not outside.

Her insides would never be the same, however. Fiona mentally paused for one complete second to consider the loss of her virginity, then shrugged it aside. It had been nothing more than a fact of life, not something to treasure, nor yet an encumbrance. As she had no intention of seeking out any other liaison, preserving any physical innocence was pointless. On the other hand, the thought of going out and sacrificing her maidenhead on the altar of experience or womanhood with any other man was, as she'd considered earlier, still antipathetic.

Wandering through the dining room, empty kitchens, drawing room and music room, Fiona couldn't deny that the revelations of the late night had changed her. They had changed her *mind*, her perception of how her life was ordered, of what could be and caused her to rethink what she might want in the future.

Having shared such a night with Alden Swenson and Oliver Morewell, Fiona couldn't imagine withdrawing to treat them as extended family, of pretending a polite but distant interest in their affairs, of deliberately hurting them by turning her back and permanently distancing herself. Yet, she knew quite well that she could not disclose to them where she had spent her hours two nights earlier, not without Morpeth or Canning's permission. Complicating the situation further was the simple fact that they would now know she had not spent that night, two nights earlier, with a lover. How long would it be, she wondered, before Oliver's intellect snapped into place and he put together her friendship with Young Canning, Anthony Morewell and Martin Morewell and came up with the diplomatic bureaucracy as an answer?

How much did the pair of them actually know about her facility and education with languages?

Fiona found the bell pull in the kitchen that would presumably summon the couple who cared for the house. She considered, remembered Alden, too, had escaped the bed and decided to leave the pull. Although at Lennox House she wouldn't have hesitated from retreating to the formality of the dining room at breakfast with Carrington's comforting presence to provide a polite distance, pursuing such a tactic here was likely to backfire, and she had mentally committed to spending the day with them anyway.

Inevitably she'd have to face that awkward first moment alone with them.

Not yet, though. She wandered into the music room at the front of the house, opposite the drawing room and immediately felt her heart swell with appreciation. The room was clearly a room used and loved. Oliver's treasures were much in evidence, with a portrait of Alden hung over the fireplace. Long windows at the far end of the room looked over a flowering expanse of garden. A fine pianoforte with a dark oak patina, highly polished, occupied the entire end of the room with neatly organized sheafs of sheet music behind the glass doors of a nearby cabinet. Instead of paintings, long glass cases held fine instruments on the walls—bassoon, oboe, three varieties of clarinet, a cello and a violin. Set neatly between the two bay windows and seats that faced the forecourt was a giltwood harp, with a matching music stand beside it.

Fiona sat, stared and drew a deep breath, settled into the window seat and wondered.

She remembered every inch of Winchester House, where even her mother's chambers seemed terribly impersonal, having been decorated by Fiona's grandmother. She thought about her sister, Abigail, in Warwickshire, where Abigail's private rooms had been decorated to her taste and for her express needs. She thought of Gloria and Clare's location of the nursery near the master suite, at Gloria's insistence, instead of by custom in the highest floor of the house, and of the drawing room for which Gloria had been shopping while she'd been in London. She remembered even Genevieve, separated from the man who married her to keep her safe, who'd created a studio and private space in his mother's house that suited her perfectly.

Alden had given Oliver the time, resources and support to create this room, this home. He shared more than a bed with Oliver. He shared interests, finances and connections. Alden allowed Oliver to decide his sartorial appearance, though Fiona had seen Oliver defer to Alden on several occasions, looking to Alden for leadership or advice. They even shared their families, both the good and the bad. They had a full life, together.

What would it be like to be so important to someone else? What would it be like to be so important to Alden and Oliver, to be part of that intimate sharing of everyday experiences, defeats, successes, and even quiet moments?

With a wry smile on her lips—and the question in her mind—she moved to the pianoforte. Doubtless it would draw Alden even if it didn't wake Oliver. But she would do the deed gently. She needed to eat, and as they were her hosts, it was up to them to organize breakfast for her, at least until she understood the life into which she had fallen.

* * * *

Alden frowned at the bare top of his desk. He hadn't bothered to pull down a book or to disguise his idleness with a blank sheet of paper. Instead, he simply sat.

Oliver didn't generally play sonatas in the morning, and this particular one was unfamiliar to him, not something he would have expected Oliver to choose on what would undoubtedly be an emotionally difficult day. In fact, he was bothered by the notion that Oliver was playing the pianoforte at all. Oliver hadn't come into the room to bid him good morning as he usually would have, before ringing for Mr. and Mrs. Janzen, and the music might wake Fiona before she was completely rested.

With the combined library and study tucked between the master bedroom at the back of the house and the music room at the front of the house, Alden knew he could hear the crescendos and lilting melody far better than Fiona would in the next room. At the very least, he could join Oliver, and check on his state of mind.

Alden was far too flummoxed to be able to sort out his own head. The hours in that bed had, in retrospect, been bewildering. The moment when he'd pressed his finger past Fiona's virginity had turned his mind upside down, first by lust and now by a deeper consideration. While he and Oliver had, once in years past, made a decision to turn their backs on the expectations of society and live on the edges of it, they had no right to deny such acceptance to Fiona, or to any children that might eventually be born of an extended affair. Even worse, Alden was alternately proud and ashamed that he'd relieved strong, decisive, *gently bred* Lady Fiona of her virginity. From now on, he thought, he would always be responsible for looking after her, unless she married another.

The thought that she might actually wed someone else sent a shooting pain through his gut. He wanted to be the one responsible for her. The duty did not belong to his father, nor to her mother, nor to Anthony Morewell, nor Meriden. It was not even solely Oliver's, though Alden was thrilled that Oliver wanted to nurture and care for her, too, in his own intense way.

He grimaced as he opened the music room door and realized the music was not Oliver's. In the instant before he saw her, he detected the difference. Fiona played flawlessly, her eyes on her hands as she ran her fingers over the ivory keys. But her brows were pinched together in concentration where Oliver's face would have been full of expressive emotion. There was something distinctively different between her performance and Oliver's.

With a dip at the corner of her lips, Fiona sighed, glanced up at him and ended the piece, shrugging her shoulders and practically leaping to her feet. "We were all required to learn an assortment of pieces, to perform at house parties and in the drawing room after a dinner party. 'Tis a requisite skill for a young lady," she dismissed. "And this is a beautiful instrument."

Alden raised his eyebrow but nodded. In his world — in Oliver's world — music was not only a skill, but an expression of the soul. How did Fiona express hers, if not through music? Clearly he should not read anything about the state of her mind from the state of her music, as he might have done with Oliver. "How are you?" he asked, instead, taking both her slender hands inside his big palms and pressing them together.

Fiona, whom he judged to be charmingly garbed in her dressing gown and perfectly presentable without even the benefit of washing up, frowned as she hesitantly met his eyes.

"Don't prevaricate," he suggested. "Just answer."

Lifting her hands farther, he kissed the back of one then the other. He waited to hear that she was sore, or stiff, that she needed to bathe. He wondered if she was hiding in the music room because she wanted nothing to do with the dishonorable rogues who had seduced her. He wondered if she wanted to return to London, immediately. If she would be writing to His Grace of Lennox immediately to inform him of his son's perfidy. If—

Instead, Fiona blurted out quite bluntly, "I'm hungry."

Alden couldn't help but smile at the flush that rose on her cheeks. "Come, then, *roosje*," he chuckled, tucking her arm inside his. He never hesitated to touch Oliver, but there was some nebulous insistent demand inside him to keep her within the shelter of his arms. He tried to squash it, knowing she wouldn't appreciate any protectiveness or paternal superiority, but by the time he introduced her to the Janzens, Alden realized he couldn't completely suppress it.

Instead, he seized on it and determined to demonstrate every ounce of pride he felt at the thought of her beside him. *The better to seduce her to staying at my side. I wonder if she will ever come to me as willingly as Oliver does.* "*Mevrouw* Janzen, *Meneer* Janzen, let me make you known to Lady Fiona, who would very much like to break her fast." He smiled down at the top of Fiona's head. "Lady Fiona drove out with Oliver and me last night. She'll be staying the day, and I know you will be as pleased having her in the house as we are. *Ze is erg belangrijk voor ons.*" She is very important to us, he repeated, willing the kindly housekeepers to see the treasure he and Oliver had found.

"*Ja*," Mrs. Janzen agreed, bobbing a curtsy and pushing her husband back toward the kitchen even as she spoke directly to Fiona. "You have the *heer*, my lord, sit you down at the table, *ja?* I shall bring you tea and food and will cook more breakfast."

Alden obediently escorted her to a chair beside the head of the table and took a seat next to hers, contemplating her quiet surprise. "Carrington's father was the caretaker for several years after we left for Amsterdam. He'd retired from Lennox House but was restless and this place suited him, until he died in January. We sent the Janzens in March to take over and open the house. Of course, we knew by then we'd be moving back and were already working to that end. In Amsterdam, Mrs. Janzen ran our household and Mr. Janzen was Oliver's driver."

Fiona blinked at him, her eyes curiously rounded as if she was trying to solve a perplexing problem. "Oliver has a personal driver?" she asked faintly.

Alden shrugged. "He did in Amsterdam. When we moved there, he spoke Dutch adequately, certainly better than I did, but his sense of direction was hopeless. He lost his way within two blocks of home three times the first week we were there. It was a necessity, for his own safety." He looked more closely at Fiona, surprised at her frown, but explained, "He's perfectly fine here, and we have only one private servant in Lennox House—a gentleman's gentleman, who sees to our wardrobe and personal business. I'm much more likely to need a driver than Oliver, what with the business."

Shaking her head, Fiona blinked again and peered at him intently. "Why are you talking so much?" she asked directly.

Surprised, Alden quieted, but even if he was outwardly pondering an answer, he already knew what it would be. Lowering his voice so that it wouldn't carry to the kitchens, he murmured reluctantly, "As you were brave enough to trust me — us — with your fair self, it's imperative I return that trust. So, the truth is that I'm speaking because Oliver isn't here to do it for me. Or, perhaps —" He paused and tightened his lips. "I have always been reticent around people, except Oliver — and now you."

"I see," Fiona acknowledged, her response cut short by Mrs. Janzen's busy, chattering personage as she delivered tea. While she set out the dishes, along with a plate of sweet-smelling cake and a tray of sliced apples, she inquired about a bevy of household arrangements, all of which Alden decried any knowledge. Fortunately, just as she snorted and was ready to retire in defeat, Oliver entered the dining room.

Alden paid careful attention to Fiona's face as Oliver greeted her in his usual effusive way, deliberately keeping silent. He had been surprised by Fiona's question. What did it mean, that he had spoken to her so easily and at length? Oliver glanced at Alden, but wrapped his hands around the sides of Fiona's face and kissed her thoroughly, despite the presence of Mrs. Janzen, who shook her head wearily. Eventually, he drew back, but only after saying, "Good morning, my treasure."

Fiona, Alden noted, appeared dazed, but she recovered quickly, her eyes sharpening in their direction, as Oliver bent his head to Alden.

Alden tilted his head and welcomed the caress, tasting Fiona's tea and the paste Oliver had used to clean his teeth. He loved the firmness of Oliver's mouth and the shared intimacy, an experience they could not share in the Lennox breakfast parlor. "Good morning," Alden murmured.

"A very good one, love," Oliver returned, meeting Alden's gaze. The complicated brown hues of Oliver's eyes were lighter than usual, evidence of his satisfaction.

Mrs. Janzen distracted him almost immediately. Alden sat back and watched Oliver answer all the housekeeper's questions with barely a blink, reassure her then send her back to the kitchen with a smile.

Alden almost shifted nervously. He knew, simply *knew*, that it would not be as simple as it had seemed this morning. And he had a difficult question to ask Fiona, one she would dislike. He didn't imagine that she would fall into their harness simply because she'd spent one night in their bed, even if the night had been beyond spectacular.

Oliver raced ahead of him, as usual, speaking even before he poured his tea, "So, Fiona dear, in case last night wasn't evidence enough, we're keeping you. Apropos of that, exactly where did you spend the night before last, if not with a lover?"

Fiona, to her credit, did not spit out her tea, but she had to struggle to swallow.

Alden shook his head, sighed, put his head down and concentrated on the cake before him. Fully expecting Fiona to lambast Oliver, he held his counsel and waited.

Instead, Fiona said mildly, "I take it you slept well."

"Marvelously," Oliver agreed, raising an eyebrow and waving his spoon in Fiona's direction. "As you well know, as you were able to leave our bed without waking me."

Fiona smiled, absolute innocence reflected in her features. "You needed your rest," she returned pertly. "And Alden was already up and about."

"I was," Alden agreed briefly when Oliver glanced at him.

"Yes, the man always rises at dawn." Oliver gestured dismissively. "I can't break him of the habit, and he has some senseless notion about not waking me."

"He's grumpy when he's woken early," Alden contributed drily, "and this is early, for him."

Fiona snorted. "It's after nine, and lovely outside. The afternoon looks to be warm." She paused. "And it's a drive back to London."

"We're not going back. Not today," Oliver returned calmly, sitting back in his chair and meeting her gaze.

Whatever Fiona planned to say in response was delayed by the arrival of Mr. Janzen with a coffeepot. He poured a cup for Oliver, another for Alden then disappeared through the baize door to the kitchen.

"Actually," Fiona corrected Oliver, "we're returning this evening for the Egyptian lecture at the Society of Antiquaries. I suspect you've forgotten it, but if you expect to have an ongoing relationship with me, as you've just laid claim, then you'll need to adjust your expectations to include my tuitions. I came from Northumberland for the lecture, if you remember."

Alden remembered, but he hadn't been satisfied even then that she'd come to London for a lesson in hieroglyphics. Now, with all that had happened in the short few days since they'd met, he was even less inclined to believe her claim. However, he had no contradictory evidence to say she was telling anything less than the truth.

"I remember," Oliver agreed. To Alden's senses, highly attuned to Oliver for years, the words were reluctant. Oliver, too, had doubts. But Fiona had made them no promises, either for the day or the future, and

Alden was aware that they had virtually abducted her from the home of a senior government official. No doubt there would be many watching to see if she did appear, and to check on her well-being.

Thinking, Alden sipped at his coffee. "We can dress early, dine here and return to town. I'll leave you both at Somerset House and send the Lennox carriage to await the conclusion of the lecture."

Oliver considered Alden for only a second, then turned to Fiona and watched her perfectly composed features for a moment. "It will do," he agreed, though his reluctance was now obvious. He pointed a spoon in her general direction. "So long as you agree that we—the three of us—are now together, and Alden and I do have a right and the privilege to look after you."

Fiona, quite obviously not the submissive maiden stereotypically modeled as the ideal English lady, gestured back with her spoon. "Only if I have the same right and privilege to look after *you*," she returned, then glanced at Alden. "And you."

Alden, amused, knew his lips twitched revealingly.

Oliver, however, frowned. Had he seen something in her face that Alden had missed? But no, Alden realized, Oliver just saw the trap more clearly than he'd seen it. "Exactly how do you intend to look after us?" Oliver asked directly. "Because I have to tell you, we will insist on your safety and on your health."

Fiona sighed, but declined to directly answer. She seemed relieved, even, to see Mrs. Janzen come through the door again with a tray of plates of ham and eggs. Fiona looked at it appreciatively and spoke to the housekeeper in beautiful, flawless Dutch.

Oliver stared. Alden couldn't help the sudden hunger he felt, and it wasn't in his stomach. Watching her performance, knowing she was doing it purposefully, made no difference. Without compunction, she thanked Mrs. Janzen for the meal and proceeded to ask the older woman what she needed to know about the two of them. Alden, who spoke exceptional — if not native — Dutch, was just able to follow the rapid-fire conversation. Oliver, with his more limited Dutch skills, patently couldn't follow it at all.

"What won't they tell me?" Alden did catch that, quite clearly.

Mrs. Janzen's answered even more rapidly than Fiona had spoken — at length.

Alden turned to Oliver, raising his brows in a clear warning. "She's showing off — and finding out how to look after us," he informed Oliver, smirking.

Oliver stared at him, openly aghast. "Perhaps we should take her for a walk in the gardens after breakfast," he muttered. "Away from Mrs. Janzen."

"You know very well that Mrs. Janzen dotes on you." Alden smiled at the two women, and grinned when the housekeeper launched into another exposition of how pitiful Oliver had been when he'd needed nursing through the measles at the very mature age of twenty-eight.

Her story made Fiona laugh openly, but Fiona switched to English to say prettily, "Thank you so much, madam, for the excellent advice. I'm sure it will be indispensable."

Oliver looked distinctly worried. He pursed his lips, swung his head and fixed Mrs. Janzen with a basilisk stare. Unperturbed, she served him his plate and clucked her tongue against the top of her mouth in a gesture Alden found comfortingly familiar. "Master

Oliver, no need to take a temper. I just tell the good lady how to manage you."

Alden thought Oliver actually paled at that announcement and beside him, Fiona chuckled.

As soon as Mrs. Janzen disappeared, Alden assumed control of the conversation. "So we'll return to London for the evening." He fixed his gaze on Fiona's fine black brows, which seemed more apt to reveal her inner thoughts than her composed lips and attentive eyes. He'd noticed that she had trouble controlling them when she was indignant or amused, and studied them as he spoke. "Tomorrow we'll return here to the villa for two or three days, as we need time to adjust to being with each other. You may bring Lucy if you insist, but I suggest leaving her in London. There is a room in the attic she could use, but Oliver will want to pamper you, and frankly I'm not entirely sure she approves of us, let alone the three of us."

As he'd anticipated, her brows arched as she considered. "I don't have my engagement book," she prevaricated finally, "and I just can't remember if I've already accepted an invitation from Princess Esterhazy for afternoon tea tomorrow or if I missed the opportunity when I was out yesterday afternoon. I have the invitation on my desk."

"Perhaps it would be advantageous for Fiona to appear at a function or two tomorrow," Oliver agreed with Fiona, surprisingly. "As much as I'd like to keep her here," he continued, "people will wonder, as she disappeared from Canning House and some must have noticed. If she attends the lecture tonight with me and a luncheon and tea tomorrow, the matrons will see and take note. If questioned, she can simply say that she felt suddenly indisposed or developed a migraine and we took her home. We can return here tomorrow evening."

Alden shrugged his shoulders. Oliver was better at managing society's maze of subtle proprieties and unspoken rules. Oliver had been raised to live and breathe the rules of society and a variety of European embassies, while Alden had been raised in isolation in Wales by nannies and a bully of an elder brother. He'd always understood the basics, of course, but the judgment of matrons and *grande dames* made him infinitely grateful for Oliver's guidance. "I am clearly outnumbered." He nodded his head, then studied Fiona. Something about her face still bothered him, but Alden knew well that he couldn't know her well enough yet to discern the reason behind her abstraction. Perhaps the difference between how she'd been until last night and now was simply the outcome of how she'd spent the dark hours between them. "Now then, how do you feel?"

Fiona set down her fork and pondered his question.

"I thought you might like to soak in a bath," Oliver ventured.

Fiona blinked. "Yes," she agreed, "but I think I'd like to walk in the gardens first. There's no sense in bathing twice and it's a warm day. I saw the gardens from the music room this morning, and if I hadn't been so hungry, I'd have been exploring them already."

"Let's plan on a cold collation for lunch and explain our early dinner plans to Mrs. Janzen. I'll help you dress, then we can walk after and even have lunch on the terrace. The elder Mr. Carrington and now Mr. Janzen take great pride in the gardens," Oliver noted. "And, of course, it's the perfect time of year to appreciate the greenery and the flowers." Oliver's enthusiasm was almost contagious, and for a moment Alden absorbed his welling joy.

But he hadn't forgotten Fiona's reticence, her reserve, which could hide both happiness and secrets, and he hadn't forgotten her unexplained absence the night before last.

At one time, he'd loved at first sight, and he'd been right. But Fiona was no young boy, innocent of anything but pranks and full of trust in his own siblings. She was an adult woman, with a full life that had not included Oliver or Alden for very long at all. Alden knew very little of her or her capabilities, and he was certain that there was more to her than a simple desire to learn about hieroglyphics or attend Princess Esterhazy's tea.

Chapter Nine

Fiona fiddled with her spoon and tried to look inconspicuous. Lunch, touted as a cold collation, was clearly within Mrs. Janzen's formidable skills. She'd served a delicious cold berry soup the men obviously knew well. Named *watergruwel*, it was wonderfully refreshing. That had been followed by a proper cabbage salad — *koolsla* — and duck she'd obviously roasted all morning, with a generous cheese platter to finish. They'd been able to smell the delicious aroma of the duck from the terrace when they'd finally set off on their walk.

Fiona had commented on it. Alden had seemed distinctly hungry and Oliver's eyes lit like a child's as soon as they smelled it. But they had stayed outside and allowed her to explore several acres of flowers and flagged paths, patiently waiting for the luncheon bell and slowly building an appetite as they wandered.

Gradually, the unusual stiffness in her lower back to the backs of her thighs had eased and disappeared.

She decided to whisper a suggestion in the ear of Lennox House's chef regarding roasted duck, particularly since Oliver oversaw the menus. Why hadn't he suggested such a simple dish when he so clearly loved it? Perhaps Mrs. Janzen would be willing to share it, for the good of the men that the housekeeper openly mothered.

It had been delicious, along with everything else on the table. But now she was faced with knowingly returning with them to that large bedchamber at the back of the house, where, in full light and with her wits fully about her, she'd put herself into their hands—or as she understood it—primarily Oliver's. He was very direct in his plan to 'improperly' pamper her. By improper, he meant that he intended to touch, explore and learn her as closely as possible.

Despite the remembered pleasure of the night before, she had no illusions. Fiona was nervous. Even worse, she was guilty—guilty of deceiving them, guilty of planning to deceive them.

If there was anything she'd learned from the disaster of the Winchester marriage, it was that a web of lies started with the first and only got more complicated. Fiona herself was the product of her mother's first lie, and her sisters and their complicated marriages and lives had followed, along with scandal. Eventually, Winchester's understandable bitterness had turned to madness and he'd actually killed a British officer in pursuit of Fiona's sister, Gloria.

The only reason he hadn't hung was the title, and even that would go back to the Crown when he died.

So when Oliver looked at her curiously, set down his knife, and asked, "What's bothering you, Fiona?" she actually had something to talk about.

"You know about my father?" she began, glancing at Alden. After all, her father was a former lover of her mother's, and Alden's father was her mother's current lover. The word *awkward* popped into her head.

"Which one?" Alden responded bluntly.

"Winchester won't be a part of your life again," Oliver said, but that didn't reassure Fiona even a bit. She hadn't been talking about him.

"I rather think she's referring to her natural sire, not her legal one," Alden corrected Oliver, though he continued to watch Fiona carefully. She felt them, felt him examining her, weighing his words. "I know about all your mother's legal affairs, convoluted as they are. In the absence of her brothers, she's named me as the executor of her estate," he finally said.

"So," Fiona began, then trailed off.

Alden shrugged. "So Lennox intends to care for your mother and all four of you for your lifetimes. Your mother's estate is relatively small, primarily composed of the assets your uncles kept protected in trust on her behalf. It's a living, but she doesn't need it. She'll be welcome to live out her lifetime in any of the Lennox households, including the London house, and my father has put aside the funds to care for her."

"That's not what I meant," Fiona said defensively, then sighed and glanced at Oliver, who was watching them curiously. "Do you know my father?"

Alden shook his head. "I can't know him. He's dead," the man stated.

Relieved that she didn't have to further explain her relationship to Abigail and the earls of Meriden, Fiona raised her chin slightly and asked the question that meant more than the first. "Does it make a difference to you that I'm a bastard?" she asked bluntly.

Oliver's eyes narrowed as he stared at her, and Fiona's nerves returned tenfold. She wouldn't have said she cared what anyone thought, but every hour with Alden and Oliver was revealing confusing aspects of her personality she'd never stepped over before. "A difference?" he finally asked. "Of course it does."

Fiona's heart sank and she felt the blood rush from her head.

"I'm frankly *relieved* that you are part of a family that adores you. Your mother and Lennox both made it clear to me that Meriden dotes on you. Even his mother, who had more cause than any to resent you as a new sibling of her late husband, thinks you are precious. What can be said of that importance from Winchester's family, after all?"

Fiona flinched, drawing in a deep breath. "Actually, Aunt Betsy and her sisters were all Winchester's half-sisters," she allowed. "So Libby and your brother Anthony are not really my cousins."

"Gammon. Have you turned gaumless?" Oliver broke in, obviously irritated. "No one gives a devil's bollocks—"

"Oliver!"

"Who your parents are—either of them." Oliver ignored Alden's sharp reprimand and berated Fiona, practically out of his seat as he leaned over the table and pinned her.

"Society cares," Fiona retorted. "Maybe you don't realize it, but when I first came out of the schoolroom and Mother took me about in society, the *haut ton* treated my mother as if she was an arbiter of fashion and behavior. People sought her out. Abigail followed, and Gloria, and she was practically a queen of the Marriage Mart, even though none of us were the least bit close to marrying. But then Abigail's engagement to Meriden was announced and the web of lies she'd told for two decades started unraveling, even in public, a bit at a time. And everything changed, for her and for us."

Oliver's face darkened, but Alden was staring at her, listening, so Fiona looked at him steadily as she spoke.

"At first it wasn't too terrible," Fiona admitted. "But there's no help for it now, you know. I'm perfectly acceptable as an amusing companion, a dance or whist partner. But there's no question that I'm no longer considered suitable. Gloria is beautiful and Clare has an heir, Abigail was already married to Meriden, who was an outcast himself and Genevieve is already married, even if it's a marriage in name only. But I was out before the scandal began and I still am—and I know the difference. My bastardry does make a difference, a subtle one, but it's still there."

"That's a cartload of shit." Oliver stood now, his voice rising as he got to the last word, thundering it out. "If it's true or even if it's a product of your fanciful imagination."

"Oliver," Alden interrupted harshly, but Oliver held up a hand and shook his head.

"You'll have your say, Alden, but I need to make a point."

"Kindly do so without the crudity," Alden murmured mildly. "Check."

Oliver snorted. "Fiona, you know damned well that Alden and I are from two of the oldest, most well-born families in England. The bloodline of the Morewells is so pure that it practically screams Norman lord, and every Morewell to hold a title back to the one who crossed the Channel has married with the approval of his father to a female who is just as wellborn, usually into the French aristocracy. Over the generations, these Morewell wives, from early on through the next duchess in the person of my sister-in-law, have faithfully produced a battalion of noble warriors and statesmen. But despite all that good, morally superior blood in my veins, when I needed the support of my family, all I received was a threat and a superior sneer. That's the sort of family that one doesn't need on one's side in the drawing rooms of London. So maybe your family tree isn't in unblemished condition, but they have not abandoned you or mocked you and they'd be here at the faintest intimation of trouble in defense and support of you. The de Rothesay sisters, the Earl of Meriden, his mother, your mother, His Grace of Lennox, Alden, myself and your aunts in-name only are a far superior breed of family to anything yours truly has ever had at his back."

Fiona squinted and frowned at him direfully. "There's no need to shout," she huffed, a bit peevish at his indignation. "And whether it's right or not makes no difference in the eyes of society. Once I was considered wellborn, the daughter of an earl. Now the matrons of the best families no longer consider me an eligible *parti* for their eldest sons, nor even for their second sons who are destined for government posts the world over. You can't change that by pointing out that it's not right, or that I should be happy about it. I'm hardly dangling after any of their precious progeny, but I understand that if I was a young, beautiful debutante, they'd cut me direct. It's only my ape leader status and my association with Canning House that keep me on London's guest lists." She glanced at Alden's still face and swung back to Oliver. "I don't want to cause more problems for either of you by our association. Your mother won't approve. She intensely dislikes even a hint of association with Martin, and she resents my friendship with Libby and Anthony. I know Lennox doesn't disapprove—how could he?—but I'm still a reminder to him that Mother had a very *active* life before she ever knew him."

"The devil take it, you're still the daughter of an earl." Oliver slammed his palm down on the table and stood, now glowering at Fiona. "And in any event, why do you *care* what those old biddies think? You're too bloody intelligent not to see them as the small-minded, prudish, back-stabbing bitches with nothing more productive to do than sit in judgment over others who want nothing more than their kindness."

"Checkmate," Alden murmured grimly, standing.

Fiona watched Oliver glance at him, startled. She sighed. "Never mind. I just wanted to clarify that being with me isn't going to cause the outrage you think. The matrons may talk and there will be gossip, but it's not as if you've ruined me. I'm on the shelf, my mother is an infamous adulteress, and my natural sire is a public mystery at least. My fall from the ranks of the virtuous spinsters won't cause much of a ripple."

She watched, fascinated, as Alden's fixation on Oliver turned to her. Disapproval etched the lines in his face. Alden moved around the table toward Oliver, though, even as Oliver's face reddened with outrage. He shrugged off Alden's hand and chased down Fiona instead, dragging her out of the seat and clasping his hands around her upper arms and shaking her just a tiny bit, but enough for her eyes to meet Oliver's and stay there. "Don't *ever* belittle yourself like this again. You are a *lady* and society will treat you like one. For the love of God, I will spank you until you can't sit if you even suggest that anything less is acceptable from anyone."

"Fiona is not the only one who won't be able to sit," Alden said decisively, locking a muscular arm around Oliver's lean waist. "Because you are hardly acting the gentleman, with that filth coming out of your mouth. I know you aren't often in a temper, but I won't tolerate the language, especially to Fiona. Both of you are coming with me. We're going to address this privately. *Now.*"

With his other arm, he drew Fiona against his opposite side and directed his two miscreants down the corridor toward the bedchamber.

Fiona, typically, couldn't bear to be manhandled without speaking to it. "There's no reason to rush," she complained. "It's not as if we've an appointment."

"Oliver has an appointment," Alden returned, pushing the man forward a bit. Oliver took the hint and opened the door, so that Alden could guide Fiona through. Behind him, Oliver closed and locked the doors, leaving the key carefully in the lock. "And I think you should watch as he and I have that appointment. If you'll just sit here," he directed, guiding her to an armchair near the empty fireplace, "Oliver will bring me a hairbrush—indeed, let him bring me *your* hairbrush—and we will take care of it immediately. You see, Oliver and I don't often disagree, but if there is one bad habit from his youth that I have always detested, it's that he forgets to control his tongue when he is aggravated about something."

Oliver came up beside Alden then, a bit of color in his cheeks at the criticism.

"And you might remember that I warned him," Alden added, turning his head and holding out his hand. Oliver's breath hitched, but he handed Alden the beautiful wooden brush and frowned. "Twice, though I let it pass last night when I knew he was in *extremis*. Why don't you tell Fiona about our agreement?" he proposed to Oliver. "I want her to understand why we're here."

Oliver shifted awkwardly, biting his lip. Alden watched him, a small smile on his lips. Fiona remembered how he'd reacted to her own anxiety the night before and shivered. Alden derived pleasure from Oliver's dilemma, and presumably from Fiona's nerves, too. Still, Oliver was Oliver, and he soon began to speak, sinking to his knees beside Fiona's chair, seemingly so that he could see into her face more closely.

Alden listened carefully, taking a temporary seat on the chaise as half his mind considered how Oliver's appointment would be conducted.

"It started when we first moved to Amsterdam. Alden's never liked that I curse, but of course I did it so the other schoolboys didn't think me any more of an odd duck than they already presumed. But once we left Oxford, and later England, I didn't have that excuse anymore, and adjusting was hard. Alden was forever noticing how impolite I was, especially to him. He began to say that I was being disrespectful to him, and I suppose it was. I only ever spoke English with him, and of course what little Dutch I knew didn't include any cursing so it stood out when my bad language was only ever directed at Alden. One day, he told me to stop. I was in quite a temper about something—I can't remember what—but when he told me to stop, I asked him how the fuck he thought to stop me."

Oliver paused at Fiona's widened eyes, but he only squeezed her knee. "Right. It was disrespectful. Alden certainly thought so. He grabbed me, pushed me down onto the bed and said either he was going to fuck my mouth until I remembered to think before I spoke or he would spank me. I was enough of an idiot to respond that he'd have to do both to make that sort of impression."

Fiona jerked and looked to Alden, who shrugged. "He's the one who made the challenge."

"Anyway, after he did both — and quite thoroughly — I didn't say one word out of turn for days. Finally, Alden sat me down in the office and asked me how I was feeling, and I said that if I got so out of control of my mouth again, he should repeat the lesson. It worked, after all." Oliver grimaced and blushed all in one lovely expression. Fiona tried to be serious but was somewhat amused by his confession. "And he did warn me. The first warning was last night. This morning, when we were in the dining room, he said, 'Check'. He meant that as a warning — to get control of my mouth, if not my emotions."

"So he's going to spank you," Fiona said faintly.

"Yes, and it's going to hurt dreadfully, be unbelievably loud and look unbearable. It does help me, you know. It's not so much that I won't ever curse again, but it's perfect to remind me to be in control of my voice and my speech. I don't want to hurt either of you with a lack of self-discipline."

Fiona reached out and brushed a stray hair from Oliver's forehead, then leaned forward to kiss it. "Thank you, for including me in what must be a difficult experience, both physically and emotionally."

Oliver turned his face and kissed her lips, wrapping his hands around her scalp. "Never fear, dearest. Before we're finished, you won't just be watching."

Fiona scrunched up her face for a moment, but immediately realized what he meant. She extended a hand toward Alden almost mindlessly as she shook her head.

He took it, urging her out of the chair to his side. He drew her down onto his lap and Fiona almost sighed with the wonder of his large frame, hard chest and heat against the side of her body. "Ah, yes. Fiona—*roosje*—we have a small matter to address, the one of your pride and stubbornness. Running away instead of confession. Ignoring your safety. Avoiding Oliver and I. But do not let Oliver's plight worry you. When it's finished, you will be a sorry girl, but it won't be what Oliver described. Indeed, perhaps it would be best if you went first, so you aren't terrified. His spanking would be unbearable on your fair skin."

Fiona's heart beat harder. She knew her hands fluttered and wanted to hide the telltale emotion from Alden. They'd shown her unbelievable pleasure, true, but this was more than sharing a bed with them. "I-I-I don't know if I can—"

"Of course you can," he returned, his low voice extraordinarily gentle as he wrapped his arms completely around her and squeezed tightly. "Getting a spanking isn't about what *you* can do or what *you* can bear. It's cathartic without grief or loss or tragedy. I know you feel guilty about keeping secrets and sneaking out, if not outright dishonesty. Let me help you with those feelings."

Fiona resisted the almost violent urge to submit to Alden's masculinity. It surrounded her, holding her in his arms and on his lap, his lips nestling against her temple, his scent filling her mind, the taste of him in her memory. She fought the urge inside her, the one that insisted she lean against him and simply agree. But despite her best intentions, a small whimper escaped. To Fiona, the sound echoed in the room.

"Talk to us, Fiona," Oliver murmured, clasping her knee. She looked up. He was on his knees in front of Alden, close enough that she could feel the heat of his body through her arm and under his hand. Her summer gown was thin and offered little protection, and maybe, Fiona thought, that was a good thing.

"I can't break my word," she whispered. "And I won't. Gentlemen always speak of their honor, but women have it too, and I made a promise. I can't tell you where I was or why I keep slipping away. It's not nefarious or immoral. It's not even dangerous, but I made a vow." She looked between them, eyes narrowed. "I was never chastised in the nursery, but I believe it would have made me even more recalcitrant. I suspect the same would be true now."

Against her arm, Fiona felt the chuckle in Alden's chest before it came out of him and she glared. He cleared his throat quickly, and smiled serenely in response. "Perhaps, *roosje*, we should consider this matter in a different manner. I will not try to coerce you into a confession. You will keep your secret for now, and we will agree that you will have your secret and that we are aware of you having this secret. In return, you will refrain from running away, worrying us or otherwise avoiding us. Will this secret will require your time again?"

"You can't be serious," Oliver interrupted. Fiona turned her head quickly, frowning at Oliver's surprise. "You're going to allow this...this—"

"What would you recommend, then?" Alden asked, squeezing Fiona comfortingly.

Comforting? The man was going to spank her, and Fiona was taking comfort in his hug.

"There are many who say a woman cannot have honor, you know, that her very nature—"

Faster than she thought she could move, Fiona shot out her hand and covered Oliver's mouth. "Think very carefully, Oliver Morewell, before you finish that sentence," she warned in a soft voice, suddenly tense. "Once certain words are spoken, they cannot be unsaid." She'd heard the theory, advanced by some gentlemen whose superiority was threatened by female scholarship, that a woman's only honor was in obedience to father or husband. She felt such a position was not even worthy of debate.

Oliver grimaced and kissed her palm before drawing her hand away and clasping it between his. "As I was saying," he continued, "some say that her very nature is deceitful, and has been since she was created. But of course she was created by the same Maker who made man, so she must have the same concept of honor."

"Very clever," Fiona returned dryly.

Alden smiled, and before Fiona quite realized, Alden shifted and so did she. Shrieking briefly, Fiona landed on the chaise. Beneath her, Alden shifted and suddenly her legs were across his lap. "Just because we have negotiated a cease fire instead of a surrender does not mean you are free from any consequences," Alden cut in. "I will always take you to task for endangering yourself, and you've done that several times this week, *roosje*."

Fiona started to respond, twisting her head, but Oliver was right there beside her, on the floor so their eyes could meet. When she opened her mouth, instead of speaking, Oliver kissed her, and by the time he released her lips, Alden had pulled up her skirts and was smoothing them over her waist.

"So pretty," he rumbled, cupping the bare flesh of her backside.

Fiona squealed. He'd touched there the previous night, of course, but that had been in the dark, in passion. This was in the light of the afternoon, with the windows open to the back garden, and Oliver looking on eagerly. Obviously wanting to participate, Oliver reached out and arranged the flowing material, draping it out of Alden's way, while Fiona warmed to Alden's hand. He rubbed, soothing her, until Fiona sighed and sank into a relaxed stupor.

It was heavenly, before a firm swat landed across her rear.

Fiona yelped, jerking her upper body. Oliver' cupped her cheek as she began to turn around. She opened her mouth, wanting to tell him to stop, but Oliver was there first.

He kissed her, his tongue pushing into her mouth and the tip tracing her teeth.

Alden smacked her bottom again, and Fiona started.

Oliver withdrew his tongue but whispered against his lips, "It doesn't hurt, does it? It's only your pride that is at stake. You can trust him—us—with your pride."

Oliver was correct, so Fiona dug her fingers into the fabric of the chaise and grunted when the third spank landed, this one harder. To her surprise, Alden continued spanking her steadily, the swats landing over the base of her bottom.

"Breathe deeply and stay calm," Oliver encouraged, tucking a strand of hair behind her ear. The juxtaposition of his gentle caresses with Alden's palm regularly hitting her backside was difficult to reconcile, but Fiona tried to follow his directions, at least until Alden spoke.

"Why do you fight so hard to prove you are independent?" he asked. "We know you do. We were warned you would."

"Who said that?" Fiona demanded, kicking her feet a little and feeling suddenly childish.

"Everyone," Alden said shortly.

Oliver stroked her cheek and nodded. "It's the single thing absolutely everyone says about you. *Oh, you haven't met Fiona yet? She's wonderful, but so very independent.*" His voice deepened a bit as he ran through the litany. "*A wonderful woman, but too independent by half. Her mother should have done better with that.*" He smiled and went on, "*Lady Fiona is so kind. I'm sure you'll appreciate her independent nature, she doesn't want to be a burden to anyone.* But my favorite was your sister Abigail. *I love Fiona dearly. I just worry that she won't let anyone close. Someday she'll need something, and she won't know how to ask because she insists on doing everything on her own.*"

Fiona gasped, stiffened and immediately regretted it when Alden's hand continued smacking. Against the tensed muscles of her rear, his palm stung her skin. She tried to relax, but the damage was done. The spanks were hurting more, and she didn't want to answer.

"I'm going to keep this up until you say something I believe," Alden warned.

Oliver was watching her closely, too, and Fiona knew he'd want to hear her response. She didn't want to think about it, especially what Oliver had said of Abigail.

"I can ask for help," she claimed. "I let you help me last night."

"You didn't ask. I insisted." Oliver winced slightly as Alden smacked his hand down yet again, this time even harder, hard enough at Fiona made a small noise of distress.

Alden paused, rubbing his palm Fiona's skin. Her bottom was hot, she realized. But she liked when he rubbed it. "Why can't you ask for help, Fiona? You haven't even asked me to stop spanking you. Can you even ask me that?"

"Yes," she shot back decisively. "Yes, you can stop."

"No, not yet," he returned calmly. "That wasn't a request. Why do you insist on proving you're not answerable to anyone?"

He smacked again, this time harder, and Fiona squealed. "That hurt!"

"Good," Alden muttered.

"You're not *answerable* to anyone," she returned. "I won't believe Oliver smacks your backside when you get a bit too puckish with him."

Alden chuckled, but kept up the spanking. Fiona wanted to moan as the heat in her bottom began to turn into an uncomfortable burn. To her surprise, he answered, "I am answerable to my father, to Oliver, to some extent, your mother. I need to take into account their beliefs, their hopes, their fears and if I make a decision that conflicts with them, do so for a damn good reason. And now I'm answerable to you, too. Maybe Oliver doesn't spank me, but he can take me to task quite thoroughly when he chooses."

"I make him explain himself, in public," Oliver confirmed. "Sometimes even at length."

Fiona sniffed.

"Last time," Alden warned, beginning the spanking again.

She whimpered, because the smacks were hard now, each one crashing into her rounded bum painfully.

Her skin was stretching tightly, so each swat stung painfully on the abraded surface.

Despite the pathetic noises that seemed to be coming from her throat without the permission of her mind, Alden didn't stop. He kept spanking.

She tried to hold out, to wait patiently for him to decide she'd had enough. She twisted, she squirmed. Fiona even wriggled. Her breathing sped, her nose itched and she fought the urge to sniffle.

"He won't stop, you know," Oliver whispered. "He'll keep smacking that adorable arse until you give him an answer."

Alden had to stop. He simply had to. The noise from his hand impacting her backside rang in her ears. She tried to listen to Oliver's breathing, to watch his gaze wander over her face, to Alden, to Alden's hand rising and falling, but that made her think of the pain in her backside and her whimpering became shameful cries with each smack.

"I've always been my own person," Fiona finally whispered. "Able to make responsible decisions. All of us girls have."

"Of course you have," Alden responded. "I'm not asking about that. I want to know why you won't be vulnerable enough to ask for help."

Oliver sat back on his heels, a look of comprehension on his face that worried Fiona. Alden stopped spanking, sliding his fingers between Fiona's thighs.

Horrified, she squeezed them together, but he simply pushed those fingers more firmly against her labia, finding and rubbing the moisture there into her skin. "Ask him, Fiona. Ask him to help you."

Alden moved his free hand from the small of her back to the sore skin of her rounded bottom. He traced the curves, using the tips of his fingers to stimulate and tease the skin along the cleft between her cheeks. She arched and stretched, wishing she could experience that magical bliss from before, wanting to insist Alden help her.

Wanting to beg that he help her.

Of course she wouldn't beg. She'd never beg, not for anything. He inserted a blunt fingertip between her lower lips and teased the quivering flesh that wanted more from Alden than his finger.

To her horror, Alden lifted the hand on her bottom and smacked down again. The strange newness of pain alongside the pleasure of his finger startled her. "No!" she cried out. "Stop!"

He smacked again. And again. Fiona bit her lip to keep from crying out, but her determination did no good. Alden left his hand in place just inside her and smacked over and over with his other hand. The angle was awkward, but Fiona was already sore.

Alden grunted, and Fiona felt him shift, then felt his erection rubbing against the fronts of her thighs. Thanking the fates that he was susceptible to the experience too, she shifted against him experimentally.

To her shock, he paused for a moment and completely withdrew his hand. Before she knew it, a heavy rain of swats came down on her arse.

Fiona would have said she saw stars, but she was certain that was she actually saw was a physical manifestation of bliss. As soon as they faded, though, the spanking became the worst pain she'd ever experienced, as though she could no longer absorb pain into muscles that had been inundated with pleasure.

"Please stop," she finally gasped. "Please, please, just stop."

And, of course, Alden immediately did.

He gathered her up, turning her, carefully sitting her so that her bottom hung between his thighs, and held her as close to him as possible. "Good girl, Fiona. Good girl."

* * * *

She lay on the *chaise* and watched as Alden directed Oliver to bend over the armchair across from her.

Her skirts had been smoothed down and a pillow tucked under her head. Oliver had put a blanket over her, despite the heat, claiming it would comfort her and he'd been right. Beneath her skirts, her bottom still burned. When she closed her eyes and thought about it, it throbbed in time to her heartbeat.

She'd never felt so full of emotion in her entire life, and she wasn't sure she if she liked it—feeling emotional. Fiona did not want anyone to think she had endangered herself, but without telling them the truth, she was certain they could not be convinced. She also knew exactly why she always had to prove she was independent and responsible. Being responsible, not being selfish and reckless, had been the only way to comfort her mother after the Worst Day. Some day she would tell them about the Worst Day, though they probably already knew. But Oliver would want to hear it from her lips, and Alden would want to comfort her. Now was not the time. Now was Oliver's time.

Oliver's chest and feet were already bare. He clenched his fists on the opposite arm as he bent down. Alden used his foot to push apart Oliver's feet, then reached around him and unfastened Oliver's trousers. Alden pushed them down to Oliver's knees before he brought his hand back up to Oliver's manhood, which was already half-stiff with the events of the afternoon. "Enjoy this now," Alden said roughly. "You know once you've been properly chastised, this will have to go without, at least until tonight."

"Yes, sir," Oliver responded, biting his lip.

"This reprimand will remind you of your manners then, at least for a few days," Alden added, picking up the hairbrush. He tapped it against his hand, then glanced over at Fiona as Oliver answered again with the same words.

Alden kept his gaze on Fiona and said softly, "You may not interrupt, understand? Comfort him if you want or walk out of the room, but don't try to stop me. I might accidentally hurt you or Oliver — or both of you."

Fiona felt her chin firm. Maybe she was a touch stubborn and blithely oblivious to the world around her, but she knew Alden would never forgive himself if he unintentionally caused her harm. Obviously, he could do it intentionally without a qualm, but he had a small dose of pride, and she had been challenging him since the evening they met.

"I won't interrupt," she assured them both. "I promise."

Alden nodded seriously, turned and bent his head down to whisper in Oliver's ear. She couldn't hear what he said, but Oliver sighed happily and nodded. "I know."

Turning Oliver's head, Alden kissed him for a brief moment, then stood and walked behind Oliver.

He didn't hesitate. With Fiona's dark walnut hairbrush in hand, he reached out and laid a smack, full force, on Oliver's rear.

Oliver nearly howled, but Alden gripped him around the waist and repeated the strike, again and again. He was fast but didn't rush, giving Oliver no time to recover before hitting him again. Oliver's howls turned quickly to stoic grunts, then to whimpering. Alden continued, on and on, until Fiona understood why Alden had spanked her first.

She would have been terrified. Alden hadn't spanked her nearly as hard nor as long, and no sadistic piece of wood was involved.

Only when Oliver seemed ready to burst into tears did Alden begin to question him. "Is this the first time we've had to address this issue?"

"No," Oliver whimpered. "Not the first time."

"Are we going to address it again?" Alden asked.

Oliver didn't answer immediately as a particularly painful smack of the brush caused him to jerk and cry loudly. But he held his position—Fiona would never be able to stand still—and managed to answer a moment later. "I hope not, sir."

"Good, that's an honest answer," Alden said dryly. Nevertheless he kept up with the brush, until Oliver was moaning, biting so tightly into his lower lip that Fiona was sure his mouth would be bruised as much as his ass.

Finally, Alden stopped, but it was only to ask another question, "Why shouldn't you let your speech get out of control, Oliver?"

Oliver breathed slowly, shakily. Fiona, who had remained utterly still, was momentarily distracted by the vision of Oliver's chest moving in and out as he caught his breath. His words were slow, and it took her a moment to process them. "Because when I speak without thinking, I hurt someone I love."

"Two more minutes, fast and hard," Alden said, glancing at the fireplace and the clock above it.

Oliver groaned, but tightened his grip on the chair.

It was at least ninety seconds before Fiona worked out who Oliver had been lashing out at in the dining room.

Someone I love.

It was too soon for love. Much too soon — unless she'd loved them nearly all her life.

Chapter Ten

Oliver had just finished dressing Fiona in a midnight blue gown and pirouetted her before Alden when Fiona's expectations for rescue were finally met. Oliver still moved a bit stiffly, but Fiona was left with a glowing warmth that she found quite interesting, and she continually reached out to touch Oliver, Alden or both.

She'd had a lovely soak in a hot bath, and she'd desperately needed it, while Oliver had dressed Alden in a dramatic turquoise waistcoat with a subdued dark gray jacket and dove gray trousers. Alden was going to take them to the lecture at Somerset House and return to Lennox House. Oliver understood that he would need to allow her to leave with Young Canning, and she would be watching carefully to see if he could follow through on what would be very difficult for him.

Afterward, Oliver had set Fiona on the dressing room bench and gone to work. He'd plucked at her eyebrows and examined her toenails. He'd carefully polished her fingernails, and brushed her hair until it was dry and shining. He'd arranged it carefully in an elegant updo on the back of her head, leaving a frame of curls around her face. He'd obviously rifled through her jewelry box and found pearl drop earrings and a matching necklace and broach. He'd applied her cosmetics, and when she asked how he had learned such things, Oliver had smiled and told her about the wives of his musician friends in Amsterdam, who had been delighted with all the questions he'd asked, tutoring him in how to care for and dress a lady. He'd helped her don a chemise, petticoats and a demure evening gown of plum silk, approved of her half-boots—no dancing slippers at Somerset House—and helped her don them.

She waited patiently as he quickly dressed himself in a dark gray jacket and trousers over a black waistcoat, and smiled when he refused her offer to tie his cravat. They held hands as they strolled the few feet from the bedchamber to Alden's study, where he'd waited.

Alden had been standing, a book in his hands, when they entered. He laid it down and held out his arms, his smile full of emotion that Fiona desperately believed could be satisfaction—or even joy. Oliver didn't hesitate but went to him immediately, pulling Fiona along with them.

When the door to the study opened violently, Fiona's fingers were wrapped around Alden's neck and she was clutching the back of his hair. Her lips were attached to Oliver's, and both men had an arm around her waist.

Fiona heard only the words, "Fucking hell," before Alden was spinning her behind him and Oliver.

Not that there was any chance of violence. Morpeth, she noted, was the one who had spoken, and he had a pistol pointed directly at Alden, which of course caused Oliver to try to move in front of the bigger man. Martin had a pistol too, but it was thankfully pointed at the floor, and his head was tipped to the side as he studied them. Young Canning pointed his back and forth between the two men, but his eyes were wide with surprise and confusion.

Morpeth held up his hand. "I don't want explanations, clankers, or ridiculous excuses. We've come for Lady Fiona, and we're taking her back to London. Step aside." He paused. "Unlike those other two, you know I'll happily put a bullet in you, Swenson."

Fiona, unable to push Alden to the side, helped shove Oliver in front of Alden and stepped around him, then took three steps to the side, out of Oliver's reach. She crossed her arms over her chest and frowned. "How tidy," she disparaged. "Coming in here with pistols and expecting bloodshed. I did expect Martin and Young Canning to affect a rescue, but I honestly thought you would be civilized and ring the bell."

Martin snorted. "We might have, but Lucy told us you weren't expecting to be whisked away, and Oliver there packed a few of your things. She is worried about you."

"And we've taken her to Canning House," Young Canning added. "Where you will be staying for the foreseeable future. You won't have to defend yourself against these brutes again. Harriet is anxious to have you stay."

Fiona rolled her eyes. "The gentlemen and I have worked out an agreement. They will not prevent me from pursuing my duties and will refrain from insisting I speak of what I have vowed to keep a secret, so you have nothing to fear. We were just ready to return to London, as it happens."

"Then you can go in the closed carriage, and directly to Harriet," Young Canning insisted.

"What game are you playing now, Oliver?" Morpeth asked suspiciously. "We know you're not a top diver. If you're prigging —"

"I thought someone at your level of government would refrain from such foul language," Alden cut in, glowering. "Fiona, come here where I can protect you."

"We're not leaving without her, Swenson," Martin said seriously. "We won't hurt or dishonor the lady, but we're taking her back to London. Lady Fiona, do you need anything?"

"No, I was already prepared to leave," Fiona said calmly, watching Oliver and Alden carefully. Alden was angry, but Oliver was...thinking. He was actually studying his brothers. She had to get them out of the house, before Oliver said anything inflammatory — or perceptive. Looking to Alden, she asked, "Alden, Oliver, do you remember our agreement?"

"Of course," Oliver replied immediately, and Alden nodded.

"I'm invoking it. *Vertrouw me,*" she added, the last two words softer than she'd intended, at least with the other men in the room. *Trust me.* She didn't know if Martin and Morpeth spoke Dutch, but Canning didn't, while Alden and Oliver did.

"As for the three of you, I will accompany you. But, at the end of our outing, Mr. Canning and Lord Martin will return me to Lennox House, as is proper. Lord Morpeth, I know you think you know what's best and have good intentions, but I won't be locked up by anyone, for any reason. You have no reason, via family or government, to have my welfare or wishes be your priority. That pistol in your hand proves my point beautifully."

Morpeth shook his head, the pistol in question still aimed across the room at Alden, despite Oliver's position firmly in front of his lover.

"Are you certain?" Martin asked.

"Yes," Fiona said, making her voice unmistakably firm.

Morpeth finally moved his eyes around the room, but he still objected. "Bloody hell, they're fucking dirty sodomites."

Fiona sighed. Still, she walked directly up to Morpeth, stood in front of him, and suddenly reached out to grab the barrel and shove it to the side at the same time that she lifted her other arm and rammed her elbow into Morpeth's stomach. His grip on the pistol loosened and Fiona relieved him of it as he doubled over. Not satisfied with his grunt of pain, she raised a foot and slammed it down on the top of his leather shoe before shoving him backward. Shocked, Morpeth stumbled up against the back of a chair and sat in it abruptly, while Fiona turned and handed the pistol to Oliver. "I trust you'll only use it if he attacks you or Alden," she stated evenly, raising an eyebrow at Alden's befuddlement and Oliver's wide grin. "Because he's not welcome in a closed carriage with me. Martin and Young Canning are more than adequate chaperones."

"You have my word, dearest Fiona," Oliver agreed. Expertly—more expertly than Fiona expected—he twisted it around and aimed the barrel casually at Morpeth's shins.

Grimly, Martin offered his arm and Fiona accepted it. "Hopefully he can convince them to refrain from calling the local magistrate. How humiliating it would be for Lord Morpeth to be arrested for burgling his brother's Merton house," she commented. "Of course, if he expects to live comfortably in London the rest of his life, he needs to find a way to keep a civil tongue in his head."

On her other side, Young Canning took her arm. "Do you think they'd trade him for you?"

Fiona smiled, twisting her head to look at Alden's stunned expression.

"They don't need to trade for him. You aren't holding me hostage, are you?" she asked.

"No, no," Young Canning said hastily. "You know we're just borrowing you! We need to finish tonight. Everything we've heard elsewhere indicates something is going to happen—and soon. We really do need your help, Fiona."

* * * *

"Why?" Alden asked in a strangled voice.

Oliver grasped one of Alden's biceps, thankful that Alden was such a rock. Still, he was surprised that Alden hadn't realized. "She'll be fine," he tried to reassure Alden.

"How the blazes do you know that?" Alden exploded.

Oliver raised a slow eyebrow. His ass still hurt from Alden's lesson earlier, so Alden's brazen curse word didn't impress him. To his astonishment, Alden blushed.

"I know," Oliver explained, "because I suddenly understand what she's doing. The key is the cast of characters. Secretary Canning, of course. Anthony Morewell, the master translator, who Fiona was purportedly delivering documents from. Martin

Morewell, who runs the documents library in the Foreign Office. Morpeth, the ass and undersecretary. And Young Canning, who is his father's shadow and enforcer inside the FO."

Alden tipped his head, frowned, shook it.

Oliver sighed. "She's translating for them, secretly. Either it's an emergency or an ongoing arrangement that has become an emergency, but it's something they won't risk sending in a dispatch box to Northumberland. Logically, it's time sensitive and a relatively obscure language. Otherwise, they'd have someone on the staff do it or send it to Anthony. They wouldn't have come here with pistols and risk exposing her role. What if we'd had company?"

"Is it dangerous?" Alden asked.

Oliver smiled tiredly. "It means she's in possession of a state secret, and that's always somewhat dangerous." He thrust the pistol into Alden's hand and sent a disgusted look in his brother's direction. "Watch him. I need to get the bags so we can drive. We will want to be at Lennox House when she stumbles in. And Morpeth will be uncomfortable enough riding on the tiger's seat, without you driving in full darkness." He paused. "What do you think my father will say when he finds out that the treasured Morpeth has returned home tonight in the company of His Grace's worthless second son?"

"Damn you, Oliver," Morpeth muttered.

Oliver laughed.

* * * *

Oliver kept the pistol concealed in his jacket pocket when the three men went up the stairs to Weymouth House. "Why," Morpeth muttered angrily, "are you putting me through this? You know the fucking servants will tell my wife and our father of this travesty."

Oliver waited until the men stepped inside Morpeth's study, closing the door behind him. "Once upon a time," he said quietly, "Alden's brother made it impossible for the two of us to stay in London. Alden wasn't suited to the life of an idle gentleman, and Lennox was unable or unwilling to completely distance himself from March. I suppose he kept alive a kernel of hope that his eldest son would repent and redeem himself, and become a responsible, dutiful son. But he didn't want to lose Alden either, so he put him in charge of the shipping company he owns and organized a home for him in Portsmouth."

Beside him, Alden stiffened, but it couldn't be denied. Their history was their history. Oliver watched Morpeth pour a drink and sink into a chair before continuing, noting his brother's lack of hospitality. "We were there a few years, had purchased the Merton villa for when we needed to come up to London. It was a pleasant location. We were comfortable—perhaps too comfortable—until one night there was a knock at the front door. I opened it myself, the butler having already retired. On the steps was a man I thought was my brother. Of course I understood his anger, maybe even his *disappointment.* I could have even accepted misguided expressions of shame and disgust. He could hardly claim any moral high road, after all. It's not as if he was without sin himself, and we'd been raised in the same nursery."

Morpeth paled, gulped back his drink.

"Do I need to go on?" Oliver asked quietly. He'd been shoved aside roughly, landing against a foyer table and falling to the floor, his head hitting the wall. Morpeth had left him and charged into the library, where he'd pistol-whipped Alden. Alden, unprepared, had not immediately defended himself, and even when he had, Morpeth had the uninjured advantage. Alden had ended with a serious concussion, but the servants had arrived in response to Oliver's frantic bell pulls. Together they'd managed to expel Morpeth from the house.

But the damage had been done. Alden and Oliver had decided the only safe course of action—aside from being armed day and night and guarded by burly bodyguards—was to leave England. Lennox had come from London as soon as Oliver's message had reached him, and agreed. They'd left for Amsterdam nearly as soon as Alden had recovered, separating Oliver from any sort of relationship with Anthony and Martin, and separating Alden further from his father.

Morpeth shook his head. "March showed up at Weymouth House and told Father you two were still living openly together, in Portsmouth, despite what he'd done to you in London. Mother cried, of course, because you'd been writing her secretly all along and she'd been careful not to let the Duke know. March was clearly being vindictive and petty. I was there, too. It was ugly, and I was angry. By the time I drove to Portsmouth, I was so far beyond angry that I couldn't even function." He looked up, wiped the back of his hand across his forehead and sighed. "I dislike everything about your life, Oliver, but I had no right to attack either of you like a brawler. You were right to dump me in the street and let me fend for myself." Sadly, he looked down into his glass. "You'd better go, though, before the butler brings reinforcements to remove you."

"Your pistol will be at Lennox House when you're man enough to come and get it," Alden finally said quietly. "And no, we won't return it to Martin."

Oliver looked at Alden, at the tired lines in his face, and ended the painful encounter for all three of them. "Goodbye, Morpeth."

Without another comment, he turned and left the room, knowing Alden was behind him. Silently, they returned to the phaeton and Alden tossed a coin at the boy holding the horses. Both jumped up and Alden set the horses to trot slowly down the street. They were close to Lennox House, so Oliver stared hard at the macadamized surface and pondered what to say.

There was nothing to be said.

Alden didn't speak either, not until they returned to their suite, until the servants withdrew, until Oliver had played the entire second movement of Beethoven's Symphony No. 6, including the complicated quail calls in the cadenza.

"My father does not expect me to marry," Alden announced, leaning against the wall near Oliver's music stand. He watched Oliver carefully. "You know that. Did you know why? Did you ever know that my father once loved deeply too, before Johna?"

Oliver blinked. "No," he said carefully, setting the oboe carefully in its stand. By his estimate, they were hours from Fiona returning. He was likely to play again.

Alden nodded. "His name was Robert Twicken. His nephew is the current Duke of Richmond."

Very carefully, Oliver watched Alden's face, remembering Lennox's compassion when Oliver was beaten by March as a young man down from Oxford, and the Duke's anger when Alden was attacked by

Morpeth a few years later. "They must have kept it very secret."

"Perhaps not as secret as my father wanted. Lennox was married, of course, though my mother did not come to London. I've wondered before, if that was why they led separate lives, if she knew. Uncle Robert was known to have fathered a natural son on one of Eynon Castle's housekeepers, after I went up to Eton. Later Robert fathered another child, and that was kept secret. Very secret. Her name is Gloria."

Shock nearly caused Oliver to stumble into his desk. He jerked to the side, then grabbed the back of an armchair and nearly fell into it. Alden didn't hesitate, but continued his story. "I didn't know about that last bit, of course. But Uncle Robert was His Grace's close companion all the time of my childhood. I jokingly thought of Robert as his chamberlain. He often stayed here at Lennox House while he was in London, and that was frequently. He was always invited to Eynon Castle in the summer, and he frequently did business on the Duke's behalf. Years ago, of course, old Richmond convinced him to do the Twickens a service and be their face in the Napoleonic War. He died in France. My father was devastated. I didn't understand until much later—until March beat you nearly to death in that alley—exactly how heartbroken he was. He told me the story while we waited for the doctor. He told me he understood why I didn't want to live a secret life even though he thought we should be discreet, that he wished he had not treated Robert's affection as a shameful skeleton in the closet that he couldn't acknowledge."

Oliver continued to stare at him.

Alden sighed. "The solution is ever so simple, Oliver. You need to marry Fiona. My family, my father, is at peace. Your family is not, and I know what's coming next. Martin and Anthony will face off to Morpeth and your father. Your mother will be sick at heart, your sister-in-law, Melissa, will be a witch and Olivia and your nephews will avoid the Morewells religiously to avoid the tension. They don't deserve to live in such a state, and you, dear Oliver, will take too much responsibility on your own shoulders and accept that it's all your fault, even though it's the Duke who is to blame. The solution is simple. Marry Fiona."

Oliver drew a shaky breath. His mind spun. "She would probably prefer to marry you."

"I'd prefer if all three of us were legally bound so tightly that neither of you could ever leave me. You already know I am such a controlling arse that I'm secretly thrilled you're financially dependent on me. It's a balm to those childhood insecurities that say you might abandon me too. I am worried that if I was married to Fiona, I would somehow break that fierce independence that is so much of her. But she can come to depend on us — for companionship, for affection, for encouragement, for love and in time she'll accept financial support from us. Besides, I do not want anyone to think I am angling myself for the Duke's title or even children to reduce Eynon's income. Eynon is welcome to it, despite his current tiny size. She can't marry both of us, but she can marry you."

Oliver held his breath, but the images and possibilities whirled through his mind so fast and so vividly that he had to struggle to speak evenly. "I only know I want you both."

Alden smiled, a gentle gesture so full of love and tenderness that Oliver felt the pain in his chest all the way to his stomach and down into his groin. "Oliver, come here, and let me show you how much you mean to me."

Oliver groaned, but drawn by Alden's steadiness, he stood immediately to his feet and approached. "Good," the bigger man rumbled. "It's going to be hours yet. Let me give you something to think about while we wait for her to come home to us."

The noise in Oliver's chest turned into a low growl. Oliver's knees hit the floor as he found the buttons on Alden's trousers. Alden had the right idea. They both needed the distraction.

* * * *

It had not taken long for Fiona to find evidence among the papers removed from Count Lieven's office of a plot to kidnap and assassinate the tsar. His death would supposedly propel Russia to withdraw from certain agreements among the Great Alliance of Russia, Prussia and Austria-Hungary. The leader of the Russian empire was known to be distrustful of his advisors and courtiers, and he apparently had reason to be. His people felt he had betrayed them and his lifelong ideals, angry over the Austrian Metternich's influence, and Alexander's agreement that Russia should participate in the Troppau Protocol.

She now understood more about the difficult relationship of Countess Lieven and Princess Esterhazy, both Patronesses of Almacks, than she'd ever wished to have known. The barrage of innuendos and accusations ratcheted with sets of letters between the Countess, married to the Russian ambassador to London, Prince Metternich, the Austrian foreign minister, and Princess Esterhazy, who was married to Prince Paul Esterhazy, who had served as ambassador to London from Austria. The Russian empress, now Elizabeth Alexeievna, but Princess Louise of Baden by birth, had bluntly suggested that Countess Lieven refrain from slandering the well-mannered and formal Princess. Metternich had reminded the complaining countess of Austria and Russia's ongoing powerful relationship through the Great Alliance.

But following those letters were other letters, written to the Count and Countess, and left unsigned, which suggested that a change in leadership was coming. Would the Lievens continue to represent Russia under a constitution? Alexander's own guards, the Semyonovsky regiment, had rebelled once already, and plots abounded to remove him from the throne and eliminate Russia from the hated Troppau Protocol, which granted the Austro-Hungarians and Prussians a right to interfere in Russian self-governance in the event of a revolution.

Most damning were the recent letters, written to the Count Lieven under the name of the Union of Salvation. They came from two different authors, outlining two different plans, both ending in the deaths of Alexander I, his brothers, Constantine, Nicholas and Michael, their families and Alexander's wife, the ailing empress. One promised that the tsar's last living sister, married to the King of the Netherlands, would be spared, but the tsar's other nephews would not be allowed a claim to rule Russia. The other letter suggested Constantine and his Polish wife would be permitted to become emperor under a constitutional republic modeled after Britain.

The intrigues, disguised in the formal language of the Polish Kashubians, left Fiona with a lead weight in her stomach. Revolution would endanger not just Alexander I—a disillusioned reformer turned autocrat—but also so many others who had no expectations or desire to rule the cold empire.

Fiona wondered briefly if the Kashubian Pole who had been tasked with translating the letters and burning them would be discovered secreting them out of Russian hands instead. She sympathized with him, bound to a Russian emperor who had established a constitutional government for Poland but not for the Russian people. He'd come to the English, not to betray the Russians, but to protect Alexander.

Still, mostly, she just didn't want to be a part of the Court intrigue.

The realization, doubtless brought on by fatigue and the sick stink of treachery, disturbed her. She had worked hard, loved languages, knew she was being trusted with tremendous secrets and appreciated that she could finally put her learning and intelligence to good, useful purposes. She would never betray Canning's trust, of course, but it had been easier when she was simply providing secondary translation, rather than hurriedly trying to verify the tale that the Pole had apparently brought to Morpeth.

As for Morpeth, she glared at him through the darkness as she settled her skirts in the carriage, Young Canning beside her and Martin next to Morpeth on the opposite seat. Morpeth's hands were clasped tightly together and his face was hidden in the shadows.

"They are taking advantage of you," he began. "You're a virtuous young woman and they are twisting that to their own immoral purposes. You'll never be first. They will always put themselves before you. I can get you out of town tonight. Martin can—"

"One way or another, I'm going to Lennox House. Whatever foolishness you, or you and Martin together, have thought up to keep me apart from your own brother and Alden, won't work. I've made my choices, and I won't change them. They are not dishonorable men, and they do not dishonor me."

"I won't pretend that I understand any of this Morewell family drama," Young Canning interrupted, his voice harsh in the darkness. "But the lady wants to go to Lennox House, and that's where we are taking her."

"I agree," Martin added. "I have no part in Morpeth's intrigues, Fiona. Morpeth, you have more to worry about than Lady Fiona. Young Canning and I will make sure she comes to no harm. You need to follow up with Canning immediately and decide how to warn the tsar that his life and many others are in imminent danger, without letting him know of our source within the Russian embassy."

"It's as if we're part of that damn Protocol, and we didn't even sign the agreement," Morpeth muttered. "If we warn him, we're interfering in their internal affairs. If we don't warn him, the ultimate outcome could be a war that spreads across Europe. Damn it."

"If you don't warn him, many innocent people will die," Fiona said sharply.

"Your job is finished now, Lady Fiona," Morpeth shot back. "This is a decision *I* have to make."

Fiona felt her heart wrench a bit at his condescension. Luckily, Young Canning cut in before she said something she might regret later. "Actually, this is a decision my father will make," Young Canning warned. "If Alexander is informed of the danger, he may retaliate and take out innocents in his desire to purge any traitors from his ranks." He rapped the top of the carriage with his cane, and from above him, the carriage driver opened the flap to the top seat. "Canning House first, my good man. Then Lady Fiona and Lord Martin to Lennox House. You'll wait for Lord Martin there and return him to Canning House."

"Aye, Master Canning," the coachman agreed, closing the flap and returning his attention to the horses.

Fiona remained silent. She had nothing further to say to Morpeth and was still slightly disturbed by the other two. Young Canning she could easily forgive. He was the least knowledgeable of the Morewell dramatics, and he hadn't had cause to know that Fiona was drawing closer to Alden and Oliver. Martin, however, had known, and he was still sitting across from her when Morpeth and Young Canning departed the carriage.

"I am so sorry," he said immediately.

Fiona bit back her sarcastic comment and waited.

"It was the Pole, of course. He insisted it was imminent, and we were desperate to know the details, but it had to be from someone we trusted. That was you, and we had to find you."

"I see," she offered after a moment of silence.

"No, I don't think you do," Martin argued. "What else could we have done, Fiona? Waited until you came back to London? For all we knew, they were taking you to Wales, permanently. You disappeared from Canning House. Lucy told us that Oliver had packed your things, and we were in desperate straits. If I had known for certain you had gone with them willingly, if I'd known when you were returning or if I had known that imminent meant sometime in the next few months and not next week, I might have tried to stop Morpeth."

"I don't trust him with Alden or Oliver. I never will," she said softly. "And for their sake—not just my sister Gloria's—I'm glad March is gone, too."

"They love each other," Martin finally said quietly.

"Yes, it's one of the reasons I enjoy their company."

"You can drop the formal reserve, Fiona. I know that you've shared a bed with one of them, maybe both of them."

"Together," she informed him bluntly.

Martin winced and held up his hands. "I don't need details, please."

"I would do the same thing again in a heartbeat," she added.

"I don't want to see you hurt, Fiona. You are a good woman. And I don't think they're using you, at least not in the way Morpeth does. But I am worried about you. If push comes to shove, they will choose each other instead of you."

Fiona's mouth twisted. She felt it twisting, and a rough laugh escaped. "Martin, don't you understand?" She leaned forward, and said it again, or maybe for the first time, "I don't want them to pick me over each other. I want them both."

Martin sighed and shook his head. "I was afraid you would say that."

"Why?" she asked, completely lost.

"You would have made an excellent ambassador's wife, Fiona. If you were married to Oliver, you could have had that."

"My God in heaven, you really don't understand," Fiona exclaimed. "Oliver doesn't want to be taken back into the family bosom to become an ambassador or to work in the Foreign Office. He wants his family back so he can appreciate his brothers and his nieces and nephews. It's not about his *career*. It's not about money."

"I hope you're right about that," Martin returned, looking away as the carriage came to a halt. "Because you're here, as you asked. I hope they are here, too."

"They will be," Fiona assured him.

* * * *

Fiona was honestly surprised that they weren't waiting for her in the drawing room. Or her sitting room. She frowned and looked down at her crumpled evening gown. She supposed it would be best to change before looking for them, so she headed into her dressing room and exchanged her evening clothes for a nightdress and dressing gown. She had nothing illicitly charming, as Gloria and Abigail did, but it didn't matter, she told herself even as her shoulders slumped in disappointment.

She'd much rather have had Oliver's help in disrobing.

Sighing, she slipped back in the sitting room. They weren't in Oliver's office, but the door to their sitting room was open. She explored there and in both men's bedchambers as well. Oliver's clothes had been tossed onto the floor of his dressing room, so she knew they'd returned to London, which eased her speeding heart a bit too much.

With a sigh, she stumbled back into her sitting room as her clock quietly chimed five times. Wherever they were, presumably they hadn't heard her return or her conversation with Carrington in the front hall.

She needed to sleep.

Of course that's where they were.

Asleep in her bed.

Naked, with the blankets shoved down to the footboard.

Fiona stared at them, remembering Martin's concerns. She wasn't surprised that Alden had wrapped his arms tightly around Oliver, or that Oliver was on his stomach, one hand on Alden's hip. In the quiet room, Alden's breathing was slow and silent, but Oliver snored slightly, and his hair fell loosely over the pillows.

Was there room for her, too? Silently, she approached the bed, telling herself they must have expected her. They were in her bed, after all. The room was dim in the dawn, but their skin shone with a faint glow. She drifted to the head of the bed, looking down on them, wondering if perhaps she should go elsewhere —

"About time," Alden mumbled, stretching his long legs over the end of the bed as he opened his eyes and saw her. A smile crossed his face, and he sat up, gesturing her around the bed. Curious, she went to his side, noting that Oliver still slept heavily. Alden unbuttoned her dressing gown and the nightdress, sliding them down her form. Instinctively she caught at the fabric and frowned.

"I haven't bathed," she whispered, blushing.

Alden was clearly confused by her objection and tugged on the material. "It's too hot to sleep with extra clothes on," he muttered, standing to forcibly wrench the cloth away and push it to the floor. "Into bed," he murmured, patting her on the bottom.

Fiona watched for a moment as he moved to the door. She wondered where he was going, leaving her with Oliver, but he only locked it. She scooted into the center of the bed as Alden returned to the bed as well, and Fiona fought back a tellingly happy sigh when he pulled her against his chest, tucked her head beneath his chin and reached over her to press a hand to Oliver's hip. "Goodnight," she whispered.

"Good morning," he mumbled. "Rest now. There will be time to talk after you've slept and eaten. Just don't run away."

"No," she answered. "I won't."

"Good girl," he said, and above her his breathing evened out, until she knew he was sleeping.

When she woke up, a sheet was drawn up over her bare form. The window coverings were pulled back, allowing a morning breeze of London soot to drift in. Fiona frowned, a large part of her wishing that she was still in Merton with Oliver and Alden. Of course, then she wouldn't have been so useful to the Foreign Office.

She supposed her ambivalence was precisely how a gentleman with a government position sometimes felt—unable to pursue his own best interests or amusements because he had a greater call on his time and energies.

Rolling over, she stretched and sighed, reaching for her dressing gown and ringing for Lucy. She didn't know where the men had gone, but they couldn't have ventured far.

They didn't appear when Lucy came in with her washing water or when she had a hot, luxurious bath, or when she dressed in a perfectly acceptable if vivid chartreuse morning gown and sat down in the family dining parlor to eat a hearty, but late, breakfast.

Carrington brought her the answer, in the form of a stiff card with Fiona's first name scrawled across the front. Without a single change in his expressionless face, Fiona knew even Carrington was perplexed.

"Who is it from?" she asked, taking the card from the salver and looking at it closely.

"It is Lord Alden's handwriting, miss. Lord Oliver asked that I deliver it as soon as possible. Both returned to the house approximately fifteen minutes ago, and Lord Oliver came down from their suite just a moment ago, with the card in hand."

Fiona turned it over and stared. "Thank you, Carrington," she said, already distracted. The back of the envelope was sealed with a fine Lennox fob, which could have barely hardened.

Her fingers shook as she broke the red wax. The stiff card was simple. Alden wrote only, '*Vertrouw ons. We zullen op je wachten.* Come to us when you are rested'.

Fiona didn't want to wait. The reservations that had kept her running and hiding from them had been broken down by Morpeth and Martin's indiscreet rescue attempt. She'd been fascinated by them long ago and now as an adult, she could admit she was completely captivated. Together, they made her feel as though she were a Greek goddess, instead of a dismissed English spinster, instead of a bastard daughter.

Could she have them *and* her work with the Foreign Office? A few days earlier, the idea had seemed impossible, but Oliver wasn't intimidated by the idea in Merton, and Alden had written *Trust us* in his note. She set the card on the table and stared at it as she sipped her tea, and wondered what life might be like, in a house with her mother, her mother's lover and two intense men determined to watch over her at every step.

Ten minutes later, she pushed open Alden's study door.

Both looked up, Oliver from the armchair before the desk and Alden from the seat behind it. Oliver's smile was a grin, eager and happy. Alden's expression was more inscrutable, but hungry as his gaze roamed over Fiona's figure. She shivered at his expression, and opened her arms to Oliver's boisterous hug. Almost immediately, Oliver kissed her, coaxing her to respond then taking her tongue into his mouth until Fiona clutched his hair.

"My turn, *roosje*," Alden rumbled, taking her from Oliver almost as soon as she was free. Still shivering, she nevertheless opened her lips for Alden, who took her mouth to demonstrate his desire. He wanted her affection, too. He cupped her bottom through her gown, lifting her onto his chest and cradling her.

Somehow, when she looked up, they were sitting on the bench beneath the window at the end of the room. She was on Alden's lap, and Oliver knelt between Alden's knees, pressing his body against Fiona so that she was firmly between them.

Oliver didn't waste a moment. It felt as if he never did, as if he always went directly for what he wanted from her. "I understand why you couldn't tell us," he said, tugging on the chain around her neck so that the medallion beneath her gown came tumbling out. "If I had ever seen this around your throat, I would have known. You aren't doing more than translating, are you? I understand what Martin's position entails, so I suspect I know how you are contributing."

"No, that's it." She frowned. "Of course I am often invited to events at the embassies, and at the patronesses' homes and other European dignitaries, because I am able to speak with the diplomats and their guests in their native languages. But those are social events. I am not *working* while at a dinner with Countess Lieven."

"Why at night?" Alden asked abruptly. "It is your health and safety with which I am concerned, of course. Why shouldn't you perform your duties during the day?"

"Morpeth doesn't want the mandarins to know that a woman is among them, perhaps even reviewing the work that a *man* has done. Not only would it reflect on the state of linguistics in London, gossip would inevitably get out and that would damage Fiona's standing in society. She would also be ostracized — or at least treated with a marked degree of caution — by the diplomatic wives and the ambassadors themselves. They would watch every word they spoke in her presence. Even if she is not actively spying for the British, if one of them said something that fit in with what documents she has seen, Fiona is bright enough to put the threads together and report it to Martin, even if he hasn't asked." Oliver supplied the answer so easily that Fiona gaped at him. He shrugged. "Not every piece of knowledge gathered by the Ministry is obtained through nefarious channels."

"That's the part I don't like and that I wish we could somehow fix for you, *roosje*," Alden grumbled.

"So you don't object to me doing it? To putting my learning to good use?" Fiona asked, looking between them. Oliver shook his head without hesitation. Alden smiled slightly and tugged on her earlobe with his thumb.

"Not as long as you choose it," Alden clarified. "But do not feel as if you must do it for the income or any nonsense of that sort. I may be a second son and Oliver a disinherited one, but we have managed quite well investing my earnings, expectations notwithstanding."

Fiona smiled. "I do not expect either of you to support me," she declaimed, shaking her head. "It's not as if we're married—"

"Ah but we will be," Oliver interrupted. "And the sooner the better, I'm thinking, although of course we will have to wait until His Grace and your mother return to discuss it with them. It's inevitable that others will find out. We will watch you too closely, and we are not at odds with each other."

"I will not choose one of you over the other," Fiona objected fiercely, squirming in Alden's lap. He held her tightly and Oliver grasped her hands, kissing the back of each of them in turn.

"Of course not," Oliver agreed smoothly. "Alden can't marry anyone without sparking rumors that he might be preparing to usurp Eynon's inheritance. And if he did marry you, the ducal succession would demand that you carry a babe immediately, then all of London would speculate on its parentage.'"

"Not that I would ever let you leave us, despite the difficulties," Alden said hastily, as Fiona began to frown.

"On the other hand, marrying me would bind the three of us together for the rest of our lives," Oliver explained patiently, still holding her hands tightly in his. She stared down at them, her head starting to spin. "We would live here, the three of us, in Lennox House. Alden's need to care for us would be met by providing us all with a home and pampering you ridiculously. I would continue to run the house and you could continue your studies." He paused. "And your work."

"And the Morewells would no longer have the leverage to harass him, even if his father and Morpeth never come to see their wrongs," Alden cut in.

Fiona jerked, but smiled after a moment. "True. It would almost be rescuing you."

Oliver managed to turn the glare he was sending Alden into a smile for Fiona. "In private, of course, the three of us would be together. In the absence of His Grace and your mother, Alden would have you as an official hostess until his regency is at an end and Eynon takes control of his title. We know it is some years away, but someday we three could have our own home here in London, travel, retire to the villa or purchase a country house somewhere."

"I would still spank you and make love to you both at every opportunity," Alden clarified.

Fiona's heart beat hard.

"What about my mother? Your father? And Meriden?" she demanded. "They will not believe any nonsense about the two of you splitting up, Oliver marrying me, and the three of us living together in Lennox House."

Oliver frowned, but Alden smiled. "I doubt anyone will believe that bit of nonsense," he reassured her. "As for your family, my instinct is to get the two of you wed by special license before any of them find out. But on a more practical level, I will sit down and tell everyone precisely what I told Oliver earlier, Fiona. I love you—both of you—and I will always be at your sides to do whatever needs done to make you both happy."

Fiona felt her throat close with heavy emotion. "So is this a proposal?" she whispered.

Oliver inhaled sharply, but straightened his back out and rose to the occasion grandly. "Lady Fiona, I would be absolutely delighted if you would do me— no, us—the singular honor of being my bride, the love of our lives, the wife of our dreams and the lady of our hearts."

"Yes," she agreed, turning her hands to grasp Oliver's in return, and laying her cheek against Alden's. "Yes."

Epilogue

Fiona laughed. It was not a laugh she'd enjoyed much until the last six months, but Oliver and Alden seemed to coax it from her more and more often. At first it had been small things, like the carved wooden box on Alden's desk that contained a sapphire and diamond engagement ring. They'd taken it to Asprey's in the early morning and the jewelers had cleaned and polished it until the Lennox heirloom had shone, but they had completely forgot about the jeweled ornament when Fiona had come into the room. Their stumbling horror at the oversight had brought out her first laugh.

Then there had been Abigail's shock that had been followed by her shout of delight. "You scheming thing, both together. If they are as good as my Charles—"

"They are," Fiona had interjected dryly.

"Heavens, how can you even walk?" Abigail had asked, and Fiona had laughed again.

Fiona's mother had returned from Wales with a smile. Her carriage was more erect than Fiona had seen in at least two years, and Fiona had recognized a lightness in her face that had not been present for far too long. She had clasped Fiona warmly in her arms, eyes wide as she'd admired the ring, wider when Lennox confessed it had been his mother's, given to Alden instead of included in the dukedom's jewels. Oliver had swept up behind her, claimed her for a proud kiss and had turned her into Alden's arms with an elegant bow. Lennox's mouth had fallen open and Fiona had laughed, joyously, as he'd kissed her cheeks.

Fiona had even laughed, outrageously, at her wedding. They had hosted a family-only event at the Merton villa. If the priest performing the ceremony had wondered why Lord Alden Swenson gave away the bride instead of his father, the Duke, or why Lord Alden had been their only attendant—Oliver's best man and witness—he hadn't had the audacity to ask. Alden had remained standing immediately behind Fiona as Oliver and Fiona were married. Oliver had kissed her and spun her to Alden, and Fiona had laughed in utter joy when Alden had brushed a tender kiss across her forehead.

Afterward, she'd even laughed at the males of her family, congregating as a pack. Alden, Oliver, Lennox, Clare, Meriden, even Anthony—all of them frowned at Genevieve, who glowed with happiness and wouldn't surrender her husband for anyone to interrogate. What had begun as a marriage of convenience with Sir Peter Devon had clearly been undergoing a fundamental change over the months of summer and early autumn.

But six months had passed, and laughter now came almost every day. She'd laughed when Oliver woke her in the mornings, tickling her sides as he slid on top of her. She'd laughed when Alden chased her down a corridor after threatening a spanking. She'd laughed when Oliver rushed to dress himself in staid, reserved colors so that he could spend extra time deciding on what outrageous matching outfits Fiona and Alden would wear out to an evening engagement. She'd laughed when they arrived and she had been on Oliver's arm, and when she'd left on Alden's.

She laughed this morning because she was vomiting in a chamber pot, Lucy holding her hair away from her face. Fiona had just realized why she was so strangely nauseated.

"We've never even discussed it," she admitted to the maid.

"No time like the present, ma'am," Lucy answered pertly. "And plenty of time before the little lass comes along, too."

"I do think we'll say it's a girl. That ought to properly terrify them," Fiona agreed.

Lucy frowned. "What about your afternoons at Canning House?"

"I suppose we'll have to see if I'm well enough." Fiona sighed.

Soon after Fiona had begun wearing the engagement ring, Alden had summoned Martin to Lennox House for a serious discussion of logistics. In the end, everyone had agreed, Fiona included. Her usual chamber at Canning House had become a small parlor and office, where she spent some afternoons with Martin and Young Canning. She could arrive respectably in the Lennox carriage and depart in plenty of time for tea and dressing for her evening engagements. And if a red dispatch box occasionally arrived at Lennox House with Oliver's name on it, none but Fiona and Oliver would know who actually had the key and opened the contents.

But now, Lucy was right. Chances were that Alden and Oliver would be overbearingly protective, once she told them. She was already cossetted and pampered to within an inch of running away on a weekly basis.

"If they kidnap me again and remove me to Merton, be sure to pack those new negligees, would you, Lucy? And as it is still February, I suspect you should be certain that there is a heavy pelisse and my half-boots as well." Fiona sighed, rising and wobbling on her feet. Lucy agreed as Fiona brushed her teeth and rinsed the telltale taste from her mouth, then walked to the door.

She might as well face the music immediately.

It took a full half hour to corral them into the same room. Oliver had been discussing fabrics with the draper, as he and Johna were refurbishing the drawing room. She'd waited until he was finished and had taken his arm, leading him forcibly up the stairs. Since that maneuver sometimes ended with Fiona on her knees and Oliver's cock in her mouth, Oliver had only pretended reluctance. He sauntered into Alden's office, a partial erection already beginning to lift the fabric of his trousers.

Fiona smiled at him patiently and waved him to a chair. Alden was absent, so she had to hunt him as well, smiling as she found him sketching out yet another realignment of their rooms. Alden was convinced that Fiona's office ought to connect directly to his, probably so that he could watch her through the doorway. "Come," she invited, "I have something to discuss with the two of you, and it may impact your architectural achievements."

Alden looked at her curiously, but set aside his pencil and the long strip of drafting paper spread out on the table. He took her hand. "Is it about the bedroom again?" he asked. "We certainly don't need three of them, especially if we each have a dressing room."

"I do think there should be two bedchambers and three dressing rooms," she confirmed. "But that's not why we need to talk."

Alden raised an eyebrow, following her through the maze of rooms and into his office. She waved him to the chair beside Oliver's and leaned against the desk in front of them, wrapping her arms around her waist.

"What do you need, *roosje*?" Alden asked immediately, glancing back and forth between Fiona and Oliver.

Fiona's lips curved just slightly. She didn't look at Oliver, kept her gaze firmly fixed on Alden, and said plainly, "A nursery."

Alden's eyes widened momentarily, and Fiona snuck in a look at Oliver as Alden turned to him. "You want to have a wee lad? That's wonderful," Alden agreed, a sudden smile on his face.

Oliver's face was utterly blank. "We do?" he asked faintly, looking back and forth between Fiona and Alden uneasily.

"I think she'll be a wee lass, not a lad, but that's beside the point," Fiona corrected.

"We want to have a baby?" Oliver asked. He drew in a sharp breath. "Of course we want Fiona to have a baby."

Alden examined Fiona and fastened his gaze on her abdomen. "It would be a miracle to have a tiny version of one of you in our home," he agreed. "Or a half-pint. Half you, half Fiona." He held out his hand to Fiona, urging her onto his lap.

Fiona never refused such an invitation, so she went onto his thighs then cradled close against his chest. "I shall confine my attentions to Oliver's body and your mouth," Alden offered, kissing her temple. "So you can be sure—"

"No," Oliver interrupted. "Why do you assume I am to be the father? Maybe Fiona was inviting you to set up a nursery with her. You'll be a wonderful father, Alden, and—"

"Both of you should be quiet. Immediately," Fiona stopped them, holding up her hand. "I love you both and both of you will father wonderful children. I do not give a pence to even know which of you her father is, and I expect you both to be her fathers. Any questions?"

Alden, this time, understood first. He tightened his arms around her, almost painfully. "Fuck."

Fiona laughed. Alden still hated Oliver's cursing, so that single word falling from his lips was evidence she could treasure.

"That is how it happens, yes," she murmured. "Although it shouldn't surprise you terribly. You were both educated well and are bright men."

Oliver came out of his chair, a shout of joy erupting from him as he launched himself at the pair. Once he had his arms around Fiona, he spoke. "Holy hell, you're already with child," he whispered, bending to kiss her stomach.

Fiona laughed, lifting Oliver's face and pressing his lips to Alden's. The men kissed tenderly, but drew away from each other to stare down at Fiona until her heart rate increased and she inhaled quickly.

"You're beautiful," one said.

"And ours," the other murmured.

"Yes," she agreed.

About the Author

Elle writes stories to entertain her friends and amuse herself. Over time, the stories have got better, and she hopes romance lovers everywhere will love them as much as she does.

Elle lives among the redwoods in the very great state of California with a devoted Mr. Sabine, one golden-headed daughter and one loving, eternally young pup. Yes, those are her curls and part of her study bookshelves!

In her spare time, she loves to explore fairy circles, climb to high places to see the Pacific and look at the bottom of the Golden Gate Bridge.

Elle loves to hear from readers. You can find her contact information, website details and author profile page at http://www.pride-publishing.com.

PUBLISHING

www.ingramcontent.com/pod-product-compliance
Lightning Source LLC
Chambersburg PA
CBHW030133180626
46812CB00002B/669